WIZARDS AT WAR!

Dashing, panting, Gull and Greensleeves cleared the meadows and rocky reaches, gained the edge of the village, the first houses.

Too late.

With a roar, twoscore or more red soldiers mustered on the ridge, reinforcements brought to the fore. They raised their short swords, bellowed again, and charged down the ledge slope. The centaurs paced them at a gallop. To Gull's left, the blue barbarians sent up a hiss and surged forward, curved blades and clubs slashing like sickles after grain.

Gull and Greensleeves were caught square in the middle.

Look for
MAGIC: The Gathering

Arena

Whispering Woods

Shattered Chains*

Final Sacrifice*

From HarperPrism

*Coming Soon

WHISPERING WOODS

Clayton Emery

HarperPrism
An Imprint of HarperPaperbacks

HarperPaperbacks *A Division of* HarperCollins*Publishers*
10 East 53rd Street, New York, N.Y. 10022

Cover illustration by Kevin Murphy

First printing: January 1995

Printed in the United States of America

HarperPaperbacks, HarperPrism, and colophon are trademarks of HarperCollins*Publishers*

❖ 10 9 8 7 6 5 4 3 2 1

Dedicated to my brother Ben, the Loner

CHAPTER

1

CHAPTER
1

An explosion like thunder made Gull look up.

The sky was clear, blue and deep. The sun was high and spring-warm. The Mist Moon, a dull white, was a fingernail paring over the western trees.

There was something else in the sky too. All Gull had ever seen aloft were moons, clouds, and birds, yet now . . .

A big lumpy ball like an inflated bladder drifted in the blue.

The woodcutter stepped away from the tree into a spot he'd cleared that morning. He hopped up on the stump to see better. He and his team were no more than half a league deep in the Whispering Woods. Whatever that . . . flying thing . . . was, it was close to his village. Above it.

"What in the name of Chatzuk . . . "

His mules snuffled uneasily. Gull shushed them and strained to hear.

The round bladder-thing was encircled with ropes,

and from them hung a basket full of tiny scruffy fig-
ures, all arms and pointed heads, all jabbering. They
struggled with something, making the basket sway
jerkily. They were hurling things.

At his village?

There came another thunderclap, louder than the
first. The stump under Gull's feet jumped, then trembled.

His mules nickered. Flossy, with her gentle disposi-
tion, minced in her leather hobble, seeking shelter
under a chestnut tree. Knothead, stubborn even for a
mule, lowered his head to chew through his hobble.
Gull hopped down and yanked on his ear. The mule
snapped at him with yellow teeth.

"Not now, Knothead!" he griped. "I need help, not
hindrances!" Tugging at the mules' collars, he started
to lash them together so they couldn't wander. But
something made him stop: a premonition that he
wouldn't return soon.

Like most muleteers, he talked to his animals as if
they understood, for often they did. "Stay here, you
two. I need see what's happening. And where's
Greensleeves . . . Ah!"

His sister had wandered off, as usual, but the explo-
sions had brought her scurrying back from the depths
of the forest.

Greensleeves was built the opposite of her brother—
small, so scrawny you could count the bones in her
hands and arms. Yet she was obviously related, for her
eyes were green, her chestnut hair wavy and untidy,
her cheekbones wide and mouth narrow, her skin
walnut-dark from a lifetime outdoors though she was
just sixteen and not full-grown. She wore a faded
linen smock dyed green with lichens, and a tattered
shawl peppered with sticks and leaves. She wore no
hat, and never anything on her feet, even in winter

snows. As always, her hands were dirty, her wrists
stained green from rooting in the soil and plucking at
grasses. Her mother had named her Greensleeves for
those stains.

Not that it mattered what her name was, for the
girl barely knew it or anything else.

Frightened as a squirrel by the noise, she ran to her
brother and grasped his brown hand. She gabbled in
her animal tongue, chattering like a squirrel, chittering like a badger, spilling incomprehensible questions
as she wrung his fingers.

Gull spoke to her the same as to his mules. "Stay
here, Greenie. I'm going"—he couldn't say "home"
lest she feel deserted—"to see about something. To see
a man. Stay here. I'll be back soon." She still looked
worried, and he wondered how much she understood.
He pried her fingers off his hand.

His mind aswim with questions—What was happening to the village?—Gull slung his quiver and bow-
case over his shoulder. He carried them for hunting,
but now he might have to drive off those little . . .
creatures in the sky. He looped his mulewhip around
his belt, then hefted his big double-bitted woodcutting
axe. "Best be prepared, though I don't know what for."

He turned to find Greensleeves close behind him.
Maybe packing his weapons scared her. "Stay, I tell
you!"

He wanted to run but forced himself to walk,
stretching his legs for the mile and a half trek to the
forest's edge. He couldn't run more than a hundred
feet anyway. Three years ago an elm tree had jumped
off the stump: elm was a man-hating tree that let go
without a warning crack. It had crushed his right knee.
All winter had passed before he could walk again, with
a permanent limp. His knee ached in damp weather,

too, so he could predict storms.

It didn't ache now, despite the thunder. What could it mean?

Nor was a limp his only wound in a lifetime of wrestling trees. An oak had pinched off the last three fingers of his left hand. Though he was barely twenty years old, his legs and arms were scarred from branches and his own misguided axe cuts, but they were huge and brawny too, for what the forest had taken away it had replaced elsewhere. Because he was forever tearing through brush and chopping branches, Gull wore no cloth, but only leather, kilt and tunic. Even his long chestnut hair was drawn back with a rawhide thong. He wore clogs of hickory he'd carved himself, good protection for his toes, though they clumped mournfully on wood or stone floors.

Life in the forest had hardened Gull in other ways, though he scarcely knew it. Working alone, cutting and felling and solving problems the day long, he'd developed his own way of doing things, and was apt to ignore advice or compliments. In fact, the village wags said, working with mules had made him muleheaded. And as for keeping company with a simpleton, it was hard to tell which was which.

Now Gull veered down a brushy deer trail that would take him to the meadows sooner. And keep him hidden. All this strangeness meant trouble.

They'd been expecting it.

One moon ago, the villagers of White Ridge had tumbled out of bed to a ferocious warbling hiss. Dashing outdoors, everyone had seen the streak of yellow-white fire burn the night. Then a crash to the faraway northwest had shaken the ground, and flames had lit the horizon. A distant reach of forest had burned for days, a column of smoke blackening the sun. Finally late winter rains had doused the inferno and the smoke stopped.

Folks had not spoken of the event and had silenced the children's queries—everyone recognized an omen, a portent of disaster. And day by day, people cast glances over their shoulders, waiting for it to arrive.

Today was the day. Two thunderbolts close together, a weird floating bladder of jibbering rascals. What . . .

Gull whirled at a slithering behind him. A snake . . .
No, his sister.

Greensleeves clutched her ratty shawl and chirruped like a raccoon, a question full of fear.

"Damn it!" her brother snapped, for the noise had startled him. "I told you to stay!"

The simpleton bobbed her head, flinched as if he'd struck her. Tears ran down her cheeks and wet her lips.

"Oh, very well. Come along. But quick, now!" Gull never could resist her crying. But half the time he couldn't guess what she wanted.

Gull brought Greensleeves to the woods each day to keep her from the village. Between her uprooting gardens, shielding animals from harm and work, poking in the bread ovens, filching babies from their cradles, and otherwise being a pest, everyone agreed the woods were best for her. There she was happy, could poke and pry and play with animals to her heart's content while Gull watched over her—as best he could. By unspoken agreement, and the brawn of the brother's arms, no man in the valley would molest her, and strangers were rare, but sometimes Greensleeves would be gone for hours, and Gull worried. Otherwise, he found his sister no trouble, welcomed her company as he would a dog's.

Yet, that the two prospered in the Whispering Woods was another sign of queer natures. No one else in White Ridge ever ventured near. The leaves and trees were too full of talk, of "whispering," for normal folk to abide: they hinted the voices came from monsters or devils or elves or other dark beings. The unending mumble and chatter and hush of the leaves had bothered Gull as a boy, but now he scarce heard it. It touched Greensleeves with less effect than rain.

Now, seizing his sister by the hand, he led her from the woods to see what was after their village, the only home they'd ever known.

Brush and briars grew thickest along the edge of the forest where the sunlight was strongest. Standing at the end of the trail, they were flanked by bracken taller than their heads. Shielded, Gull thought, and a good thing.

The valley called White Ridge was a crazy quilt of colors. Where the forest broke, running in strips here and there was meadow, tall yellow-green grass dotted with blue and yellow wildflowers. Between and all around were stretches of mossy rocks and hardscrabble ledge. Down the center were the only fertile tracts, pockets of rich riverbed loam left from when the valley's stream had been a mighty river. The stream ran still, circling rocks and rippling over streaks of lime that gave the divided village its name. Thirty cottages stood far apart, each surrounded by hip-high rock walls that protected the scanty gardens from animals. The cottages were stone, with roofs of thatch or shingles or sod. A mill astraddle the stream creaked to the south, and an alehouse trickled a plume of white smoke. A bony road ran from the northern ridges,

crossed the stream on the one-cart bridge, then sank
into the bogs to the south. Along its eastern edge, the
valley sported another forest called the Wild Woods,
yet one the villagers would visit.

All of Gull's twenty years, White Ridge had been a
quiet place, where the biggest fight all year would be
from Seal's sons stealing one of Bryony's hogs. No one
knew what today would bring. The woodcutter saw his
hunched father, Brown Bear, his back broken by the
same tree that had crippled Gull, and the thin shape
of his mother, Bittersweet. Ranged alongside were his
brothers and sisters. Gull waved his axe, but his family
didn't see. They watched the northern ridge, as did
Gull.

Atop the lime-streaked ridge where the road
dipped, perched like a herd of wolves, was a collection
of colorful characters such as Gull had only heard of in
legends.

Foremost was a stout woman in a robe of brown
with jets of yellow along the sleeves and hems. Her
head was bare, black glossy hair combed straight back.
The woman raised beringed hands and pointed to an
empty reach of meadow on her right.

Though Gull had never seen one before, he knew
what this woman was. As the elders prayed, "May the
gods keep us hale and hearty, and spare us the ravages
of any . . .

" . . . wizard."

Alongside the wizard, lining the ridge, were two
dozen soldiers in armor like fish scales. They wore
tunics and kilts of red, and red-plumed helmets. Each
carried a round burnished shield and short sword, and
a javelin slung at his back. Gull had only seen three

soldiers in his life: a motley diseased trio that passed
through the village when he was young. The elders
had hefted clubs to keep the rogues moving, but even
so, a piglet and two chickens had gone missing. These
red-garbed soldiers on the heights were different, looking strong and quiet and capable, deadly as snakes.

A force like that, Gull realized, could kill every person in White Ridge before they drew three breaths.

Yet odder still was what appeared in the meadow.

At first Gull saw nothing. Then Greensleeves
chirped. Something . . . grew . . . amidst the grass.

Grew very quickly.

As Gull watched, a figure no taller than a child
flickered among the nodding blue wildflowers. Then it
was shoulder-high to them, then waist-high.

And in seconds, the figure was—Gull tried to
guess—twenty feet high? A giant, something from the
old stories. Fat around the middle, thick-legged and
flat-footed, the giant wore clothing stitched of faded
patches, most yellowed, but some painted with stripes
and even a red dragon. In each enormous knotty
hand, the giant carried a scarred tree branch for a
club. Two clubs, thought Gull, to go with its two
heads.

The heads were bald, sallow, slant-eyed, veined.
One head frowned at the wizard. The other watched a
murder of crows take off from the Wild Woods. Gull
could see that this being was slow to think.

Yet there were more wonders, appearing all over
the valley, until Gull thought he'd been brained by a
widowmaker and dreamed it all. Yet no dream could
match this amazing scene.

Cantering from the Wild Woods, in matching strides,
came a pair of half-horse, half-humans. Centaurs, the
word came. Their flanks were roan, reddish white, and

warpainted with handprints and runes. Their torsos were hidden by fluted, painted breastplates and helmets. They carried feathered lances longer than their long loping bodies.

High above the army on the ridge, drifting on the wind, went the round bladder-and-basket thing and its jabbering crew. Screaming like monkeys, the rowdies let loose a rain of missiles, iron spikes. They jutted into the ground well short of the ridge, and red-clad soldiers hooted and waved their swords. The bladder sailed on, sinking lower, until it struck trees to the north. The minute warriors quarreled as they spilled through the trees. Even Gull could see they contributed little beyond amusement.

But if they were *attacking* the red soldiers, then who had loosed them?

Greensleeves bleated, and Gull gaped elsewhere. The festival on the ridge was only half the show.

Southward, nestled against the Whispering Woods, was another entourage equally as strange.

At the forefront was another gaudy wizard. This one had a head of stiff yellow curls and a brushy mustache, and a robe sewn in layers, dark blue at the bottom shading to yellow at the waist, then flowing like a rainbow to pink and red at the stiffened shoulders. Gull had the random thought: Where did wizards have their clothes made?

Behind this wizard was a wagon train like a gypsy camp. Five wagons formed a circle with retainers huddled at the center. Gull could pick out a fat woman, slender girls bright as birds, and hard men, armed, who leaned against the wagon seats to watch the action.

The muleteer noticed something had gone wrong. The horse and mule teams had been loosed from the traces, probably so they wouldn't panic and dash off with the wagons, then led out of harm's way farther along the wood's edge. Yet there were two smoking craters where the thunderbolts had struck. Stony soil and moss had been blasted clear down to bedrock. At the lip of one crater lay a dead horse, white, and the hindquarters of a bay. Of the other mounts there was no sign. Bolted, probably. Or blown out of existence.

There was more strangeness to come. In fact, Gull guessed, it had barely begun.

One of the floating bladder teams had already left the ground. Three more vehicles bobbed just above the ground, tethered like balky horses. Around them squabbled two dozen green-gray jokers with shocks of black or gray hair.

A weird cry ululated across the valley. The striped wizard held aloft a stone jar from which spiraled a vapor that slowly, slowly coalesced into a figure, a big one like the giant to the north. Yet this figure refused to take solid shape, remaining cloudlike, misty. And as the sky blue figure wafted over the stony mossy ground, it sprinkled cloud drops from its fingertips. Where they landed, there arose bluish warriors, male and female, with long white hair and curious curved swords or black-studded clubs: barbarians. A dozen, two dozen, three.

Beside Gull, Greensleeves made a chittering noise like a question. She had noticed a mousehole at their feet and bent to investigate.

Still, Gull answered her, framing his thoughts. "A fight. There's going to be a big fight. A war. That's what wizards do, war on one another. And death and destruction follow in their shadow."

He caught Greensleeves by the shoulder and tugged her upright. "And we've got to cross to our family before all hell breaks loose. Come on!"

Clutching his axe in one hand and his sister's arm in the other, he loped from the woods. In the distance, his family finally noticed them, and villagers cheered encouragement and hope. Dashing, panting, they cleared the meadows and rocky reaches, gained the edge of the village, the first houses.

Too late.

With a roar, twoscore or more red soldiers mustered on the ridge, reinforcements brought to the fore. They raised their short swords, bellowed again, and charged down the ledge slope. The centaurs paced them at a gallop. To Gull's left, the blue barbarians sent up a hiss and surged forward, curved blades and clubs slashing like sickles after grain.

Gull and Greensleeves were caught square in the middle.

The woodcutter skidded to a halt, too breathless to curse. They'd gained the village, but the only place to safely cross the stream was the bridge, and within minutes the red soldiers would pass it.

Nor could they stay in the village long, for the blue fighters closed.

"Bells of Kormus! Back! We've got to get back!" The woodcutter whipped around, aiming for the sheltering woods. Greensleeves skipped and jogged alongside, half-flying.

It wasn't a hundred yards back to the woods, and Gull pounded flat out. Yet something twinkled in the air before him, like rain dropping through sunshine. A wall of it, glittering brighter, then turning dark and murky. Brown, like muddy water.

Before his eyes, a wall of thorns cut off their retreat. It wasn't an orderly wall. It was more a mound such as overgrew a ruin or barrow. But it was high, taller than Gull could reach with his axe, so thick he could not see through it. Brambles, they were, gray-brown and dead near the roots, curling green and soft in the upper branches. Impassable to anything larger than a chipmunk.

Swearing bitterly, the woodcutter hunted a way around. But the wall zigzagged from the northern ridge to the river's edge. The wall even hooked along the ridge face, behind the red soldiers, cutting them off from their wizard. *The southern striped wizard must have conjured it*, Gull thought. *He's boxed them nicely. And us.*

Now where?

Gull cast about. He could hide in a stone house, but instinct told him that would be unwise—even a rabbit dug two bolt-holes. He could splash across the river, but he'd have to drag Greensleeves, and she hated swimming.

With a roar and clatter, the armies clashed not a hundred yards away.

Even Gull, who knew nothing of wars except what he'd heard in stories, could see that the red soldiers were professionals and the blue barbarians untrained savages. The red soldiers maintained a tight phalanx, two deep, that bristled with steel. They tramped to war, in unison, round shields forming a wall, and chanted a war song as they marched.

The blue fighters, who Gull saw were both dyed and tattooed blue, were long-jawed and tusked, with long white hair in various braids. Men and women alike wore tanned hides painted in fantastic patterns. Their mode of attack was to outshriek one another, slash the air and then their opponents with curved swords, or else bludgeon them with obsidian-headed war clubs.

Yet their blood ran scarlet. The red soldiers worked in teams, one partner covering the other. Gull saw a blue warrior lock on to a round shield, slice low for a red soldier's greaves covering his shins. The soldier's partner delivered a short stab to a blue throat that sprayed blood over all of them. At the same time, the first soldier shot his blade to keep back another blue warrior, who lost a hand to the partner's quick chop. That laid two blue fighters on the turf with no damage to the red.

So it went up and down the line. The blue valued bravery and bravado, the red cold-eyed teamwork. One blue barbarian leaped like a deer to clamber over the shield wall. Rather than resist, red soldiers in the front rank ducked, fobbed her high in the air, delivering her to the soldiers behind, who sank swords in her belly. Yet even dying the blue barbarian fought, and her black stone war club slammed a red-clad neck. The stricken soldier was propped by his fellows in the rear as blue barbarians fell like wheat.

Gull feared the red soldiers would dispatch the barbarians, then fall on whoever else was near. He didn't waste time gawping, but grabbed his sister again—she pointed at something in the sky, murmuring—and dragged her south along the wall of thorns. They could make for the river, try to cross, or perhaps find a gap in the thorn wall, a pocket to hide in.

Except Gull discovered what Greensleeves found so interesting up above.

Iron stakes rained on the ground before them. Spikes bounced off rocks with clangs, quivered in dirt, chopped thorns. Gull looked up.

Not thirty feet above were two flying bladders. Up

close, Gull saw contraptions that were ill assembled, with the bladders much patched, the ropes badly spliced, the baskets dinged and splintered from rough landings. Gray-green titches with pointed ears, some bald, some gray-haired, dressed in crude hides from goats and raccoons and skunks and others, leered at them. Scrawny and ugly as they were, Gull couldn't tell if they were male or female or neither. They'd dumped a wicker basket full of spikes, which dropped straight as arrows to pierce a victim's skull—had they bothered to aim.

There were six or more goons in each basket. Goblins, Gull thought, mischievous villains from children's stories.

A basket immediately above found trouble. A pointy-headed goblin raised a stake to hurl down, but pierced the bladder overhead instead. Other goblins shrieked at him, slapped his head, wrestled for holds in the ropes, screamed as the bladder deflated.

Abruptly, it split, a long rent zipping to the top. The jury-rigged mess collapsed. It crashed half on the wall of thorns, spilling wailing occupants like chicks tumbled from a nest. The other bladder floated serenely away, its crew jeering their fallen companions. One even threw a stake into their midst with a laugh, and another leaned overside to piss on them. Yet that one screamed when someone behind booted him half out of the basket.

Gull could only gape in wonder. These idiots were more dangerous to their own side.

He changed his mind quickly.

Tough as wildcats, the handful of goblins bounced and recovered, then snatched weapons from their belts: flint knives and knotty clubs. One bony female pointed at Greensleeves and shrieked.

"Meat!"

CHAPTER

2

Small, stupid, and squabbly they might be, but Gull found that these gray-green goblins were fast.

Bounding like a fox, a fiend leaped onto Greensleeves's breast. Clutching at her shawl, the goblin bit at her neck. The girl screamed and beat with fluttering hands, and both fell.

Gull swore. He could hardly swing an axe at his sister. Instead he caught the goblin by the neck, tore the thing off the girl. He could smell the creature now, musty as an old haystack or worm-eaten carcass. Her hairline was dotted with fleabites. He waggled the goblin, twisted, tried to snap her neck like a chicken. But the goblin was tough as rawhide, and raked filthy claws down the woodcutter's arm. Shocked, he let go.

More goblins rushed, most from behind.

"Greensleeves, stay down!" he roared, and prayed she'd obey.

Whirling in a circle, the woodcutter swung his axe. The heavy blade sliced the air—and three goblins.

The first tried to dodge and had an arm nipped off. Rolling over and over, howling, the wretch sprayed greenish blood. The second ducked but lost the top of his skull. He reached up a questing hand and touched leaking brains. The third was cut clean in half, and left her legs standing while her trunk flopped behind.

The remaining four didn't pause. They ran like rats in all directions. One plunged straight into the thorn hedge, half-impaling himself.

Greensleeves trembled like a rabbit, whimpering. Gull didn't bother to console her, just jerked her upright and ran.

Noise and stink filled the valley. Warbling war cries rang out, and a horse's scream. Through a thorn hedge Gull heard more goblins squabbling, and a heavy, steady thumping he couldn't identify. He smelled blood on the wind, and the acrid tang of sweat. And everywhere, smoke that was not cooking fires.

Dashing along the thorn wall, Gull hoisted a leg over a stone wall around Beebalm's house. Thorns had buried one corner, but he hoped to slip behind the house and get out of sight. Fumbling with his heavy axe, he caught Greensleeves around the waist and lifted her over the wall.

And cursed. He'd interrupted a pair of goblins gutting a brown goat.

The animal's glazed eye blinked as the pair hacked out its dripping innards. Anger flooded through Gull. That goat had been a pet of Beebalm's, raised by hand when its mother was taken by wolves. The woodcutter kicked at the goblins, but his bad knee betrayed him and he crashed atop the wall. Stones rolled underfoot and he landed on his rump. He hoped he hadn't snapped his arrows and bow. Fuming, he struggled to his feet.

The goblins had grabbed their bloody dinner and run. Gull was so angry he spit. "Run, you thievin' bastards! Run, you louses!" What right did they have? These goblins and giants and soldiers and the bastardy wizards that fetched them? What right did they have to destroy a village that was home to so many good folk?

A thrashing, crashing, crushing of thorn bushes broke into his thoughts. The sky went black, as if a thunderhead passed.

A towering foot like a tree trunk stove in Beebalm's house.

Gull gawked. Rearing above him, tall and long as a barn, clomped a . . . wooden and sheet iron horse?

Was it alive? From underneath, it looked like a walking millworks. Instead of guts, the thing sported wheels and gears and leather straps over pulleys. A mechanical heart turned camshafts that rotated the legs at the hips, then fistfuls of couplings Gull couldn't follow. Nor did he see any power source: no steam, no fire, no falling water. Or anyone controlling it.

Yet the thing walked like a stiff-legged horse as it tried to pull free the leg trapped in the crumpled house. It must have been monstrously heavy, for its flanks were slabs of rusty sheet iron. Its head resembled a blunt-nosed horse, though the eyes were articulated cones. For the life of him, Gull couldn't tell if this clockwork beast had a brain locked in its boxy head or not. Could magic alone move something so massive?

Then he had to dodge, for the beast tore loose of the wreckage, sending shingles and dusty rafters flying. With clicks and whirs and hums, the mechanical monster stumped away toward whatever its part in the battle might be.

Red soldiers sent up a shout. They splintered their phalanx, for there were no more blue barbarians, only blue bodies leaking red blood.

With mounting horror, Gull watched the soldiers charge anew. Straight for the villagers on the eastern shore.

"Noooooo!!!!"

Villagers shrieked and scattered, some to the Wild Woods, some toward the village, others to random houses. Howling soldiers slashed at the first to come near, cutting them down without regard for sex or age. An elderly man, a child, a goodwife collapsed like wheat before scythes. A young woman who tried to defend them was yanked off her feet by her yellow hair, then belted senseless. Gull recognized her too: Cowslip, Badger's daughter. He yelped and roared helplessly.

Gull craned to glimpse his family, but saw only panicked people dashing every which way. He prayed for his father, who couldn't run with his damaged back, and prayed for his mother, too, who would never leave her husband's side.

And what could he do? He still had Greensleeves, and no place to hide her. And he himself couldn't run, for his bad knee was apt to cave in. Yet he must aid them. Desperately, he looked for shelter. Would Beebalm's root cellar be intact?

He spotted a hole torn through the wall of thorns by the clockwork. Whole bushes had been uprooted, forming shallow pockets. One would do.

"Come, Greensleeves!" He tried to think of something to reassure her, but even her befuddled brain noticed shrills across the river. "Come, Sister! We'll play hide-and-seek! Here!"

Cursing, juggling his axe, yet gently lest she bolt like a deer and run to slaughter, he guided his kin to a gap in the wall. The smell of thornbush sap was bitter and green in his nostrils, the smell of fresh earth like an open grave. Pushing and cooing, he folded Greensleeves into a pocket like a baby rabbit.

Oddly, he noted the soil here was red, red as a sunset.

He caught her chin to make her focus. "Stay here! Understand? *Don't* come out until you hear my voice! Or Mother's. Or Father's. Understand?"

The eyes stayed vacant as a cow's. Gull could have wept, but there wasn't time. "Stay!" he finished, and turned.

Back to battle, whatever it brought.

Trying to watch everywhere at once—he'd seen more monsters and myths in a day than he'd heard of in a lifetime—Gull scuttled from house to house. He knew them all, and their families: Catclaw's, Snowblossom's, Toad's. He'd played in these houses as a child, slept and eaten in most of them, fought boys and chased girls and been taught by their parents. The people of White Ridge were more than a village, they were almost a tribe, where debts and allegiances and feuds ran back generations.

Yet all this history might be wiped out today at the hands of wizards and their minions. Red soldiers fanned out after the villagers. Their only goal could be rape and slaughter, for the villagers owned little but their bodies and lives.

Gull raced to another house, his knee twanging at every jolt, stopped by the house of Snowblossom. Through an unshuttered window he heard a girl hissing and cursing. And a man's laugh.

In the dooryard before the tiny house he saw the
scale-armored back of a soldier. He held a girl's hands
aloft while another soldier tore at her clothing. The
girl kicked, writhed, tried to bite, but the men were
too strong for her to wriggle free. Growling in anger,
Gull made up his mind.

He settled his long mulewhip in his weaker, finger-
lacking left hand, for he'd learned to rein with his
right. He caught a fresh grip on his slick-sweaty axe
handle.

He'd never killed a man before. He prayed for the
strength to do it now.

Rehearsing in his mind, he spun around the corner,
hopped to get the proper distance. Two paces behind
the rearmost soldier—the stretch from his sledge to
Knothead's ear. Right, then . . .

"*Hya-yah!*" He shouted his muleteer's cry to bring
the man's head up, and slashed his whip. Braided
blacksnake sliced the air, looped around the man's
neck. As the tail wrapped a second time, Gull set his
brawny wrist and yanked.

Taken by surprise, suddenly strangling, the soldier
was hoicked clean off his feet. Loosing the captive, he
clutched for his throat, then Gull jerked him onto his
back. He crashed with a metallic jangle.

The captive was Cowslip of the yellow hair,
snatched across the river and dragged here, for her
gown's hem was wet to the knees. Red-faced from
screaming and snapping at the soldiers, she looked as
stunned as they at the rescue. Then the red soldier
behind her, black-bearded, bronzed by a distant sun,
snatched at her hair and his sword pommel.

Gull could guess his plan. Use Cowslip as a shield.
The woodcutter shouted, "'Slip, get down! Drop!"

Recognizing a friend, Cowslip threw herself flat.

The soldier's hand closed on empty air. He roared an obscenity and squatted for his shield, propped against a hitching post.

But Gull was ready. Flicking his heavy axe over his shoulder, he pegged it square. Blade and haft whirled end over end, then one face of the double bits thudded into the soldier's chest.

Under different circumstances, Gull would have grinned. Tossing his axe was a favorite trick, something to while away rainy hours in a barn, something to awe children.

Never had he imagined he'd kill a man with it.

Incredibly, the soldier was not bowled over. He stood stunned and immobile, put a hand to the steel blade that split his armor and breastbone. Confused, he pushed at the blade and only shoved himself sideways.

A jerk pulled Gull half-over.

He'd forgotten the soldier at the end of his whip.

Like a monstrous scaly pike dying on shore, the man tugged wildly to free his throat. Gull had been so absorbed in the axe trick, he'd slacked his sweaty grip. But mostly he was astonished at having killed a man. The idea took getting used to.

The soldier didn't give him time. Thrashing, he rolled to his knees. Strong fingers had loosened the whip. Rasping, he rose and unsheathed his short sword, murder on his blackened face.

And Gull stood empty-handed.

Could he kick the man with his hickory clogs? His knee would buckle and he'd fall. Would that save him?

The soldier grinned evilly, drew his arm back for the stab, that quick death stroke that had felled the blue barbarians.

But the soldier never finished his stroke.

Instead he grunted, half turned, and fell.

Cowslip stood over him, grunting herself. She'd snatched up the other sword and plunged it two-handed into the man's back. The man twitched, cried out, clawed to get away, but Cowslip leaned on the pommel, shoved it sideways to slice his liver and lights. The soldier dropped like a poleaxed steer. Cowslip ripped the blade free and whacked him alongside the ear, splitting skin to the bone. But he was dead.

Behind her, the axed man had finally fallen. Stepping around the protruding haft of Gull's axe, Cowslip took aim and chopped his throat. A farm girl who'd slaughtered pigs and chickens and cows had no qualms about spilling the blood of a rapist.

Blood ran off the sword like a butcher's blade. Cowslip faced Gull, then clutched her shorn gown together, blushing. She and Gull and all the village youngsters had always bathed nude in the swimming hole below the ledge, had seen each other naked a hundred times, but Cowslip was suddenly shy. She asked, "Are you all right?"

Gull averted his eyes from her torn bodice. "I, uh, should ask you that . . . " Funny, he'd known Cowslip all his life, yet had never noticed how pretty she was, how strong and capable and smart. He had the odd thought: She'd make a fine wife.

"I'm fine. Better than them." She spit on the whipped man, but Gull thought she did it rather than face him. "But what shall we do now?"

Gull blinked again. Oh, yes, he remembered, there was a battle on. Two battles: wizards' army against army, and the villagers against all. Shaking his head, he retrieved his whip and axe. There was a nick in the blade's edge, and he felt again that irrational anger. He'd forged this axe himself, and the soldiers had spoiled it. And rats were digging in Snowblossom's barn! Where were the dogs that should have killed them?

With a start he recalled his family. His mind was wandering, like Greensleeves's.

"We must . . . " he tried to sort through confusion, "I don't know, gather who we can and hie for the woods, I suppose." Cowslip clutched her new-won sword and ragged dress and waited. Why, he wondered, did she attend his ideas? He didn't know what to do. "These wizards will ravage the village, fill it with death."

A sizzling in the sky cut him off. Both craned to look.

Up on the ridge, above the new thorn wall, the brown-and-yellow-robed wizard raised a curved horn like a ram's. The wizard called something, then blew into the mouthpiece. From the bell belched a fireball big as a melon. The sizzling sounded again. Gull and Cowslip tracked the burning path. Gull recalled two earlier fireballs had blasted dirt from bedrock, killed a brace of horses. Where would this fall?

A whiff of smoke floated to his nose. Sap, bitter and green, burned. A crackling sounded close.

Gull dashed around the house.

The wall of thorns was afire in three places.

"*Greensleeves!*"

Gull dashed headlong for Beebalm's house, galloped around to the mangled thorn hedges. Fire crackled amidst brambles. He felt its heat on his sweating cheeks and forehead. Smoke choked him, burned his eyes. He kept his axe aloft lest he blunder into his sister fleeing the fire.

"Greensleeves! Greenie, where are you?"

Thorns scratched his hands and arms and legs. They stung on his forearm where the goblin had raked him. Cursing, fumbling, he swatted at smoke and shorn branches to find the hollow where he'd hidden his sister.

She was gone.

It was the right hollow, for stooping showed her footprints. But where she'd gone he couldn't tell. There weren't even drops of blood from thorn pricks.

Gull backed from the smoke, wiped streaming eyes. What now, by the gods? Where to look? What to do?

As if the gods answered, thunder rolled. Gull glanced up. Clouds had swept in, thickened, deepened. This thunder was real. Maybe the rain would douse the fires. Maybe the town could yet be saved.

Yet the gods today were mischievous, vindictive, out to bedevil him. The earth under his feet jumped.

Distant screams, close-by crackling, the bleating of a goat all ceased.

Gull breathed low in the quiet. He'd felt this before. Once, as a child.

Groaning sounded all around. Pebbles by his feet jittered and danced. The groaning became a grinding, and the world trembled.

Earthquake!

The ground trembled so hard Gull could barely keep his feet. He felt his guts rumbling, his teeth chattering, imagined his spine crumbling and brain swimming. Then the earth bucked harder and he fell. Yet as he landed, the soil stopped moving.

How long could the earth shiver like this before it crumbled entirely?

Shaking all over, Gull scrambled upright. Of all the frights he'd ever endured, this was the worst. If the very earth could turn traitor, what could be counted upon?

Silence rang in his ears. A child cried out once and was hushed. Was there more, or . . . ?

The full force of the quake hit.

The ground jumped as if someone had snapped a carpet. Gull flipped completely over onto his rump. He dropped his weapons and clutched the quivering soil. A roar like a waterfall threatened to drown him. The stone wall around Beebalm's smashed house spilled apart. A crack opened near his foot. Another crack rippled by his hand along the edge of the thorn hedge.

In a flash Gull understood something of magic: the wizard had not merely conjured the thorn hedge, he'd actually transported a stretch of brambled earth from some distant place to here. Part of another village, another valley, had been shoehorned into his. Thus a crack erupted where the local black soil met the hedge's red soil. What power these wizards controlled!

Including the power to move the earth.

Gull could do no more than cling like a fly to a cowpat. He looked around for anything solid, but even the sky shook. Or perhaps his eyes jiggled in their sockets.

Above the primeval roar came the splintering of house beams and the ringing of roof slates crashing on stone. The woodcutter recognized them: house beams rending. Stones rumbled, roof slates shattered like glass.

Then it was quiet and still.

A temblor or two rippled by, but that was all.

Gull rose, but had to clutch his thighs. His legs

shook as if the earthquake still lingered in his bones.

He cast about, to see how the village had fared, what damage there was.

But the village was gone.

Of thirty cottages scattered throughout the valley, only one or two still stood. A few more made of wood had their roofs stove in. But most were heaps of rubbish, stone and wood and thatch mashed together. Stone walls were scattered over gardens and pathways and dooryards. Cracks in the earth ran everywhere, some a handspan wide, some long and deep enough to swallow a cow. Even the river was gone, the watercourse dried to a trickle. The quake must have split the riverbed somewhere north of the ridge. And they needed water badly. Cooking fires shaken by rubble set many houses smoldering, then fanned by a rising breeze, ignited.

White Ridge, his home, was no more.

In white-hot, impotent anger, Gull clutched his axe haft so hard it should have broken. Wizards had done this, destroyed his home in their senseless battle.

Raising his tool-turned-weapon, Gull swore, "On my *honor*, I will *kill* any wizard I meet, without *pause*, without *mercy*! You hear me, you mercenary bastards?"

As if in answer, lightning split the sky, yellow forks scattered 'round the compass. Rain slashed down, cold and hard, drops denting the ruined earth.

Yet the battle raged on.

Through a gap in the thorn hedge, uprooted and tumbled and jumbled as everything else, Gull heard a frightful banging and clanging. Dazed, he turned to see through the haze of hard rain.

The two-headed giant had run into something its own size, the clockwork beast. Rain soaked the giant's clothes and ran rust down the iron flanks of the construct. A club in each hand, the giant pounded the sheet iron and wooden monster as if flailing grain. The beast ignored, or did not feel, the blows. With no offensive weapons of its own, it could only march at the giant and butt with its boxy head. It mashed its nose against the giant's middle, where particolored sails were clumsily stitched, and shoved. With two legs against four, the giant gave ground, both heads frowning, clubbing all the while. He bashed off a jutting wooden ear, splintered a beam along its spine, but did little other harm. The mechanical beast pushed and pushed, four legs churning and clumping, internal gears whirring, and the giant was steadily backed toward the Whispering Woods. Every blow of the tree-club on the iron flanks rang like a gong.

Then the clumsy giant slipped on mud or wet grass. Off-balance, he crashed heavily. The clockwork beast mindlessly walked over him, heavy wooden hooves mashing. Struggling to rise, the giant latched onto a leg just above the fetlock, near a complicated joint. Wrenching, he tried to pull himself out from under. But the joint broke and the leg came free.

Rain running in his eyes, Gull watched, fascinated, as the clockwork beast stepped off the giant. Three-legged, it clumped away. Mindless, it described a vast circle like a beheaded chicken. The giant, a foot trapped in a cleft, tried in vain to get up.

It was set upon by a six-headed dragon that swooped from the concealing rain.

The woodcutter gasped, unconsciously moved to a heap of rubble for shelter. The dragon was all gray, as if carved from stone. It was fat-bodied and spraddle-footed, and slow. Gull had always heard dragons were called worms, or wyrms, or even snakes, for they had long sinuous bodies. And only one head.

Then he recalled the old story. Barktooth Warbeard had fought a multiheaded beast. A hydra.

Fat and slow, the beast was still deadly as three pythons. The trapped giant had time for one cry before a fanged head struck. One enormous hand disappeared into the hydra's maw. The giant screamed from both mouths. Another head sank fangs into his wrist. Another bit higher, into his biceps. The powerless giant howled as its arms were shredded.

Gull shuddered. He felt sorry for the giant, for he could sense no malice in it. Anything that thick-witted could hold but little hate in its heart. Yet it had agreed to fight for a wizard, and now would die by another conjured monster.

Rain intensified, and the combatants were lost to sight behind the dense wet curtain. Gull turned, scanning. He had his own problems. How to find his sister? How to help his fellow villagers, now that the village was gone?

A great despair settled, like a yoke of stone dropped on his shoulders. He almost asked, Why bother? With the village wiped out, whither the villagers? Yet he ignored the gloom and plodded away. Find his sister. Plenty enough to do.

He called against the darkness and rain, "Greensleeves! Greensleeves, where are you?"

Hissing and the drip of rain sang in his ears.

"Greennnnsleevvvvvessss!"

"Here! Here I am!"

Gull stopped in surprise. What? His sister couldn't talk.

Hobbling—his bad knee had been wrenched twice and now there was rain too—he limped around the ruins of another house.

Square into a pack of soldiers.

CHAPTER

3

"We know you've got it! Dig it up or eat cold steel! *Now!*"

Hefting his sodden whip and slick axe, Gull picked his way around a barn. Who had called out? Who was shouting.

Peeking through a knothole, he saw.

Another moral of the old stories was that soldiers were greedy. These were no exception. A half dozen had rounded up twenty villagers at swordpoint and herded them among the ruins. The drenching rain edged their silver scales with rust, made the red hairs of their horsetail plumes stick up in clumps. Swatting and jabbing, the soldiers barked harsh orders. "Dig up your fortunes and you won't be hurt! Disobey and you get this! *Move! Move!*"

One soldier with epaulets of gold braid pricked Seal in the back with a rain-rusting sword. Seal was a big-bellied man, a lazy bully, a lifelong foe of Gull's. Yet threatened by strangers, Gull viewed him as a brother.

There were more, too. Gull's family was here. His mother Bittersweet, his hunched father Brown Bear. His sisters Rainfall, Angelwing, and Poppyseed. His brothers Lion and Cub. But where was Sparrow Hawk? And where Greensleeves?

Their enemies dead, the heartless mercenaries had fallen to looting. They knew villagers buried their few coins, usually out back, but sometimes within the house itself. They'd kill a few and set the rest to digging.

The woodcutter pondered what to do, then suddenly jumped so high he almost rapped his head on the eaves of the barn. Someone had touched his wrist.

Sparrow Hawk.

The boy grinned nervously at his big brother. Sparrow Hawk had his mother's impish sense of humor, her infectious grin. Tousled red hair was plastered over his head by the rain, and rivulets ran past his freckled sunburned nose. He whispered, "What are you hiding for, Gull? Aren't you gonna get them?"

Rather than set down a weapon, the woodcutter wrapped a huge arm around the boy's head and squeezed him close. "Hush up, bonehead! We need a plan!"

"What?" The boy squirmed to see through a crack between boards. "Can't we just rush 'em? I've got a weapon too!" He held up a rusty spike, one dropped by the goblins.

Gull almost sighed. Eleven summers old, and the child was ready to take on the world. Gull couldn't condemn him, nor his enthusiasm, but he did have to keep him from harm.

"Look, Hawk. Take that pigsticker and circle around, way 'round. I'll charge them from this side, and you can be the reserve, pink one in the back—uh oh!"

Looking through the knothole, Gull saw a soldier suddenly snatch a boy, Chipmunk, by the hair. He laid his sword against the lad's forehead and bellowed, "I want your silver! Or the child loses his scalp!" Chipmunk yelped as the soldier sawed. Skin parted in a crimson line. Rain washed blood into the boy's tight-shut eyes. A mother shrilled.

Seal, normally a coward, stepped forward to defend his son. But a soldier poked his sword into Seal's fat gut, and laughed as he gasped. Seal's wife, Feverfew, protested, and the soldier slapped her with the flat. Another raised his blade. "Kill a few! That'll move the rest—"

Gull swore. "Get moving, Hawk! Go way 'round!" He shoved his brother, who took off along the back of the barn. Then he charged around the other side, swinging his axe behind him. "Join me! Arm yourselves! *Yaaaaaaahhhhh!!!*"

As he'd hoped, his sudden attack stunned the soldiers, so some did nothing. Yet older veterans moved like lightning. Four slid together, back-to-back, and scuttled behind the villagers to determine the source of the menace.

The young soldier holding Chipmunk balked, tugged for the shield slung on his back. Streaming wet, huge, and screaming, Gull leaped within striking range and swung. Belatedly, the killer raised his sword, and Gull slammed him under the armpit with the full strength of his felling axe. Knocked three feet sideways, the soldier grunted and folded over the blade. Heart stopped, he slumped and slid off the axe head.

There's one, thought Gull, already swinging. *Five left*.

One soldier kept backing away from the fallen one, ready to run. Perhaps this one didn't like axes. Without delay, Gull hoisted his rain-slick axe and charged the knot of four soldiers. But now they were prepared. They'd assumed their double rank without crowding, as Gull hoped they might. They swung their shields into place, a wall of steel.

I'm going to die here, Gull thought. *But at least my family is safe. I hope they find Greensleeves.*

Changing tactics, he braked in the mud, stopping just out of sword range, croaked another war cry, and switched his swing overhead as if splitting cordwood. He had some advantage. They'd expected a sideways swing they could deflect with their shields. And at the end of his axe haft, he had the longer reach.

The sun-bronzed men in front grimaced, anticipating pain. They were fast, and strong, and raised their shields to block. But this was no dandy's war axe, a thin blade and lightweight, made for cutting flesh, but an eight pound mallet of sharpened steel made for dropping oaks.

The axe struck like an avalanche. It punched through a wood and iron shield, buckling and twisting, then crushed bones in the arm behind. A veteran hissed.

With a savage grunt, Gull jerked on the haft. The blade tore free. Too fast. The woodcutter lost his balance and slammed on his rump in the mud.

Good thing, too, for the man's partner lunged for Gull's guts with his sword. He missed, pinking Gull's leather tunic. But the other front ranker skipped forward to deliver the deathblow. Gull saw the blade flicker like a snake's tongue, threw up his hands to block it, knowing he'd only lose fingers before being filleted.

But the swordsman staggered back. A stone struck him in the face. Teeth crunched and he howled. More rocks struck the soldiers, who parried with their shields.

Gull kicked the wounded man's knee with his hickory clog, then scurried away on all fours. He scrambled past his father, who directed the attack.

"Get 'em, White Ridgers!" Even half-bent, at half strength, Brown Bear was a powerful man. From the ruins of a house he grabbed a rock in each hand and pitched them against the soldiers' exposed legs. "Seal, hit 'em in the head! Badger, the legs! Bluebell, throw that beam amidst 'em!"

But the advice went unneeded. Cursing, the soldiers backed away, rocks clanging off their shields. Masked by driving rain, they faded around another ruin and were gone.

For now.

And Sparrow Hawk had circled that way, Gull thought. Had his brother met the soldiers?

A muddy hand lifted Gull by his shoulder. His father propped him up, yet half-hunched, had to twist his head to see his tall son's face. The man looked like Gull, just craggier and gray. "Good work, son! Good work! I'd have given them the same could I stand straight! You're—"

"Never mind that!" cut in Bittersweet. "Where did you leave Greensleeves? And have you seen Hawk?"

Gull explained hurriedly about the holes in the thorn hedge, how she'd disappeared, then about Sparrow Hawk—when suddenly the ground rippled underfoot.

A man yelped. "Aftershock!"

*   *   *

"Not again!" his father griped, as if earthquakes were no more trouble than gut rumbles.

Yet the earth did not snap, nor their teeth chatter, as before. One ripple was all. What did that mean?

After people breathed again, the survivors took stock.

They huddled in the rain amidst the wreckage of their homes. Chipmunk's mother, Feverfew, fussed with his forehead gash. People peeked at Seal's belly cut, but the big man only raised his belt and tightened it over the wound. He puffed out his chest, suddenly a hero. Parents calmed children, wiped noses, hushed crying, wrapped soggy shawls around their shoulders. Others gazed over the ruins of the village, seeking the missing, talked of arming and organizing a search party. Cowslip, her bodice pinned with thorns, her hair flat and lips blue with cold, stood close by Gull's family and watched him intently.

The woodcutter trotted the way the soldiers had gone, hunted for signs of his brother, and found none. He called and received no answer. Where had Hawk gone? Probably adventuring, his brother sighed. Well, he'd have to fend for himself—it was Greensleeves needed finding.

First, though, Gull returned to his family. The elders, they argued about how to proceed.

"We won't have any crops at all this year," said one man.

"We'll need to live in the woods like outlaws and savages," said another.

Bittersweet held tiny Cub against her skirts. "We'll have to move on. This devastation will bring plague. It always follows a wizards' duel, the legends say."

"Aye," said Feverfew, "they might's well plow salt into the ground."

Half-listening, Gull climbed the heap of rocks that had been Badger's house and craned for a view. Through layers of rain and gaps in the thorn wall, he could see something of the battlefield the valley had become.

Up in the meadow, the two-headed giant was still foot-caught. He rolled and twitched and moaned piteously, a high, wild keening. His right arm was chewed to an elbow stump, and streaming rain washed away his blood. Three-legged, the clockwork beast clumped along the edge of the forest as if it were a fence. Goblins dragged something like a body across a muddy field, fighting and pushing and arguing every inch of the way. Of the hydra there was no sign. A centaur or a horse flashed past a gap in the hedge. Red soldiers hacked something across the river at the north end of the village. More villagers clustered at the far south, almost to the bogs, as if afraid to set foot in the village again. They didn't respond when he waved an arm, and his shouts were drowned by the rain. Only a family of six, Snowblossom and Hedgehog and their children, skulked from heap to heap, coming slowly. Gull waved them on. But where the blazes were Greensleeves and Sparrow Hawk?

"We'll not leave!" Brown Bear's head waggled from side to side. "We'll rebuild! We'll pack together for the winter. Gull can cut beams, I can saw planks—"

From his perch, Gull gave a shout of surprise. "What . . . ?"

Snowblossom's family had disappeared—down a hole?

Hefting his axe, Gull called for someone to follow, then jogged toward the spot where Snowblossom's family had vanished.

A gaping hole, round as a well, had caved in not far from the river. From the aftershock? Why not a crack?

A head popped into the rainy gloom below, and Gull knelt at the crumbling edge. He couldn't see who it was. "Snowblossom? Hedgehog? Grab my hand!" He leaned as far as he dared. Seal grabbed his belt behind.

His hand was ignored. A head covered with dirt rose from the hole as someone climbed with strong fingers sunk in the dirt. The head waggled, shedding dirt, revealing a blue dome with tufts of wiry hair.

Gull snatched his hand back. What . . . ?

The hole boiled. A dozen, two dozen, fifty little goomers spouted from the depths like rats from a flour bin.

It was hard to see them clearly for the mud. They were knee-high, naked, blue or gray, scaly like snakes. Wiry hair sprouted from shoulders and elbows. Jutting ears, huge noses, bigger mouths. They chanted as they spilled from the hole. "Oi, oi, oi! Watcher! Gonner get 'em, gonner barsh 'em!" Gull couldn't tell if they were true words or not.

Then the things, trolls or whatever, scattered. Gull and the rest shrank back as if from plague rats, but the little goons just swarmed past. Trailing dirt and mud, they flitted everywhere, digging, shifting rocks, burrowing into ruins. Gull saw one troll burst from a ruin with a copper pot, hoisting it like a treasure.

They were scavengers! Conjured by wizards? It must be. The trolls would scour the ruins for valuables. Gull's anger, which he'd thought squelched by the rain, returned hot enough to make his brow steam. Was there nothing sacred to these wizards, that they'd callously destroy a village and then pick the meat from the bones?

Shifting his axe, Gull trotted after a troll who dug

like a dog, shooting dirt between his legs. The wood-cutter grasped the thing around its thick neck. "Hey, you! Get away! We've enough trouble—"

He couldn't lift the troll. It might have been made of granite or lead. Gull changed his grip, but the troll shrugged it off. The tiny, almost-comical troll hopped to one side, lifted a big-toed foot, and kicked Gull in the leg—the bad leg.

For once, Gull didn't fall down. But he did gasp and rub his knee. The kick was like a mule's. Beady-eyed, the troll glared around its melon nose and spit, "Gwan! Goncher gummin gaflin baglit, nosher!"

It resumed digging. Within seconds, it plucked an oilskin pouch and tore it open with its teeth. Silver and copper coins reflected the dim sky. Chuckling, the troll stuffed the treasure into a pouch over its scaly belly. Then it scampered over the heap, big feet flying, vast nose twitching.

It must smell the metal, Gull thought in amazement. So these trolls were perfect scavengers. And there wasn't much Gull could do to stop them. A hundred or more had spilled from the hole. Gull doubted an axe could even dent the pests.

Hobbling, he returned to the hole. A timid cry sounded below. Hedgehog's family. Pulled out and brushed off, they'd been trampled under big dirty feet. Snowblossom reported the tunnel went on and on, the gods only knew how far.

"One more thing to endanger the crops," Gull groused. "It'll channel groundwater away."

They limped back to the main cluster of villagers. But Seal yelped. "Look there!"

Against the wet vault of sky, a human flew.

*   *   *

The villagers had seen miracles all day, but this seemed the greatest one. What could top a person flying like a bird?

Squinting against rain pelting his eyes, Gull watched the wizard soar, arms outspread like an eagle. It was dark, for dusk approached, but coming from the north, Gull assumed it was the brown wizard, the woman with glossy black hair. At least, he saw streaks like yellow jets. The woman was no bigger than his hand, looping, yet drifting in one place, riding the ether. Gull pondered her purpose.

Then, quick as an eagle, the wizard swooped. A flash of lightning seared the sky, blinding one and all. Above the rain and wind, Gull heard skirts flap overhead, like wash on a line.

And like the breath of death, fatigue suddenly smothered the woodcutter.

Gull's bad knee buckled and he fell. His axe dropped with a thud, his quiver and bow clattered as they struck a beam jutting from behind.

His mother gave a groan and collapsed. She fell face first into the mud, like one dead. Gull gave a cry and reached for her, but it was agony to lift his arms. He had to crawl like a salamander, had only enough strength to turn her head from drowning in a puddle.

She didn't breathe.

Frantic, Gull waggled his mother's head, pinched her cheek. Her eyes were open and speckled with mud, yet she didn't blink. Calling for help, he could only croak. He couldn't even cry, he was so tired. His eyelids drooped, his head nodded. Desperate, he shook his head but only made himself dizzier.

Squinting through a black haze, he found everyone

else similarly felled. His father lay on his side, mouth open, rain dropping onto his tongue. Cowslip lay with one hand sprawled over her head. Was this the plague his mother spoke of?

Gull tried to roll, got halfway up.

A sharp blow made him cry out. A rock had banged his forehead.

Another struck his leg. His groin. His shoulder, foot, chest.

More stones fell.

A rain of stones like hail.

With a flash, Gull knew this was wizard's work. If one were flying in the sky, her enemy would conjure a stone rain to down her.

Even if it killed every living thing in the valley.

Slowly, so several more stones struck him, Gull dragged his leaden arms over his head, tried to cradle his mother. His father lay only five feet away, but it was too far. Gull was too weak.

Stones pattered all around him. All sizes, from pebbles that bounced to fist-sized rocks that plocked in the mud. Thick as rain. Deadly, as if hurled from the gods. Gull heard rocks clash on ruins, on other stones, on peoples' heads and faces. Impotent, weaker than a newborn kitten, Gull could only weep.

Then a large rock got past his limp arms. Images crashed in his brain, then plunged into a well of blackness.

Then he saw nothing, not even blackness.

Gull opened his eyes, but his vision stayed black.

For a moment he panicked. Had a blow to the head blinded him?

Then he noticed, far off and faint, a pinpoint of

light. The Glitter Moon, just rising over the tree line. He groaned with relief and instantly regretted it. Pain shot through his head like fire.

Slowly, carefully, Gull rolled over. He clenched his jaw against the skull pain, but his jaw hurt too. Exploring with a mucky hand, he found a bruise over his cheekbone, where a stone had struck. He found other bruises too. Yet that stone rain must not have lasted long. Even a few minutes of it would have killed him. Nearby, half-buried in mud, lay a rock bigger than his fist. Hurled from the sky, it would have decapitated him.

Then he remembered his family.

Shuffling, wincing at new flashes of pain, he groped for his mother. Cold mud lay all around, but something white was close at hand.

His mother's face. He was touching her.

She was cold and wet as the earth.

Tears leaked from Gull's eyes, salt burning the bruises. With clumsy sprained fingers, he brushed mud from her eyes. "Mother . . . " She didn't respond, and never would.

The others?

Crawling, he found his father cold, the same. A stone had cracked his skull above the ear.

It got worse.

Lion and Rainfall had both been killed by stones, Lion half-buried. But Angelwing and Poppyseed and Cub were alive, for Lion had covered his brother with his body, and other villagers had snuggled the girls close.

Gull enfolded Cub in his arms, grateful prayers on his lips. He shook his brother to wake him, though he'd have sad news.

Cub's head wobbled as if his neck were broken. His eyes remained shut.

Gull pressed his ear to the boy's chest. Yes. There
was life, shallow breath and a tapping heart, but slow
and quiet. The thready pulse resembled his grandmother's seizure, when she'd fallen and lain in bed,
taken a week to die.

Crawling around and over bodies, he identified
Angelwing more by her homey smell than anything,
dragged her from the clammy embrace of a dead
neighbor. He leaned close over her tiny mouth, his ear
against her teeth, her breast. He shook his sister,
called her name, but he couldn't revive her.

Wails rose all around. Cowslip and others, strong
young folk, found they couldn't awaken elders or small
children. They were alive, yet still as corpses.

Worse than dead.

Their souls sucked away.

Half-mad with grief, Gull staggered to his feet.

In the steamy dimness and chill night wind, he
realized it was deathly quiet all over the valley. The
battle was over. The soldiers and the monsters were
gone, returned to wherever they'd sprung. Even the
wall of thorns was gone. Even the clouds were gone.

Yet the village of White Ridge might have gone
too. It was smashed, burned, and leveled, its people
felled by sickness and stones and savagery.

All done by wizards.

Spreading his feet wide to keep from toppling, Gull
raised both fists to the black sky winking with stars.
He shrieked, howled, cursed magic, and wizards, and
the gods that spawned them.

CHAPTER

4

Despite a roaring bonfire—the remains of a house—
the night was long and cold and miserable. The villagers were seared on one side and chilled on the
other. No one slept much. Some folks wondered what
to do, but they were shushed. "Dawn will bring
enough evil," intoned Catclaw.

Gull pondered what he might do, but the enormity
was overwhelming. He had to find Greensleeves and
Sparrow Hawk. He had to bury his dead, and tend the
not-dead, the comatose ones. He had to . . . but he
ceased to think, and sank into a dull, wet, pain-fogged
funk.

Dawn's watery sun raised steam like fog. A squabbling first roused Gull. Vultures had come to eat the
dead. Their cousins, ravens and crows, awaited their
turn or fought over lesser spoils.

That woke him, and the resounding CLUMP
CLUMP CLUMP KABUMP squeakcrunchgrind CLUMP
CLUMP . . . of the clockwork beast. The poor creature, or

construct, still circled the valley. It had limped on three
legs all the night long, like a mill out of kilter that would
not seize up.

Another sound came to him: the scuttling of rats.
Gull lobbed a stone at a small hunched silhouette,
grunted when he knocked it off a heap of rubble. But
the sounds continued. All night rats had circled the
fire and dug in rubbish. The earthquake must have
brought them out, he thought, collapsed their dens.
Though he'd never have believed this many rats in
their village. Nor were these healthy, grain-fed rats,
but skinny scabby things.

Enough moping, Gull thought. His father, who lay
dead not a dozen feet off, had always said, "A busy
man has no time to brood." Gull could honor his
memory by following his advice. He rose and
crouched—aching in every joint, bruised and muscle-
sore—cast about what was left of the village in the
eerie dawn light, then slowly poked up the fire, rous-
ing others out of their stupor.

Awed, speaking quietly, as if the disaster might
return any moment, the survivors pooled their knowledge and divvied up tasks. Snowblossom and
Hedgehog and others would try to dig up the root cel-
lars. Seal and his sons and daughters would hunt stray
goats and cattle. Old Wolftooth got help to drag bodies into a pile for burning: there were too many to
bury. Gull offered to butcher a horse he saw yonder,
but he'd need someone . . .

As if reading his mind, Cowslip offered, "I'll watch
for Greensleeves and Sparrow Hawk, and tend the
fallen ones."

Just before last light, they'd lugged the stricken
together, close to the fire to fend off the rats, but there
was little hope they'd live long. That mysterious

life-drain had felled in equal numbers: killed a third of the survivors outright, stolen the soul but not the life from a third, and left the rest palsied and weak.

Gull smiled weakly at Cowslip. She'd spent the night close by his side, and they'd tried to keep each other warm.

With simple tasks to perform, people got moving, but they shuffled like walking dead, hollow-eyed and clumsy. The destruction of their homeland had destroyed them inside, too. They'd be a long time healing.

Hefting his axe, heavy as an anvil, leaving his bow and arrows behind, and sighing, Gull tottered across the misty morning rubble.

The woodcutter had to skirt uprooted thorns, smashed houses, cracks in the earth, the wreckage of a goblin bladder-flyer, rat-gnawed corpses of blue barbarians and red soldiers, dead dogs, and White Ridgers too.

He passed a firepit littered with long charred bones. The pit was marked by tiny footprints. Nudging his tired brain, Gull reconstructed the scene. Yesterday the goblins had hauled away something he'd thought was a body. Now he knew differently. They'd dragged off the giant's sundered arm. And roasted it.

He kept his eye on his goal.

Across a former meadow, toward the Whispering Woods, lay a dead brown horse. Bleary-eyed, Gull steered around the dead giant.

Yet the woodcutter jumped in shock when he beheld the giant moving.

Or rather, something *on* the giant moving.

Between the two heads lay a long, pulsing . . . plucked chicken?

Chicken skin-colored, certainly, and naked, but tall as Gull. It was half-buried between the two heads. The woodcutter could see skinny buttocks stitched with blue veins under transparent skin. What . . . ?

The horror compounded itself. The giant groaned, raised a cold white arm thick as a tree trunk, pawed weakly at his neck.

Gull froze. The gesture was so pathetic, and so human, like a baby trying to brush off a gorging mosquito. The woodcutter's heart went out to the giant. Though as a mercenary he deserved no sympathy. . . .

The giant moaned, shifted a huge dirty bare foot, kicked so that Gull jumped back. Despite his stupor, the giant suffered. His arm stump showed white bone and red meat rotten with dirt and pus. When it banged the ground, the giant moaned anew.

The plucked chicken picked up its head, and Gull gasped.

A long head, no hair, tall pointed ears, a lacework of blue veins, a mouth full of fangs. And red blood on thin lips.

Vampire, thought Gull.

The fiend reached out almost gently with a clawed hand, pressed a filthy fingernail against the giant's eye, jabbed. The giant recoiled, and the vampire yanked up his earlobe, sank his teeth in the flesh below. Gull, who had slaughtered animals, knew a rich vein pulsed under the ear.

But he wasn't thinking of that as he attacked.

Howling, the woodcutter snagged the hem of the giant's patched sailcloth smock, hoisted himself up, clambered across the heaving round belly. Gull acted on pure instinct. Something dead leeched off something alive. Compared to this ghoul, Gull and the giant were brothers.

The vampire whirled at the battle cry. Gull saw webbing between the fingers and under its arms, like a flying squirrel. The skin was so translucent, spider-webbed with blue veins, that wan sunlight shone through. Through belly skin, Gull saw a patch of red—fresh blood in its stomach. Gull fought to keep his own stomach, and his balance, as he hefted the axe above his shoulder.

With one blow, he'd slice the vampire from helm to crotch, and kick the pieces to the crushed meadow for the crows.

But the vampire gave a tiny leap, barely pushing off with its long toes, and was gone.

Surprised, Gull swung halfway, then fully around, searching. Where had it gone?

A weight like a dead deer's crashed on his back.

Gull fumbled his axe and watched it slide away down hilly flesh. The woodcutter slammed face first onto filthy cloth that smelled of sweat and salt.

There was another smell too. A fetid slaughter-house odor.

A hand cold as death mashed his head, lit fires in the many rock bruises and scratches, ripped his long hair aside to expose his neck.

Better to stare death in the face than take it in the back, he remembered his—dead—father saying.

With a mighty kick, Gull tried to roll over. His bad knee rang with pain. He heard the giant grunt from two mouths.

The vampire grappled him tight, though, and sank claws into his face. Fingers gouged flesh from his fore-head. One hooked and grazed his eyeball. Gull couldn't decide if he were angry or frightened. A giant leech slurping his blood terrified him. But this attack—after how many in two days?—set his blood boiling.

He snapped his head and bit at the hand, kicked at nothing, swung a clenched fist. Strong the vampire was, strong as a mule, but its thin arm let go when the brawny woodcutter slammed its elbow. The vampire snarled and lunged for his throat with long white teeth stained red.

Arms tangled, the woodcutter kicked again, banged the vampire's legs with his own—

—and knocked the two of them headlong off the giant's heaving body.

Sky, dead skin, salt-streaked cloth, mud—all flashed by, then Gull slammed on his aching shoulder in trampled meadow grass.

But the human leech still clung.

Gull felt a searing pain on his biceps. The vampire bit him to the bone. The man yelped, hammered the hairless head with his elbow. The skull felt like rock, and he only drove the wicked teeth deeper into his own flesh. Gull kicked, but one leg was hung up. The hill of a giant loomed on the other side like a cliff. Gull's head was half-buried in weeds.

Gull's anger evaporated as fear rushed in. He was helpless. He'd die here, drained of blood.

And who would find Greensleeves? And Sparrow Hawk?

Frantic, the axeman slammed his elbow against the unyielding head. He couldn't bend his arm to reach around.

Above the pain and burning itch, he heard slurping.

His blood, disappearing down an undead gullet.

Gull screamed—

—a thudding and thumping sounded close at hand—

—the sky went dark—

—and a feathered lance pierced the vampire to the ground. Black blood sprayed Gull and the giant. The woodcutter saw the spear point was wider than his hand, cut with flutings, crudely forged but sharp.

Then he was rocked by the death throes of the vampire as it thrashed like a pickerel on a hook. An elbow clipped his chin, teeth ripped free of his arm. Black blood spattered his lips, rank as ditch water. The vampire clawed at the lance shaft. It would not surrender its un-life easily.

Yet the lance wielder, mounted high on his horse, twisted the shaft to tear the fiend's vitals. Little by little, it died, fading to skin and bone, then a layer of sticks and slime.

Disgusted, the woodcutter swept off the gore, wiped his eyes, struggled to rise. The high horseman snagged his wrist and jerked him to his feet.

"Ugh. My thanks, good sir. I was trapped . . . and . . . couldn't . . . "

Silhouetted against the gray sky, he saw the horse and rider were one.

Staring down from deep brown eyes under a visored war helm, was a centaur.

"You are lucky," came a gruff but curiously whinnying voice. "Spit of Sengir Vampire is like medicine to keep blood from clot. No corruption."

"What . . . ?" Gull could only clutch his bleeding biceps and stare.

The being seemed incredibly tall. The helmet made it taller, for it sported a plume made of, of all things, a red-dyed horsetail. The face was obscured by the enclosed helm. It and the breastplate were etched with sworls, then painted or enameled. The being wore wide armbands, and had been warpainted yesterday with handprints and runes, though now the paint was runny and smudged. The back half was roan, reddish brown, and shoulders and arms sported equally red, though sparser hair. War harness and packs were slung across the back. The deadly lance was longer than the creature's body. Feathers tied to the lance with rawhide were dyed purple and white, and tattered. The lance had seen hard use.

The centaur grunted as it jiggled slime off the lance, made a human pout of disgust. "Sengir Vampire like elf. Just as bad. Travel alone, though. Fly into battle-fields always. Have you seen my mate, Holleb? I am Helki."

Now Gull understood why the voice sounded high. "You're a—woman!"

"Yes." The helmet bobbled. "And you are man. So?"

So why are you so hairy? Gull wanted to ask, but didn't. The lance hung in the air like a thunderbolt. He tested his arm and found it had quit bleeding. He'd won more scars from two days of adventuring than some men gained in a lifetime.

"So . . . I haven't seen your mate. I'm searching for folk myself—" With a rush, memories of dead and missing crashed around Gull like surf, threatened to wash him away. "I . . . we . . . our village is ruined."

Oddly, the centaur nodded in sympathy. "And our lives, I think. We should work together. Would be good."

Anger stabbed Gull to his toe tips. Work with these, who'd helped destroy his home?

"But perhaps," the centaur interrupted, "neither of us have problem now." She whinnied pure delight.

Circling on dancing back legs, she flashed away
around the hill of giant, paint-daubed tail flicking.
Gull heard her call, "You search a two-leg looks like
you? Girl?"

"What?" Gull felt stupid and thick. Like him . . . ?

Then he got it. Snatching his axe, he ran.

"Greensleeves!"

"'The gods watch over drunks, children, and
fools,'" Gull quoted.

Trotting across the meadow, dancing around craters
and cracks, came the other centaur. This one was bigger and hairier, and undeniably male, to judge by the
war club slung between its legs. This must be the
mate, Holleb.

Seated on the centaur's back was Greensleeves.

She looked fine, with chaff in her hair, briars in her
gown and shawl, dirt on her small feet. Light as a bird,
she slid off the centaur's back, chattering. The centaur
nodded absently. Probably he thought it some foreign
language, not her own animal gibberish.

The centaur embraced his mate, breastplate to
breastplate, then slid alongside to bang flanks. Both
rattled in their own tongue, and Gull could tell it was
love talk, for it floated like song.

He hugged his own sister, asked, "Where were you?"

She chittered like a squirrel, then squeaked, pulled
away, and went to the giant's side.

The monster-man had slumped again. One head lay
in a puddle, lips white with pain. The other stared glass-
eyed at the sky. The nearer head turned vaguely as
Greensleeves touched a massive shoulder, caressed the
bald creased head. She cooed in a way Gull recognized:
soothing sounds his mother had made to a hurt child.

But his mother was dead. And it was partly this giant's fault.

Roughly, Gull jerked his sister away. Anger made his voice harsh. "Leave him! Let him die!"

A patter of thumps sounded behind. He confronted the looming centaurs with their three-yard lances. Gull tucked Greensleeves behind him, balanced his axe.

The mare-woman nodded at the giant. "We should help. He is a thinking being, in pain."

Gull wanted to spit, he felt so bitter at himself and them. But like lancing a boil, he might as well get it over with.

"No. Better the sick die. And you that can leave, leave."

The horse-folk shifted their feet. The female demanded, "This is how two-legs show thank-yous?"

Words almost choking him, Gull rapped, "I grant we owe you. You saved my life. He rescued my sister. But that scarce makes up for destroying our valley as your trade. A mercenary expects not thanks but blood money. So collect it and begone!"

The centaurs danced backward, as if to gain swinging room. The male barked at the female, snorting, whinnying, and she chirped back. Then she whirled on Gull, who raised his axe.

"Know you, two-leg rat-man," she sneered, "we are no merc-mercenaries who take money to fighting. We are forced labor, slaves to wizards, made to fight without our will. Would we could return home and stay, but no. But you know all, and not listen!"

With that pronouncement, they whirled in place. Tails flying like flags, they cantered off across the meadow for the woods.

Gull was left to ponder her words. Slaves to wizards? That must be a lie. No one could be forced to war against their will, could they?

Yet he felt regretful as they pranced into the woods, ducking branches and parting brush with their lances. If it were true . . .

Greensleeves gurgled like a badger, plucked at his sleeve, dragging him toward the giant.

Gull protested. "No, Greenie, no. I can't help him. Half a hundred of our own folk need help. And he's just a mercenary . . . "

It was no use. Despite having twice her weight, he was towed along. The giant's shorn stump stank of corruption. Probably he—or they—would die shortly anyway.

The giant's left head focused. Greensleeves patted the nose, long as Gull's forearm. Wracked with doubts, the woodcutter ventured, "Can you speak?"

"Speak?" Big eyes blinked slowly. They were slanted, almond eyes. The skin had a yellow caste, too, Gull noted. The giant must come from far away—he'd heard there were men of different colors in the Domains. Judging from the wrinkles around eyes and mouth, this giant was also very old.

And slow. He finally answered. "Yes. I talk. I hurt."

Gull pressed. "Did you come of your own free will to fight for the wizard?"

"Wi-zard?" More thinking. Having a giant brain should make one a genius, Gull thought, but this giant was thick as a child. "Wi-zard make me come here, make me fight."

"Does she pay you? Feed you?" Gull was feeling increasingly stupid. And guilty.

"Feed? I hunger."

"Are you a slave to the wizard?" Gull insisted.

"Slave?" A long pause. "I must do . . . as she asks."

"Oh, my," sighed the woodcutter. "Greensleeves, I'm the simpleton."

Not long after, Cowslip and Greensleeves had cleansed the giant's wound, found fresh manure (but where were the cattle?) and packed on a poultice. Gull had butchered the dead horse, and lacking bandages, had sliced raw horsehide to wrap around the giant's stump. The giant sat up and ate every scrap of horse—liver and lights and guts—but he was used to raw fish, he explained slowly.

Cowslip asked the giant questions, and slowly they learned that he lived by the sea, fished, had fashioned his patchwork smock from the sails of shipwrecks, and was named Liko. (The single name, they guessed, meant one identity, not two. One brain in two skulls, with a wide gap between.) The left head answered questions while the right stared into space, daydreaming.

Gradually, throughout the long day, the villagers picked up. It gave them little time to mourn, though they were quiet. Everywhere Gull looked was some reminder of a life lost forever. A tree in which his brothers and sisters had built a hut, a stone where his grandmother had basked in the sun and told her stories, a stone wall he'd rebuilt with his father.

Only Greensleeves seemed not to mourn. Perhaps she didn't understand what had happened. Cooing, she puttered as always, tended people and the giant, mixed water with dandelion and burdock roots and fennel leaves for a poultice, brought comfort with her touch.

Some survivors had propped up an intact roof and cleared out underneath, and under this pitiful shelter

they laid the comatose villagers on bare earth. Some
had stopped breathing, and were buried in a far-off cellar hole. They had to set a girl with a switch to shoo
rats away, for the pests scuttled everywhere. Cowslip
showed Gull a nasty bite on the wrist: she'd shooed
rats off a wounded child. The bite flamed red. She'd
also picked up fleas from the creature, and had to
scrub them off with mud in the swimming hole. Light-
headed, she stayed game, and returned to tending the
sick.

But at one point she asked, "What shall we do,
Gull?"

"Do?" He paused at digging. They were trying to
free a root cellar under a house, one containing winter
turnips. He moved slowly because his head still ached
from yesterday's stone rain. He felt light-headed too,
probably from losing blood to the vampire. "I—I don't
know, 'Slip. Rebuild, I guess. What else can we do?"

The girl looked around the valley, brushed back her
corn yellow hair. "It will be like building on a graveyard."

Gull shrugged, winced. Questions about life and
death and afterlife had never concerned him. "The
only other choice is to leave, and where would we go?
My mother claimed the ghosts of our ancestors stayed
with us, watching and protecting. Now there are a few
more. But in fifty years, this tragedy will be just a story
to tell children."

The girl laid a brown hand on his forearm. "Whose
children, Gull?"

Gull studied her face. Despite dirt and fatigue, she
looked beautiful. With his maimed left hand, he
trailed hair away from her cheek. "*Our* children.
Because we *are* going to stay—"

Suddenly she was in his arms, hugging his chest
and sobbing. He patted her soft hair with his callused,

crippled, scabby hands and cooed, "There, there. Don't cry. We'll protect each other, Cowslip."

She turned her face up, and he kissed her.

Yet Gull's father had often said, "When the gods decide to punish a man, they do it all the way." Gull remembered that before the sun set.

All afternoon, he'd hunted cattle and goats in the woods. He'd found nothing except traces of goblins, goat horns, and hooves. This bad news he decided to keep to himself.

He felt forgiving anyway. As in any crisis, his emotions had sunk and risen overnight, soared from despair to hope in a day.

Maybe he wasn't thinking too clearly, but he didn't care. He was in love. Holding Cowslip had been the finest thing he'd ever felt, and he almost skipped through the forest. Cowslip would make a fine wife, and he a good husband, he hoped. They would rebuild a home, replant the gardens, dam the stream and bring it back, help neighbors rebuild, see White Ridge grow many generations yet. Another of his father's axioms: A man is only beaten when he quits.

He whistled as he left the woods. Far off, the makeshift village continued to grow from the old center.

But running toward him came Cowslip's brother, Gray Shoat. The boy's cry sent a shock of cold fear.

"Gull! Cowslip's sick!"

CHAPTER
5

Cowslip lay on her back, alone.

Gull blinked, stunned. He could hardly recognize her.

She had crumpled in the path not far from the victims of the mysterious weakness. She'd been fetching them water. A puddle and a broken redware crock lay by her hand. Her mouth hung open, arms flopped alongside, one foot folded underneath. Even under a wool gown, her armpits and groin looked swollen fit to burst. Her skin was dark as dusk, as if she were choking to death. Or already had.

None of the villagers would go near. Horror froze them. Fathers held their children at bay. Mothers sobbed, one of them Cowslip's.

As Gull ventured close, an old man, Wolftooth, grabbed his arm. The woodcutter barked, "Let go! I must see to her! Why aren't you—"

"Don't!" Wolftooth rasped. "It's death. Black Death! I know it from the legends! It fells a person in their tracks! Oftimes a wisewoman come to administer dies before her patient!"

Gull stared, but did not approach. He'd heard the stories, too, about whole cities wiped out by the Death. "What if she's . . . "

"She's not," interrupted Wolftooth. "She's dead. All the rest, too, all inside the house." The "house" was the roof under which they'd laid the victims. " 'Twas rat bite killed her. Poor Cowslip."

So that was her epitaph, thought Gull. Poor Cowslip, who might have been wife to Gull the Woodcutter. Tears blurred his vision of her, burned his cheeks. Clumsily, he stumbled around the path and wreckage and Cowslip's corpse to peer into the shelter.

By the low entrance lay a boy, Otter, set to shoo out rats. He, too, was swollen and black. Fleas trailed from his body, more fleas than Gull had ever seen.

And everywhere inside the shelter, tiny eyes glittered at him. Hundreds of them. Yellow teeth were bared, then the rats returned to feeding.

The horror was so great, so overwhelming, Gull couldn't grasp it. His mind shut down, walling off the terror before he went mad.

All he could think was: First his mother and father, then his sisters and brothers, then Sparrow Hawk missing, and now a woman he'd just discovered he could love.

And moments ago he'd been whistling in the woods. Suddenly he hated himself. And everything else.

Behind him, Wolftooth argued with Seal, the village bully. And others. The argument rose to a roar. " . . . We're going, and now, and that's that!"

"Going where?" Gull demanded, falling into his old ways of questioning everything Seal said. Other villagers stopped squabbling and stared at the two men.

"Away!" snarled the fat man. "This village is cursed! It's an open grave!"

"Going *where?*" Gull repeated. "You don't say *where!* You've never *been* anywhere else!"

"That doesn't matter! Just away!"

Feverfew quavered, "But Seal, do you think—"

The fat man turned to his cowering wife and slapped her head. "Fetch your pots and my jug!" He would have belted her again, but Gull snagged his wrist and squeezed until Seal gasped.

Gull snarled at the villagers. "Is this the man you'd follow when you *quit* this village, when you *abandon* your homeland? This coward and bully? *Think* of what you're leaving behind here!"

But no one answered him, or would return his gaze. They were afraid and they were running, and it was pointless to condemn them. Maybe they'll return someday, maybe not. There was nothing Gull could do about it.

So he sat on a rock not far from Cowslip's ravaged body and watched them prepare to leave.

Greensleeves talked to a ladybug on a dandelion. Rats scuttled under the propped roof. Flies droned. The clockwork beast clumped and stumped in the distance. The giant, Liko, slept with his bandaged stump in the air.

Gull sat and did nothing.

There was nothing to do. He couldn't bury Cowslip or his family for fear of corruption. Come dark, the rats would have her. He couldn't find Sparrow Hawk. The boy might have been lost in the woods, or been captured by soldiers or the wizard, but more likely he was one of the many corpses that littered the valley. Gull couldn't even think of a reason to live, except to care for Greensleeves.

One by one, as shadows lengthened, the villagers gathered their pitiful belongings. One by one, they traipsed along the ruined road, north over the ridge. A few waved to Gull, but he didn't wave back.

By sunset, the last villager, old crippled Wolftooth, had passed out of sight.

Greensleeves came to Gull and mewed, a sign she was hungry. Gull took her hand.

"Yes. Time to eat. We'll hie to the woods. That's all that's left now."

He picked up his axe and bow and quiver, took his sister by the hand, and walked toward the whispering depths of the forest.

As if to welcome them home, the forest offered up a brace of fat pheasant that Gull knocked down easily. They found the clearing he'd made—only yesterday morning? Ash branches, which burned green, caught to his flint and steel. Rather than roast the birds, he gutted them, dug some mud, encased them feathers and all, and buried them in the ashes. They could eat later. Gull wasn't hungry, and Greensleeves was wandering again, cooing to some doves in a birch copse. He thought he should restrain her, keep her close to hand, for who knew what evil still lurked. He'd seen signs of goblins. But keeping Greensleeves was like holding smoke. She went where she would. The gods would have to protect her—Gull couldn't do everything.

Flossy was glad to see her master, and even Knothead accepted scratches on his stiff mane without biting. Unhobbled, the mules had nevertheless stayed near the clearing, foraging and awaiting his return. He found that oddly comforting. Gull told them, "You've fared well, I see. Better than White Ridge. 'Tis good.

Our old home is no more, so perhaps this haunted wood is our new one. . . ."

And suddenly he was sobbing, his face pressed to the mules' necks. The poor beasts were confused, but they stood still.

Gull's grief didn't last long, for there sounded a clumping of many feet in the darkness outside the fire ring.

Soldiers! screamed his tired mind.

Frantic, more for his mules and sister than himself, Gull snatched up his axe. Where was Greensleeves, damn it? He couldn't let her wander. Things were dangerous enough—

Into the circle of yellow light tripped the two centaurs, Helki and Holleb.

They danced to a halt, tails switching gently. They planted the butts of their lances near their forefeet. With firelight glistening on breastplates and closed helmets, their upper bodies looked more like caterpillars than humans. Gull waited with his axe in two hands.

The silence dragged. Light glistened from glossy hides and Gull's axe head, reflected off white-veined leaves that rustled above. A knot popped in the fire, spraying sparks. Gull stepped on a patch of grass that flared. Otherwise, no one moved.

Helki, the talker, broke the silence. "We . . . saw you . . . talk . . . to your mules. They are fine animals. . . ."

They'd seen him crying? Suddenly Gull was mortified. Absently he rubbed his face. He was so tired and battered he could sleep a week.

Yet the centaurs' remarks weren't meant to embarrass, but to open conversation. Gull replied, "Thank you." Remembering his manners, he dropped his axe till the head rested on the ground. "Would you share my fire?"

The plumed helmet nodded. The centaurs' eyes were shadowed within, but Helki's voice was civil. "Thank you. We would. Fire is nice on a cold night."

"Yes," was all Gull could say. But they waited for more. "I talked to Liko, the giant. He too was a slave to the wizard's will, as you must be."

"Is true," said Holleb. His voice was harsher than Helki's, rough as gravel sliding down a hill.

"So," said Gull, "I owe you an apology. I'm . . . sorry."

The centaurs conferred in their own language—horse talk, Gull thought it. Finally, Helki reported, "We are sorry also. For the loss of your homeland. But we were under geas, compulsion deep in our minds that we must obey, and could not but fight."

"I understand. Now."

"Since we all speak true, we must talk."

"If you insist," Gull sighed, too tired to argue. "But talk of what? There's nothing left. You might as well return to your homeland."

"We have no way to return," Helki said. For the first time, Gull heard a catch in her voice. "It is impossible."

Gull dug up the mud-baked pheasants, broke the hard shells, separated skin and feathers from brown meat. Laying the carcasses on a stump, Gull cut them into threes. He'd offered the centaurs some. Greensleeves could fend for herself, finding mast, mushrooms and teaberries and such, in the forest. She didn't much like meat anyway, and would probably just leave it.

As he worked, the centaurs shed their armor. Their breastplates fastened in front, yet they helped one another as if they couldn't touch enough. Breastplates and helmets hooked to the harness on their backs, where already there hung haversacks for food, pouches for tools and gear, a coil of rope, a water bottle. Even the lances slid into loops along their left sides. Come what might, Gull realized, the two could dash off in a second's notice.

Yet he barely noticed this, for staring—while trying not to stare—at their fantastic shapes.

Their revealed faces were ordinary enough, even pleasant, though they had prominent yellow teeth. Covering their pates was short reddish hair that matched their bodies, though their manes continued almost to their foreheads. Their bellies were whitish, though Holleb was covered with matted hair, while Helki had flattish breasts with brown nipples that stuck up thick as a thumb joint.

Finally, the man and the horse-folk sat by the fire, the centaurs with legs tucked underneath. Even sitting they looked delicate and graceful. With his maimed hand and bad knee and axe scars, Gull felt clumsy and old. He proferred the pheasants on slabs of bark, and the centaurs accepted graciously. In return, from a haversack Holleb produced a block of dried orange fruit, pried off a slice. It was "apricot," and good.

They ate in silence a while, then Gull offered, "I understand little of what happened here, no more than an ant understands a lightning storm. How did you fall under the sway of that wizard? And why can you not return home?"

"We understand not much more," sighed Helki. "Our people live on steppes and taiga we call Green Lands near Honeyed Sea. Far to the east, to judge by sun. Ours is border country, where often are wars. We train as warriors from small child time, work as scouts for good causes. But one time wizard—not a native, traveler—hire us to survey land. We were unsure, but gave service as asked. Wizard thanked each by shaking hand. Then she gone."

"Gone? You mean she disappeared?"

"No. Mounted horse, rode off with servants. We think nothing of it. But of a sudden, one day, I and Holleb find us on battlefield, like day past. Wizard is there, now our mistress, we know not how. Geas placed on us, we must obey commands. Outside, we obey, though inside rebel, but do no good. As if had two minds in one, one rule, one submit. Fight dwarves, we did, small folk but strong, and bull-people. Then battle stall, and we home again. Like dream, except left scars." She showed her left elbow, striped with a white slash. "Happen twice more, always somewhere different. When battle done, wizard wave hands, send us home.

"Then comes day past. Scout and fight here. But when battle done, wizard is gone. No one to send us home."

"The wizard ran," growled Gull. "In those past battles, she must have won, so could tend her charges and see them home safely. But this time she got skunked, and ran like a rabbit. And left you stranded. Is that it?"

Choked up, Helki only nodded. Holleb snapped a thick stick apart, piece by piece.

"Like that silly clockwork animal out there," Gull mused, fitting pieces of the puzzle. "And those useless goblins and the poor giant with his arm shorn off . . . For that matter, it explains the soil under that thorn wall."

"Thorn—wall? What is thorn?" Despite her sorrow, Helki was curious, for herein might lie answers to their plight.

Gull explained, "That heap of briars. When I was hiding my sister, I noticed the soil was red. We don't have soil like that in our valley. I've only heard of it from travelers. So that whole thorn hedge was actually lifted from somewhere else in the Domains and dropped on our village. . . . Imagine the power to do that, to uproot part of the earth and transport it elsewhere. Look what these wizards can do! And yet they spend their time warring on one another, forcing innocent folk to fight to the death for—well, why *do* they fight, anyway? Kings fight for glory and soldiers for pay. What are wizards after?"

"Power," rumbled Holleb, startling the other two. "Power to become gods."

The fire slumped to red coals. Around them, the Whispering Woods were so still Gull had to strain to notice the hissing almost-voices that droned like summer bees.

He'd fit together a few pieces, yet the puzzle only loomed larger. If wizards warred for power, or magic or *mana* or whatever they called it, why had two of them come *here*? The only power in White Ridge had been water turning a gristmill. And there was little magic. Their wisewoman was more midwife than witch. She could bless the seeds at planting, and their blacksmith could conjure twinkles while forging steel, but . . .

It made no sense for wizards to invade their valley.

And since the battle had been pointless, his anger flared anew. How *dare* they use people like tools, then cast them aside when broken, or they needed to run?

A crashing and thrashing and snapping of branches sounded from the edge of the woods.

Gull snapped alert, snatched up his axe, looked for Greensleeves. The centaurs leaped up and liberated their lances. All three faded from the firelight.

Along with the smashing, like a tornado shearing branches, came a pounding Gull felt through his soles. He took a new grip on his axe. Whatever it was . . .

High up, branches parted at the edge of camp. Filling the firelight stood Liko, the two-headed giant. Leaves fluttered from his shoulders and spiraled into the fire. With one heavy arm missing, he listed left. The almond eyes looked sleepy, like a child's.

"Have you food? I hunger."

They had the giant sit down against an oak. The tree groaned, as did the man-thing. His twin faces were pale as birch bark, oily with sweat.

Gull asked the giant how he felt, but got only a murmur. The woodcutter turned instead to the centaurs. "What shall we do? He's a brother-in-arms, a victim of wizard slavery like you."

The centaurs talked in their own language, snarling and snapping like a dogfight, then Helki offered, "We see cattle in other wood. We could fetch one. Eats he meat?"

"He eats anything. But can you really find cattle at night?"

The man-stallion Holleb went hot-eyed. "Do you jest?"

"No." Gull was surprised. "But I searched for cattle— gods, just this morn—and found no sign."

Helki snorted delicately. "Holleb can track ladybug across lake. We fetch." Gear flapping on their flanks, they cantered off into the dark.

Since there was no one else to do it, Gull inspected the giant's wound. The giant's left head watched him curiously while the right head slept. Unwrapping the green horsehide unleashed a gagging stink. Jagged bone jutted from flesh both flaming red and rotten gray. Sighing, Gull rebound the wound.

No wonder the giant was tired, he thought, fighting infection like that. He'd have relief soon, and the peace of the grave, once the blood poisoning reached his heart. Gull kept his voice light. "Giants are made of stern stuff, I see. No wonder they tell legends about you."

He wasn't sure if the giant understood or not. With his slitted eyes and parchment skin and bald pate, Liko looked ancient and wise, yet Gull could see that most everything confused him.

To change the topic, he asked, "How did you fall into the service of that wizard, Liko? Did she shake your hand too?"

A frown. "Wizard?"

Gull's neck cricked from having to look up. Even seated, the giant's heads were four feet above his. "The woman in brown and yellow, the hand waver. Did she shake your hand?"

"No. She gave me wine barrel. In tiny boat." He raised his arms to show the length of the boat, but lacked a hand and frowned again. His heaving chest and stomach made the patched-sail smock toss like a ship at sea. "Good wine. Good friend."

And Urza's own bargainer, the woodcutter thought, to buy a slave with one barrel of wine. "Why not rest, Liko? The centaurs will bring food soon."

"I like wine, too."

"Don't we all. You'll need wait till the fall harvest."

A twig snapped behind him. Not one crackling in the fire.

Gull whirled.

A goblin was stealing his axe.

*　　　*　　　*

"Yaaahhh!!!"

The woodcutter howled to startle the thief, jumped awkwardly over the firepit.

Short-legged and weighed down by the eight-pound axe, the goblin didn't get far. Gull swatted, knocked it against a tree.

Dropping its prize, screeching, the goblin scrambled to get away. Gull grabbed a skinny ankle and hoisted the creature like a hooked fish. With a ragged kilt hanging around his arms, he was obviously male. He didn't weigh forty pounds, and had a black streak in his gray hair, like a skunk.

The wretch gibbered, pleaded, threatened, wind-milled his arms, almost snapped his own ankle with contortions. Gull shook until his head bobbled and he fell silent. "That's better. Now, do I bash your brains out on this oak? Or will you say why you stole my axe?"

"I didn't, I didn't!" the goblin cried. Normally a lichen green, his inverted face turned bright as clover leaves.

Gull snorted and walked to the firepit. Waving the goblin over the flames, he asked, "What did you say?"

"All right! I did, I stole! Is that s'bad?"

"What? Of course it's bad! It's wrong to steal! Especially from me!"

"Yes, yes, I see that now! I won't do't again! I swear!"

"Pah! Once a thief, always a thief." He shook the skinny leg for emphasis.

"Yessir, very true. But I'm a bad thief. See? I got caught! So I'll give it up!" Not killed, the goblin calmed. "If you could leggo me leg, sir?"

"Hush." Gull let the goblin drop onto his head. What to do? He should just wring his neck and throw the carcass to the ants. One wasn't much threat, but goblins were like rats or cockroaches, and should be stomped whenever possible.

A rustling made him turn. Greensleeves returned from the woods.

Burbling in a questioning tone, she put one hand on Gull's arm, the other on the goblin's foot. Upside-down, the goblin latched onto her ragged hem. "Oh, save me, sweet lady, good miss! I'm innocent, I am! This brute's seized me, a poor wretch who never done any harm. . . ."

"No harm?" Gull couldn't help laughing at the bald-faced lie. "You and your bunch tried to cut me! And eat my sister! You *did* eat Liko's arm! I ought to—"

Chattering, Greensleeves pushed Gull's arm lower. Spiderlike, the goblin scrabbled, latched onto a rock near the fire, screamed at burned fingers. "Green-ie . . . "

But with her gentle urging, Gull finally dropped the culprit. Bouncing on his head, rolling upright, the goblin shrilled. "Ha! Fooled you, white-skinned ninny! You donkey, blundering boob! I got away! Takes more than a great stupid mountain of meat to conquer Egg Sucker! Ha, ha!" His gloating was spoiled by blowing on singed fingers.

Gull took one step, and the goblin bolted into the darkness.

The woodcutter turned to chide his diminutive sister, then gave up. Her eyes shone adoration for her big brother. "That's foolish, you know. Letting a rabid skunk like that loose. But I suppose there's been enough killing . . . "

His sister glanced over his shoulder. Had the centaurs returned?

No.

Standing in the firelight, bright as sunrise, was a
man in stripes and a headful of yellow hair.

Snatching his fallen axe, Gull acted on pure instinct.
He charged.

"I'll kill you!"

CHAPTER
6

Gull was head and shoulders above the wizard, probably weighed half again as much. The woodcutter swung an eight-pound double-bitted axe at the run, while the wizard stood firm with only a child's rattle.

Nonetheless, it was Gull who veered off. A foot spasmed, and he slipped on damp oak leaves. He skidded on his side, dragging his axe.

Idiot, he cursed himself. To stumble in the face of an enemy.

Swearing aloud, he scrambled up and charged again. He carried his axe at the head lest he stumble again and gash himself. If he got near this wizard, he wouldn't need a weapon. He'd rip the man's throat out with his fingernails—

His right arm flailed on its own, suddenly cramping. Off-balance, he slid on his face, tasted leaves again.

What was *wrong* with him?

Neither howling nor swearing, but cold and clear-headed, he dropped the axe and tried to roll over and over. That way he couldn't fall. If he could knock the man's feet from under—

His thigh spasmed, a pain like muscles shearing. A knee jerk stopped his rolling.

This, he thought, was not his fault. That rattle had knocked him silly. Could he crawl, grab the man's ankle . . . ?

As Gull lay panting, twitching, a hand graced his forehead. "Be at ease. I come in peace, to talk."

Anger dropped from Gull like water running down a drain. Maybe killing this wizard wasn't a good idea. Maybe talking was better. Maybe he could help . . .

Unless, a dark part of his mind warned, he'd cast another spell . . .

Gull dismissed that idea. He knew his own mind. He was just tired from two days of fighting and running and living and dying.

"All right," he puffed. "Talk."

When his muscles would respond, Gull climbed to his feet. The wizard tucked the "rattle" into his belt. It was turned from polished silver with furrows and knurls. The woodcutter pointed. "What is that thing?"

The wizard touched the head. "Oh, nothing much. It just diverts attacks. I'd hate to bring anyone to harm."

Harm, thought Gull. Same as the goblin had denied.

The man's voice sounded young, and despite his bushy mustache, Gull guessed he was probably not twenty. Certainly his hands were soft as a baby's. His yellow hair, combed back and stiffened with limewash, was unkempt as a boy's.

His gown was some shiny material that winked as folds caught the firelight. By its rustling, it seemed sheer as ashes. The woven bands of color were no wider than a finger, from red shoulder wings to a yellow waist and dark blue hem that trailed no dust. Many things studded the belt, knobs and jewels and tiny faces, but most curious was a small brass-bound book hung by chains on his left.

Gull had only seen one book in his life, an old one from Wolftooth's travels. It showed drawings of fanciful animals and far-off cities. Gull wondered what a man might see in this book that he chained it close.

As if reading his mind, the wizard swung the book behind him. "Merely wisdom bequeathed by my teacher. You'd find it dull."

Gull found himself agreeing. This boyish wizard had an infectious smile. . . .

Or was this more spelling?

Gull shook his weary head, concentrating. "Why did you come here? Haven't you done enough to ruin this valley? There's nothing left, not even crumbs for rats." Anger thickened his voice.

But the wizard dispelled it easily as dousing a fire. "Yes, I've seen. A terrible thing. A beautiful valley, now spoiled."

"Then why. . . ?" His babble confused the woodcutter. "Why was a battle necessary?"

"It wasn't. May I share your fire?"

Unable to deny a common courtesy, the woodcutter waved. The wizard swept back his skirts (like a woman, Gull thought) and perched on a stump. Liko and Greensleeves watched him curiously.

Gull sat on a rock. Bruised as he was, scratched, dirty, crippled in hand and knee, he felt ancient and broken-down compared against this prissy wizard. He made his voice harsh. "How is this tragedy not your fault, if you were party to the fighting?"

The wizard locked his fingers around one knee and leaned back. Firelight tinted his hair white, an odd young-old look. "As with everything, there are good and evil wizards. That brown one was evil, pure and simple. He came here to enslave your village. You saw those plumed soldiers in the scale mail attack your village. He conjured that giant there, the rain of stones—"

"That killed my father."

"Exactly. He unleashes death. He summoned the plague rats—"

"That killed the woman I loved." The last word stuck in his throat. He'd never said it aloud. Certainly never to Cowslip. He hoped her soul walked easy.

"See? We're agreed. Now, I am a simple seeker of truth, good things to benefit men and women every-where—"

"Why, then, your own army? You summoned a blue cloud that brought forth blue warriors."

The wizard rocked like a fidgety child. "True. But only to protect myself and my entourage."

Gull remembered the circle of wagons with people huddled inside. Where were they right now? He glanced over his shoulder, saw only darkness. Where had the train gone after the battle, that it could return now? Or was the wizard alone?

The visitor was babbling. " . . . see that *all* my spells are defensive. I *never*—"

"Flying goblins that hurl iron spikes? A wall of briars? A hydra to bite a giant's arm off?"

Both of Liko's heads frowned. Yet if this wizard feared the giant might rise and pound him to pulp, he didn't show it. "I try to lessen the destruction other wizards cause. Remember the fire horn? I brought the rain that quenched its blazes. Surely you don't think that storm was spontaneous?"

Gull frowned. "Two wizards appeared and my home was ruined. I can only think the two wrecked it."

Mildly, he said, "I can understand. Yet if a wolf chased a rabbit through this clearing, and both scattered ashes and started a blaze, would you blame both?"

"We speak of men, not rabbits and wolves," grunted Gull. Likable he might be, but this wizard's tone was insulting, as if he spoke to a slow child. And his answers came easy and quick, as if rehearsed, though not much to the point.

The wizard sighed. "You're a hard man. Any trouble I've caused I can fix. Would a demonstration of good faith convince?"

"It might. It would beat this torrent of words you pour on my head."

The wizard rose, crossed to lay a hand on the giant's thigh. "Good evening, good sir. May I see your sullied arm, please?"

Liko probably didn't understand the words, but he raised his arm. Hands nimble as a surgeon's, the wizard unwrapped the stump and examined. "You come from near the sea, giant?"

"His name is Liko," put in Gull.

"Liko, then. You do? I recognize your caste. I've visited your land in my travels. Lovely country. There's a sea gull there sports a yellow belly, yes?"

Awed, Liko nodded. Both heads watched the wizard say, "Would you like to return home? I can send you there."

"Home?" asked Liko, and Gull's heart ached for him. The giant was like a lost child. "Yes, home. I would like that."

"Of course you would. Everyone wants to return home. Here's what I'll do. A simple spell to heal your arm, make it grow back—"

"Grow back?" yelped Gull. "A man's arm can't grow back!"

For the first time, the wizard looked miffed. "Magic can cure or kill; create or destroy."

Gull wanted to spit. He was being treated like a moron. So why didn't he wallop this wizard?

The wizard worked. One hand on the stump, he consulted the book chained to his belt, muttered an arcane phrase Gull didn't catch.

Then, a miracle.

The wound healed.

Red raw muscles coiled like snakes, knit together like yarn. Rotted flesh sloughed off like sunburn. The jagged bone smoothed to a blunt end. Then, like frost creeping across a windowpane, skin from the edge flowed until meat and bone were covered, pink and smooth as Liko's bald heads.

Gawking, Gull touched the healed stump. A miracle had occurred before his eyes. Yet he recalled—

"You said it would grow back. All you've done is sear the stump shut."

"Things take time." The wizard sighed. "First comes healing, then rebuilding. If a house falls down, you first must clear away the rubble, true?"

Gull ground his teeth. Everything this wizard said reminded of his village's destruction.

But again, the wizard rambled, deflecting Gull's anger. "His arm will regrow, because I have commanded it so. Once back in his native land, he'll be more at ease, so will heal faster."

The woodcutter laid a hand on Liko's huge arm. "Are you *sure* you *know* his native land? Yellow-bellied sea gulls might be common to many shores. He could end up stranded as far from his home as he's stranded here."

"You know little of magic. A creature conjured from a familiar place retains an impression of it, as a man walking through snow leaves footprints that point to his starting place." He turned. "Liko, will you go home?"

Looking wise as an ancient sage, twice so with two heads, the giant nodded. "Yes. I go home. Fish."

"You'll have fish aplenty," smiled the wizard. He walked to the giant's feet, placed long fine hands on the big dirty toes. "Then go, and heal quickly."

Before Gull could say good-bye, or even wave, the giant twinkled like foxfire under moonlight, or snow in a campfire, or rain—

—and was gone.

The wizard turned with open hands. "There. I've healed your big friend and sent him home. Do I side with good or evil?"

A quote from his cynical father came to Gull's mind. *A man can help others a little and still help himself a lot.*

The wizard took his silence for assent. "I'm glad we agree. Because I'd like to hire you."

"Are *you* mad? Work for a *wizard*? One of the godless fiends who destroyed my home and wiped out my family?"

Gull cast about for his axe. He'd been right all along: he should have butchered this smooth-talking fop when he first walked into camp. (But he'd tried, a thought nagged, and had fallen down.)

"I can't *believe* your gall! Me work for *you*? I'd no more trust a wizard than a broken-backed snake! I wish the gods would wipe every wizard from the Domains. *That* would be the end to *all* misery. . . ."

When he drew a breath, the man in stripes huffed. "Look, I've explained all that. I'm for good works and you can help me. Now try to listen, please?"

As Gull subsided, the wizard regained his tree stump, sat primly, and continued. "My freightmaster is dead. When we circle the wagons, we put the horses outside lest they panic and bolt. My freightmaster wouldn't leave the beasts, and was killed by a fireball. I have no one to handle my teams. I saw your mules, fine animals, well cared for and content. You'd make a good freighter, or muleskinner or wrangler or whatever you prefer to be called.

"Look around. You have no reason to stay here—a haunted wood with a helpless sister to watch. Join me and I'll pay well—"

Suspicious, Gull demanded, "How know you of my sister?"

A hand waved the question away. "I gather information. I always learn what I can about a place, and who's in it, to know what I'm defending. I saw you caught in the battle—and again, I apologize—and save your sister. It was brave how you sheltered her, and showed brains. I need a man like that.

"I'll pay in gold, two crowns a day, and board is included. You can travel and be paid for it. You can squirrel away a fortune, find some new place to settle." He laughed. "Work for me for three years and you can *buy* a village!"

Flustered by this strange offer, Gull stalled to think. He sat on his rock, stirred the fire with a stick. "Where does a seeker of truth and knowledge find so much gold?"

Another hand waved that away. "In seeking magic, venturing where few will or can, I uncover whole fortunes. Sometimes more than I can bother with.

Oftimes I barter the money to locals for more folklore, clues to more knowledge and magicks. Not something you need fret about. My followers can sink their teeth in my coin. Now. What's your answer?"

Another of Brown Bear's comments rose to mind. *Sleep on any bargain. Time enough to make mistakes.* More to his dead father than himself, Gull replied, "I need consider. I'll give my reply in the morning."

"Wise." The wizard nodded. "Very wise. You'll make a fine freighter. Smarter than poor dead Gorman. Come at dawn if you come at all. We leave shortly after." He rose to go, stripes shimmering in the firelight.

"Wait," called Gull. "*If* I come, I must bring my sister. I'm charged with minding her."

The wizard smiled. "You're good to animals and people alike. She may come along. Likely she'll eat little. I bid you good-night, and hope to see you in the morn."

Stripes rippling like flames, he faded into the dark.

Gull sat thinking a long time, his first real chance to consider the future. Only the crackling fire kept him company. Greensleeves had curled up like a cat to nap.

Should they go or no? Could they stay here?

No, for many reasons. They had no grain, no stores, and the Whispering Woods did not abound in game. They'd soon exhaust it if they camped here. Just as the plague rats in the village would eventually exhaust its food, then move into the woods like a rapacious black army. And if plague and starvation didn't kill them, winter's cold would.

For himself, he almost didn't care. But he had to care for Greensleeves.

And there was another advantage. By staying close

to this wizard, he might eventually meet up with the
other wizard, the woman with glossy hair. Then,
though he couldn't see how, he'd take revenge for the
ravaging of White Ridge.

A nagging doubt returned: what if Sparrow Hawk
returned? Yet in his heart, Gull knew the boy was lost,
probably forever.

Having decided to leave, Gull felt like an uprooted
tree. Alive, but dying slowly, hardening and rotting at
the same time.

And that was another thing he'd forgotten to ask.

Where were they bound?

Come the dawn, two humans, two mules, and two
centaurs left the Whispering Woods and tripped toward
a circle of wagons on a ridge above a ruined village.

Gull had yoked his mules to his wood-hauling
sledge and piled it with tools: two saws, two axes, a
hammer, files and whetstones, a haversack, a redware
jug, his longbow and arrows, a cloak for bad weather.
He walked in his leather tunic and kilt and wooden
clogs, and that was all he owned.

With him came Greensleeves, who owned a ragged
gown and shawl and nothing else, not even shoes, for
she'd always lost any pairs given her. A bundle of ferns
was clutched in one grubby hand. An ash leaf dotted
her messy brown hair, and her brother plucked it away.
Their mother had always tidied her hair, but now they
lacked even a comb.

The centaurs wore full battle armor, but no
warpaint, and carried their lances upright so the feathers fluttered in the morning breeze.

No one talked, though they'd discussed long into
the night.

Helki and Holleb had agreed that, while there were countless stories of ruthless wizards, there were also stories where they befriended heroes and helped to save the day. So the striped wizard—whose name Gull hadn't learned—might well be a harmless student. It might benefit to work for him.

Yet the centaurs couldn't discuss much, for they were too eager. They marched, eight feet in time, with heads high, but skittish as colts at first snow.

The wizard's entourage watched them come. As he limped across the mossy ledges, Gull studied back. The wagons were fairly new, brightly painted, the canvas yellowed but tight. The camp was neat, free of rubbish and food scraps, even sported a canvas screen around a cat hole privy downwind. The wizard didn't allow slovenliness.

Only the horses and mules tethered to the picket line looked neglected. Gull frowned at shabby coats, matted tails, overgrown hooves, and dull eyes. He was suddenly glad the freighter had been killed—he deserved it.

Seven men and more women ate breakfast in the circle. A fat cook sweated over a grill. After two days of forest fodder, the aroma of pancakes and honey made Gull's stomach squeak.

A large dark man in black leather called into a wagon, and the striped wizard popped out, smiling. He hopped over a wagon tongue and raised both hands.

"My friends! Good to see you this fine morning! Come, come! Join us! Have you eaten?"

Gull clucked his mules to a halt, stopped Greensleeves from chasing a butterfly. The centaurs stamped as if clicking heels.

"Business before we break bread," said the woodcutter. "I've pondered your offer, and we will hire on. I can see your stock need care, and Greensleeves will be no trouble. But I do ask one boon."

Having won, the wizard smiled like a king. "I'll do my best, sir. What may I grant?"

Gull waved a hand. "These be Helki and Holleb. They were summoned here by the brown-robed wizard and stranded. If you could see fit—"

"To send them home, as I did the giant?" A smile. By daylight, the wizard looked more boyish than ever, not unlike the lost Sparrow Hawk. "I'd be delighted. I've already sent some—home this morn. My body-guards caught goblins raiding our larder. Returning them to their blighted wastes will be punishment enough. I sent home that crippled clockwork, too. I hope whoever owns it can repair it."

That was curious, Gull thought idly. How could he know whence the beast came? Had it a brain? Had it talked?

"Now, may I ask . . . "

The centaur-soldiers described their green step-pelands north of the Honeyed Sea. The wizard asked many questions, listed foreign names by the score, until he mentioned Broken Toe Mountain. The cen-taurs fairly danced in place. "Yes, we know that mount! Is close to home! You have been there?"

The wizard smiled in answer. Without further ado, (or payment, Gull noted), he laid hands on their breastplates. They shied at the strange touch, but the wizard shushed them and whispered a spell.

Yet Helki bleated and backed off. Flustered, she tripped sideways to Gull. "We go. But we thank for hospitality. We remember always as friend."

"I too," said Gull, choked. It hurt to say good-bye again after losing so much. "I'm sorry I doubted your— honor."

Greensleeves caressed the centaur's glossy roan flank, offered her ferns. Distracted, Helki took the bunch.

"It's good you go home," Gull said. "It's important to have a . . . home . . . "

Tears leaking from under her helmet, Helki saluted with her lance and cantered to the wizard, who smiled like a doting grandfather. With laid-on hands, a whisper, and a twinkle like dawn starlight, the centaurs disappeared.

The wizard dusted his hands, satisfied. He patted Greensleeves's tousled head, shook Gull's hand. "I'm glad you've joined us. We need you. And welcome your sister and her gentle ways. Come, break your fast. Then you can meet the stock. As you say, they need attention."

"But how are you called?" Gull asked. "How shall I address you?"

A shrug. "We're not much on formality. I'm younger than most of you, so it'd be silly to go by 'Master.' Call me Towser."

"Towser?"

A small smile. "Aye. A name for a small dog. My father was a joker. And so is his son, sometimes."

So it was that, two hours later, Gull hitched horses and mules where the cook's boy pointed. He cinched harness and tugged straps, pronounced the teams ready. His own mules were hitched before another team to the chuck wagon. Gull rode the box with Greensleeves alongside. Inside, the cook and slops boy went back to sleep amidst boxes and sacks and barrels.

Gull clucked, got his team rolling. Others wheeled behind. Towser was fuzzy on their destination, simply ordered them into the Whispering Woods at the first gap that would take wagons.

As the wagon rattled along the ridge, Gull didn't look down. There'd be only bones in the valley now.

And he'd never see it again.

CHAPTER

7

For certain, thought Gull as he sawed at the reins, this new job would free his mind from brooding. He suddenly had a thousand new tasks amidst a company of strangers on a strange road through a haunted forest.

Good, he added cantankerously. He'd be too busy to mourn.

The wagon train lurched and bumped through the depths of the Whispering Woods. The trail was not hard. Since the trees were climax forest, so old they hardly grew, they formed a solid canopy that sheltered the leaf and mold floor, depriving brush of sunlight. Only mountain laurel or rhododendron, taller than Gull and wiry, could have slowed them, and they avoided those clumps. Mistletoe hung in curtains from oak trees, but was tender enough to shear. Indeed, the only obstacles were the contours of the land, with its rocky streambeds and drop-offs, kettle holes and ridges.

The biggest obstacle wore on the humans—the

ceaseless whispering. Gull and Greensleeves were used to it, but it got on the others' nerves.

The whispering was like the sea, old Wolftooth had said. (And how did he fare? And Seal and the rest?) Or a chorus that hissed, trading secrets and comments, like old women at the fountain or geese overhead. The susurrus bubbled at every hand, here, then there, as if ghosts gibbered behind. But turning and twisting revealed nothing except more squeaking.

The mad whispering had kept everyone from White Ridge away, which was why Brown Bear had been the village woodcutter. Bear had feared nothing, and had dragged his skinny terrified son along, until that boy too was tall and strong, and from a lifetime of felling trees that might crush him, or worse, came to fear almost nothing.

Yet Towser's entourage darted fretful glances at the looming trees and close canopy above, illuminated only by splinters of sunlight, so it always appeared dusk in the wood. Even the scout, a burly man in a fur vest, stayed within sight of the chuck wagon.

And who knew, thought Gull, but that some monster might dash out of the twilight depths. In a morning's ride he'd come deeper than ever into the forest. He'd never seen anything bigger than bears, but he'd seen some strange tracks.

With a "Haw!" he turned the team, driving them up a slope toward the scout atop a low ridge. The mules' shoes bit through leaf cover to strike loam. The wagon wheels slewed sideways, and for a moment Gull thought they might topple. But the team found purchase and the wagon straightened, and so they continued. The scout moved on, hunting the flattest passage northwest. Gull glanced behind. The other drivers followed his ruts and mounted safely.

So far they'd been lucky in finding passage. There might come a time they'd have to push, or lever the wagons up the slope, or fell trees. But that would be later, and they'd solve any problems then.

This was his life now. Freighting wagons and mounts he never knew existed three days ago. The gods surely sent a man odd twists when the whim struck.

What other surprises lay in store?

The wagons—his wagons—were well built, sturdy yet springy, high-wheeled to climb over rocks and ruts, yet narrow as an arm span, long-bodied, sides and ends sloping toward the belly so loads would shift center-ward and low. They would not tip easily. There were five wagons altogether, four canvas-topped and one a solid box. Gull drove the chuck wagon, which rattled with iron cooking pots and grills and cranes, boxes of apples and crocks of oil, bags of flour and salt. With him were Greensleeves, the fat cook, and her skinny helper.

Next came the women's wagon: six of the most beautiful women Gull had ever seen, dancing girls in swirling silks and satins, a rolling harem for Towser. The dancing girls flitted through the wagon train like songbirds, riding in different wagons, but Gull noted one or another always attended Towser.

At the center, safest from harm, was Towser's box wagon, gaudy with gold filigree and carved faces and painted scenes of the world. The wizard spent most of the day and night inside. A squint-eyed clerk in gray drove with ink-stained hands. An important man, Gull decided, since he doled out the pay.

Close behind came the astrologer's wagon, which

held, if Gull had glimpsed aright, a eunuch who acted
as nurse and herbalist; an astrologer like a withered
apple; and a partidressed female who carried a tall lyre,
obviously a bard.

Last came the men's wagon. There were four bodyguards. Each was a big man, big as Gull. Three drove
wagons, wrestling reins all day. By turns one scouted
their passage, watched for danger, and knocked down
game if possible. Mostly they existed to protect
Towser, with their lives, if necessary.

Eighteen people, Gull counted, each paid at least
two gold crowns a day (though probably Gull was the
poorest after the cook's boy). A fabulous sum Towser
laid out every day just to live in comfort and style.
He'd dismissed money as unimportant, but he could
afford to: he had heaps.

Mulling, daydreaming, or not thinking at all, Gull
drove and rocked with the wagon. White Ridge lay far
behind now. If nothing else, perhaps he could leave
some sorrow behind too.

Noon found them eight or nine miles into the forest.

The fat cook roused from her pallet, groped her way
to the front of the swaying wagon, grabbed Gull's
shoulder with burn-scarred hands and wheezed, "Find
a flat spot and circle the wagons, Big Boy. We'll eat."
The cook's boy had already jumped out the back to
gather windfalls for firewood.

Smoothly, the teams pulled the wagons around—
even the stock knew the routine—and drivers set the
brakes while everyone else hopped down to work.
Two dancing girls toted canvas buckets to fetch water
from a stream. The bodyguards consulted with the
returned scout, two took up crossbows and belted on

swords, then walked circles around the camp while the others loosed harnesses. The clerk disappeared inside Towser's wagon, one dancing girl exited to make room for another. The nurse helped fan the fire; the bard settled on a rock and tuned her lyre and sang. Only the old astrologer got to lay a blanket in the sun for a nap.

Gull also got to work. He had plenty of it.

The animals—eight mules and twelve horses—kept their collars but were turned out to forage and drink. Hoof tool in hand, Gull checked each foot for cracks or stones lodged under shoes. That was eighty hooves, and some of these formerly abused animals gladly stomped his foot when he got careless. He talked to each, patting, gentling. It would take time to win their confidence: even Flossy and Knothead would bite if they got a chance. Come evening, Gull would have to curry hides and comb matted manes, check for harness chafing or flybite infections and other problems. If needed, he'd erect a bellows and tiny anvil and reshoe. Plus he must oil harness, replace worn sections, fix broken iron, grease axles, watch wheels for cracks and splits, check leather springs for tears. Plus drive one wagon all day and fret over four more.

Clearly his days would run from before dawn to after dark. Watching Greensleeves the while.

Speaking of which, where had she gone?

Camp rang with the clanging of pots and grills, chopping of firewood, singing and plucking of the bard, chattering of the girls and women, rude jesting from the two idle bodyguards.

But no sign of his sister.

Gull fumed. He couldn't really watch her—she melted away like smoke. The gods and her native luck would have to protect her. He'd be too busy—

"Hey, Big Boy!" Sweating over the fire, the fat cook held up a plate. "Come and get it or it goes to the pigs!"

Gull shifted his mulewhip to the middle of his back and took the tin plate. Boiled salt pork, a slab of fresh corn bread, and pickled somethings. A mug of warm ale. Gull was impressed. The long winter past but crops not up, food had been lean in White Ridge. He hadn't eaten corn bread in three months, nor drunk ale in two. Furthermore, the pork was rich and spicy, the bread golden crumbly, the pickles crunchy sweet, the ale tangy brown. He told the cook so, and she smiled.

"Glad you like it. It's damned hard work. Where's your little sister? I've got her plate here."

Mouth full, Gull shook his head. "She doesn't eat, usually. She finds mast in the forest. Or lives on air, like a fairy."

The cook wiped her face with a fat arm, loaded another plate. "That's why she's so thin. I'll fix that. Hey, Bad Boy, come and get it!"

Intent on eating, Gull lurched as someone belted his shoulder. His plate plopped on the ground.

Beside him, the scarred man in leather laughed. He wore black head to toe: laced tunic, breeches, flop-top boots, arm bracers, short-cropped hair. Not much older than Gull, he'd yet been hard used. A scar ran from his left temple to his jaw. The flesh was puckered and rough, as if rasped off, and he lacked an ear. White furrows pulled his eye wide open, a sardonic glare.

He sneered at the bruises on Gull's face, as if the woodcutter had already lost a fight. "Whatsa matter? Your hands slippery with horse sweat? Move aside! I won't be smelling horseshit while I eat."

Meekly, Gull nodded, turned to go. "Yes, sir."

The bully's arm extended for his plate. Gull suddenly whirled back, slammed his elbow below the man's ribs, driving halfway into his guts.

The man heaved and doubled. But even short-winded, he whipped a knife from his belt and twisted, slashed at Gull's arm.

But Gull had moved on. He backpedaled, planted a clog against a backside.

The cook bleated as the bodyguard toppled into the firepit, glancing off an iron crane, scattering ashes into food.

Still, he rolled with the fall, spun, and threw the knife.

A *crack* snapped against the ears, and the knife flickered toward the trees like a glittery butterfly. Gull had snaked out his whip and tagged the knife in the air.

The whole camp watched, stunned, even the fallen bodyguard. Grinning, Gull looped the whip over his head, flicked. The invisible tip sizzled at the bodyguard's head like a wasp. He yelped as his single ear split.

Gull flipped again. Like a trained snake, the whip swirled thrice around his neck, settled its viper's tongue on his breast. Unhurriedly he unwound it from his throat.

The bodyguard checked his ear, found bright blood. "Next time I'll kill you!"

"Next time you *try*," Gull replied, "I'll pop your *eye*."

He reached for the bodyguard's plate, and the cook gave it. "Good enough. A man who wastes food can do without. Hey, Slow Boy, come and get it!"

Most of the camp had run to see the bully test the

newcomer. The bully picked himself out of the dust
and walked into the forest. As Gull ate, another bodyguard, wrinkled and bronzed, grinned gap-toothed and
signaled a thumbs-up.

"One friend, one enemy," Gull mused. "Not a bad
morning's work."

Greensleeves returned as Gull hitched the last
team in place. She carried something long and gray-
black. As Gull turned, it snarled.

A badger.

Despite the foaming fangs, his sister hugged the
beast to her breast, for it was heavy. It lay docile to
petting, yet was clearly wild. One ear was gnawed,
probably by a wildcat.

Leaning backward, Gull joked, "You could name it
after that bodyguard. But leave him here, Greenie. He
won't ride in a wagon."

Cooing, blathering, Greensleeves stroked the
striped head, toyed with stiff whiskers, tickled its muzzle. The animal liked the scratching. Finally she put it
down, and it scuttled belly down into the brush. Then
she yawned, wide-mouthed like a child.

Gull chuckled, caught her by the waist, hoisted her
onto the wagon seat. Inside, the cook crooned, "Ha,
there's the little darling! Come here and nap with
Felda, sweetie." All dirty feet and knees, Greensleeves
tumbled into the back to curl like a dog.

Gull limped around the wagons, checking one last
time. As he passed the women's wagon, a blob of spit-
tle landed before him. The leather-clad bodyguard
perched on the box. His ear had scabbed, but swollen
twice its size. He sneered, "You won't live the night,
shit shoveler."

Grinning, Gull put a hand to his head. "What's that? I can't hear you. There's something wrong with my ear."

Veins bulged in the bodyguard's neck. Two wagons down, the crinkled bodyguard silently guffawed.

Gull finished inspecting, then called to the clerk on Towser's wagon. "Ready to roll."

The clerk spoke into the wagon, then nodded. "Move out."

To the click of brakes and slap of reins and cluck of drivers, the wagon train uncoiled and wheeled down the trail picked out by the sheepskinned man the cook called Slow Boy. Creak, rattle, clunk, into the depths of the Whispering Woods.

Gull wondered how far the woods extended, where they ended, what came next. Then he hollered at Knothead to take the proper side of a rock, the stupid mangy lop-eared peabrained son of a blind piebald pig.

Anyone not driving was free to walk. The bard always did, toting her lyre and whistling birdcalls. The dancing girls hopped from one wagon to another, into Towser's when summoned.

Yet Gull was surprised when a white-clad dancing girl caught the edge of the chuck wagon seat. "Give me a hand!"

Gently, Gull hauled her aboard, then returned to his driving. In this stretch, he could easily scrape a tree and break a wheel. Yet he risked a glance. Penetrating the makeup, he guessed she was only slightly older than Greensleeves, still a girl. She rode in silence a way, then offered, "That was clever how you snipped Kem's ear."

Gull chuckled at the memory. "Oh, that was nothing. I flick flies off my mule's ear without a twitch. He was testing my mettle. Now we know where we stand."

"Well, ignore his threats. He only beats people who give in. He made our last freighter's life hell."

So that's why the man hid among the horses, Gull thought, and died by a fireball.

Gull clucked to urge his teams around a stand of birch. "Do you speak from personal experience?"

"Aye," she said frankly. "I slept with him once, but he hit me. So no more."

Ah, thought Gull, she was grateful he'd bashed Kem. "What did Towser say about that?"

"What? The hitting?"

"No, the sleeping."

"Oh. We're allowed to pleasure the men as long as they pay for it. We're in Towser's employ, after all."

"And what do you do for Towser?" Just making conversation, Gull didn't expect a reply.

Yet she smiled and answered. "Not as much as you'd think. He frets about his health and stars too much to enjoy a romp."

"Eh? His health and *stars*?"

"Aye." She stretched like a cat, yawning. "He has the notion—you won't tell him I said so?"

"What?" Gull looked sidelong. The girl's hair was dark, cut short at the sides to kiss her cheeks, with the rest braided down her back, twined with white ribbons. All her clothes were white with yellow and blue piping: sheer blouse, vest brocaded in flowers, pantaloons, slippers bound with more ribbons. He returned to studying his mules. "No. You can trust me."

"Hmmm . . . " she demurred, then plunged in. "Towser has the notion that working magic drains his 'vital juices.' He's always carping about 'balancing the salts' and 'maintaining electricity,' whatever that means. That's why he has a nurse in attendance, Haley, the eunuch. Sloppy green potions six times a day, poured in one end or squirted up the other. Ridiculous. And he worries about the influence of the stars, so he fetches along that witch, Kakulina, his personal astrologer. All she does is draw star charts and mumble absurdities. I should have her job. She doesn't have to humor someone who talks constantly of his bowels and his birthstone."

Amused by his boss's queer notions, Gull smirked. "You could have asked to be muleskinner."

"I should have. I couldn't be cook, that's for sure. I never learned how."

"Can't cook?" Gull gurgled. "Every child in my village learns that!"

The girl extended a slippered foot over the seat, let it bob with the sway of the wagon. Sunlight dappled her powdered face, making her look artificial and unhealthy. "When I was a child, my parents sold me to a bawdy house. Eleven mouths were too many to feed. And I was too pretty to keep. I learned how to set a table, serve tea and ale, mull wine, dance and sing, to duck a hurled bottle, to recognize disease, to hide my money so the other girls wouldn't steal it, to beg a man not to slash me. Later, when I was old enough, I learned how to arouse a man, how to fulfill his fantasies—"

"You don't need to tell me the rest."

The girl stared straight ahead. "Anyway, they never taught me how to cook."

"Doesn't sound like a jolly life."

She shrugged thin shoulders. "It's not the worst job in the world. I don't have to gut fish, or plow, or lean over tanning vats, or muck out hogs. I don't have to please six or seven men a night, only one, and Towser doesn't require much. And I've been saving my money. Someday I'll have a business of my own."

"Oh?" Gull was amused and bemused. In some ways, this woman reminded him of poor Cowslip, practical and level-headed. Yet dainty and aloof, she was unlike any woman he'd ever met. "What kind of business?"

"A shop for gentlemen and ladies. A milliner's. I'll sell only the finest hats and gloves. In some big city."

The driver nodded. "People will always need clothes, so you won't starve. It's good to see ambition. All I ever learned is how to cut wood and shape timber. And whack mules in the head. That would have been enough, too, but my luck ran out three days ago."

"Don't dwell on it, then. Be glad for the home you had. Some of us were denied even that."

They rode in silence a while, then Gull asked, "How did you come to work here?"

"Towser bought my contract a year ago. He was very queer about it, too."

"How queer?" This woman was one surprise after another.

The dancing girl frowned in recollection. "He had all us girls paraded into the main hall, then he had each don this silver medallion he took from a box. We took it in turns and never did learn why. Then he bargained for me, and my mistress let me go."

Gull could make no sense of that, just shrugged. "How are you called?"

"Lily. Towser has me dress in white. The other girls are Rose, who's sweet but dense; Orchid, who thinks she's a queen; Peachblossom, friendly enough; Jonquil, fit to butcher hogs; and Bluebonnet, such a bitch she could birth puppies."

"Thanks for the warning," Gull drawled.

Yet he brooded. The dancing girls were named after flowers, as had often been the women in his village. None of them would have been named Lily, a delicate flower grown fussily in gardens. A cowslip was a hardy wildflower that flourished in manure piles.

Then thoughts of home and all he'd lost crowded his mind, let him say no more.

In the midafternoon, the scout waved the train to halt. From a low rise ahead, he mimed Gull should walk. Curious, the woodcutter handed the reins to Lily and limped up there.

The crinkled bronzed man was taking his turn. He draped a crossbow across a knotty arm and pointed to the ground. "What d'ya make?"

Careful not to step on the evidence, Gull dropped to one knee and examined the trail. Groundwater trapped by a ledge made the earth muddy. Twin wheel tracks scarred the loam. Deep dimples were space a foot apart.

"Rivet heads on an iron rim," said Gull. "Not like our wheels. They're smooth. Someone's ahead of us. Maybe . . . four wagons?" He fingered the edge of the tracks. Sharp-cut but dry, they crumbled at his touch. "Two days ahead, I'd guess."

He straightened, tottered through a break in the trees. "They came from more north, changed their minds, hooked this way. That's why we haven't seen them before. Are they going the same place we are?"

"Couldn't tell you, bucko," chortled the man. "I don't know where we're going meself. Me name's Morven, by the way. Thirty years on the water, I was, until the sight of blue made me puke. So I hauled anchor and tacked inland, signed on with this scurvy wizard and his bully-dogs. What are you called?"

"Gull." He shook the man's bony hand. Morven had gray in his curly hair and beard. His face was wrinkled as a crab's from squinting into wind and sun. Dressed in a faded blue shirt and white breeches and sandals on crooked feet, he reminded Gull of old Wolftooth, the only man in White Ridge to have traveled.

Another squint. "Gull like a sea gull?"

"Yes. One landed on our threshold the day I was born. First and last ever seen in our village."

"Then you're fated to go to sea one day."

"Perhaps," Gull shrugged. "I don't guess the gods' intentions. They do as they will with us. I can't even guess my employer's intentions, other than keeping his livestock happy."

"Keepin' anythin' happy's enough for one man. And that includes wives. I ought to know. I've had thirteen."

Gull grinned. "Is that why you're so far inland?"

The grin shot back. "Let's say I shear clear o' seaports and let be. Come. We'll give old Puckerbutt the bad news."

They walked toward the wagon train. "Puckerbutt?"

"Tow's clerk, the pinchpenny, the nipcheese. Him as pays us, when he remembers."

"We'll see he remembers, won't we?"

"Oh, aye. But he'll never love givin' out money. Any more than Kem's going to kiss you for splitting his ear." He chuckled anew. "By the Lance of Ages, I'd give a month's pay to see it again! The look on his face! Hey, Puckerbutt! Haul your fat arse down here!"

*   *   *

Even Towser left his wagon to inspect the mysterious tracks. He decided there was nothing for it but to continue trending northwest, try to find a parallel track if possible.

And as the train got under way again, Gull suddenly knew their destination.

Northwest.

Where one moon ago, a shooting star, rocketing from the heavens, had crashed, shaking the earth and setting the forest ablaze.

A portent of doom—and so it had proved for White Ridge.

What would that mean when Gull and Greensleeves got there?

Gull lay on his side and stared at the dying fire. He was exhausted, yet he couldn't sleep.

Past midnight of the busiest day of his life, he'd only just crawled into his bedroll under the chuck wagon. He'd stowed Greensleeves in the chuck wagon with Felda, the cook, but had opted to sleep outside, where he could monitor the stock, rise quickly if wolves or bears came skulking. Toward that end, he'd hung his longbow and quiver and double-bitted axe in the axles. Then he'd collapsed on his bedroll.

And brooded on where he was.

Miles from his valley, farther than he'd ever journeyed. And every turn of these wheels carried him and Greensleeves farther away. Gull had never been homesick before, because he'd never been away from home.

Now he wondered, Would it have been so bad if he and Greensleeves had died with the rest? Would all his family be together then, in some better place?

A hiss. "Gull!"

He started at the rustle behind him, flipped quickly, and reached up for his axe.

A whiff of perfume, a slim hand pressing his mouth, then nimble fingers tugged his blanket roll open, and Lily slipped inside. Her white powdered face was ruddy by the light of dying embers, her feet cold, her body warm. Giggling, she planted painted lips on his and kissed greedily.

"We can be together if we're quiet!" she whispered. "You needn't pay me. No one will know. I'll grant your every desire!"

Blood thundered in Gull's skull like a hammer on an anvil. Lily pressed close, chewed on his lips, groped under his kilt.

"Wait!" Stunned by the surprise, his mind still far off in White Ridge, Gull grabbed her wrists.

Thinking he teased, Lily ducked and bit him on the nipple. She was drawing a reaction from under his kilt, but he tugged her hands away.

Red lips pouted. "What? Is there something else you prefer? I know all sorts of ways—"

"Hush up—honey." He'd almost said "child." She'd seen worlds more than he, yet she was so young and perky he felt like her big brother. "I don't want . . ."

Her confusion was turning to anger. "Men never know what they want! That's why they come to us! I can—"

"Heavens above! Would you *listen?*" His thoughts jumbled. Part of him knew what it wanted, but he plowed on. "It's not you, Lily. You're very pretty and very sweet. It's me. I'm . . ."

She waited, used to it. Finally he blurted, "I'm still in mourning. Being with you would be—too much happiness too soon. It'd dishonor the memory of my village, and my family. Do you understand?"

Leaning back, she studied his face, shook her beribboned hair. "I don't . . . That's . . . Never has a man given me that excuse. Too tired, or too much drink. But never . . . " She was baffled, and Gull felt a sudden rush of sympathy for her. She offered affection the only way she knew how, and he'd rebuffed her.

Yet an old saying of his mother's came to Gull's mind. "A simple hug shows more love than all the loving in the world."

And thoughts of his lost home only made him sad.

Suddenly he hugged her close, her head against his breast. Perfume wafted from Lily's dark hair. "Just let me hold you a while, please?"

Gently, carefully, she hugged him back. Finally she understood, for she was lonely and homesick too. "You're a strange man, Gull, but a good one—*Ouch!*"

Lily bleated, then screamed. Ripped from his arms, she was hauled by her hair from under the wagon.

"What the . . . ? Out of the way, alley cat!" grated a voice. "I'm here to kill your boyfriend!"

CHAPTER
8

Kem, the scarred bodyguard. Staging a sneak attack.

He must have grabbed for Gull's hair, not knowing Lily was alongside him.

Too bad he guessed wrong, thought Gull.

Dragged half-out, Lily kept screaming. Gull reached past her, clamped Kem's hairy wrist, braced his free hand against a wheel—

—and yanked with all his might.

A curse and thud told Kem's face had struck the side of the wagon. He let Lily go. A veteran of drunken brawls, she melted away under the back axles.

Still cursing, pinned by one wrist, Kem ducked and swiped with his free hand. Probably it held a knife, Gull figured. He tossed the wrist, and Kem swore as he missed slicing Gull's arm.

Kicking, the woodcutter rolled out from under the wagon toward the firepit. He wore only his leather kilt. Firelight glistened on his sweaty, scarred body. He cast around for nonlethal weaponry: cordwood, dirt, iron cookware, tack hung on the wagon. Plenty.

Kem sailed around the end of the wagon, shuffled to a fighting stance, that long dagger gleaming in his fist. "This is where we part company, Gullshit!"

Gull crooked his fingers. "You have to get close to hurt me, Lop-ear. Afraid?"

With a growl, the bodyguard lunged. Gull hopped to the side, snaked a full feed bag off its hook on the wagon, swung it at his enemy's head. Kem dodged the heavy bag, but lost his chance to thrust with the blade. Gull chucked the bag in the man's face, jumped in close, and smashed his fist on the the thug's wrist, numbing it. The dagger stabbed dirt.

Yet Kem knew how to fight, while Gull had only his brute strength. Kem let the weapon lie, slapped at Gull's crotch. The woodcutter swerved his hips, swerved back to mash the hand against the wagon. In too close, he snapped his right forearm up, clopped Kem under the chin. Locked, they breathed each other's sweat, ground hair off each other's bodies.

Kem struck like a snake, bit two of Gull's fingers like a bulldog.

Gull hissed, jabbed at Kem's eyes with his two left fingers. The bodyguard spit out Gull's hand to avoid being blinded. He punched Gull in the chest, the belly, the throat. Gull stopped that assault by whapping Kem's swollen ear. The bodyguard gurgled with pain.

Then Kem lowered his head and rammed Gull hard in the belly, shoving with both feet. Gull fetched up against a wheel. He'd been caught with his own trick, using the wagon as a wall. Kem swiped at Gull's balls, and Gull tried to knee him back, but they were too tangled to do much harm.

Then a noose floated over Gull's head and tightened on his windpipe.

*   *   *

Breathless, Gull's hands flew to his throat. He clawed for the noose, skinned his own throat, but already the cord had sunk deep. He panicked, kicked, thrashed, slammed his butt against the wagon wheel to get free. But he was held fast.

The bully had a partner, his foggy brain screamed.

Now that Gull had stopped fighting, Kem knew he had a partner, too. The scarred man took advantage. Hauling back a fist, he slammed Gull full in the belly. It rocked him, jarred his throat, but there was no way for his air to escape. Gull tried to kick Kem away, but was so close-pressed he couldn't raise his knee or foot.

The firelight dimmed, as if someone had smothered it.

That's my vision, Gull thought. Blacking out. Forever.

He let go his aching throat and lashed backward with his elbow, skinned it on rough wood, grazed the assassin's arm. He heard a guffaw. His next flail was feebler. Kem smashed his jaw, blacked his eye. But Gull had so much pain from his throat and lungs, he barely felt it.

All my troubles will end in a moment, he thought. *Who'll look after Greensleeves?*

Above the roaring in his ears, he heard a dull thunk. As if bursting from under deep water, he could breathe. The cord had gone slack.

Gull ripped the strangling noose from his neck. He retched, wheezed, gagged. Kem guessed what had happened. He hopped back to get clear.

Not fast enough.

Still retching, Gull lowered his head and charged.

His skull collided with Kem's jaw. A satisfying *clack* sounded. He butted the man again, grappled his shoulders by his sturdy leather armholes. Grunting, he spun the man.

Kem tumbled into the firepit. The cookware had been moved to one side, so there was only a stone-lined trough full of dying embers. Dying, but still hot. Trying to brace his fall, Kem drove his hands deep into ashes and red coals. He screamed.

Gull hopped up and crashed both knees onto the man's back, driving his hands deeper, buckling his knees. With both fists, Gull clouted the back of his bony skull—once, twice, again.

But when he raised them a fourth time, they proved too heavy. The black night went blacker, and he pitched over backward, thoroughly spent.

A sandaled toe prodded his ribs.

Gull opened one swollen eye. A craggy salt-and-pepper face grinned at him. Morven the sailor. "Enough playtime, children. Time for bed."

Groaning, Gull rolled over, found his feet. Kem was gone from the firepit. But a pair of feet projected from under a wheel. Gull crawled over, recognized another bodyguard, a handsome dark man the cook called Pretty Boy.

"Chad," said Morven. "A friend to Kem. Probably his only one. Quick with a garrotte, a strangling noose."

"What—" Gull coughed, swallowed fire. "What— happened?"

Chuckling, Morven hefted a crossbow. "I was cruising the perimeter, heard a noise by the chuck wagon. Figured some sneak thief was out to hook Felda's pies. Gaffed him with this. Wouldn't you know—one of our own. My blunder." He plucked sticky hairs from the crossbow grip.

Gull rubbed his throat. "Does Towser—approve of assassination—amongst his own people?"

Morven fixed his eye on a distant star. "Towser's got too many worries to bother with ours. We work out our little tiffs."

"They're—working out. I'll kill both—and then they'll be good."

"He'd just hire more bullies. Live with what you got. They'll sheer off from now on." Morven propped the crossbow on the water butt, grabbed Chad and hoisted him like a child, dumped him in the back of the men's wagon. Inside, someone protested, "Hey!"

"Sorry." Morven retrieved his crossbow and returned to guard duty.

Lily drifted out of the shadows to brush dirt off Gull's back. "You're hard to kill."

"As long as—Morven's behind me."

She knelt to brush off his legs, straighten his kilt. "More will stand behind you now. No one likes Kem or Chad."

"I'd like—to get some sleep—for a change."

Lily took his hand, led him under the chuck wagon, knelt and straightened his bedroll. "No, you'd like company. Mine."

Gull started to protest, but she tucked him into his blankets and wriggled alongside. "I know, I know. No loving. Just hugging. And maybe some kissing." She mashed her red lips on his bruised ones, slid her tongue into his mouth.

This time, Gull was too weak to fend her off.

The days that followed were all alike.

Break camp, travel, eat, travel, set up camp, sleep. Every seventh day they stayed put to rest, but that meant a full day of repairs. Gull had lived all his life in a sedate farming village, with time for naps and gossip and games. He found the rush unsettling. He wondered why the wizard moved so fast, pushed so hard. What secrets or treasures beckoned that wouldn't wait another day or two?

Gull drove, tended stock, worried about wagons, ate, slept, did it all again in his dreams. Occasionally his father or mother would loom from the mists and replay some old joke or story, and Gull awoke with an aching heart, missing them. But by then he was busy again.

As they neared hill country in the north, the forest floor grew rougher. Gentle dips turned into ravines too steep to cross, so had to be circled. Granite ledges came thicker, not just flat spans, but stepped shelves half the height of the wagons. Sometimes the wagoners had to cut saplings and lever the wagons up breaks. Rocks and rough country meant smaller twisted trees, and occasionally Gull had to lop branches, or squat and saw at ankle height so the wagons could pass over the stump. Their pace slowed to a few miles a day.

The scouts still found passage, but it took longer. Often the wagons waited for them to return, then had to backtrack and try somewhere else. They boxed the compass some days, traveling miles in a circle to make one mile northwest.

Lily rode with Gull when she could. As long as she answered Towser's beck and call, and did her camp chores, no one cared. Greensleeves wandered into the woods and back out, finding flowers and lizards and birds' eggs, yet always staying within eyeshot, as if she knew Gull would worry.

Kem drove the horses with bandaged hands, and

Chad suffered dizzy spells. Both stayed clear of the muleskinner. Conversely, others became friendly, including some of dancing girls, the cook Felda and her choreboy Stiggur, the clerk Knoton, and the nurse Haley. They wished each other a hearty good morning, excluding Kem and Chad with silence. Others remained wrapped in their own worlds, including the silent bodyguard, Oles; the bard, Ranon Spiritsinger; the astrologer, old Kakulina.

And of course, Towser.

"What *does* he do in that wagon all day and night?" asked Gull. "It must be damned rank and cramped. What keeps him busy?"

Lily arched an eyebrow. "Well, I could tell you what he does with us dancing girls, but you wouldn't learn much. His other interests are a secret. I know he has a scrying crystal. He's often so mesmerized by it, he doesn't see me enter."

"What does he see inside that?"

"I don't know. I peeked once but saw nothing."

Gull pondered that. "But what else? A man can't stare at bubbles in a glass all day, can he?"

Lily yawned, scooted sideways, pillowed her head on Gull's thigh. "You talk of men. He's a wizard. Not like us. He toys with things, or studies them. A box of stinkpots, books, little clockwork engines. He's even got a box of seashells such as a child gathers on the beach. And charms and leaves and fairy dust and such. Yet I don't think much is valuable. He doesn't keep it neat, just pokes things back in holes—they fall off the shelves and crash on his table. It wouldn't disturb him to lose the whole wagon, I don't think . . . " She was nodding off, but suddenly opened a mascaraed eye. "No, there is one precious thing. His grimoire."

"Grim-what?"

"Grimoire. His book of magic. Chained to his belt."

"Oh, that. It's full of magic spells? Does that mean if I read some—if I could read—I could do magic?"

She shook her head on his leathered thigh. "No. From the little I've seen, it's just sketches he's made. I think they remind him of spells he already knows. The way Cook has pictures on her drawer of spices."

"Ah. Oh, well, I don't want to perform magic anyway. I'd feel foolish in a striped gown."

She giggled and patted his knee. "No, your talents lie elsewhere."

"How would you know?" Gull shifted the reins and mussed her hair, making her squeal. "So far you've only suffered my kisses."

Tsking, she sat up to primp with hairpins. "A woman knows."

"Woman!" Gull teased. "You barely put curves in your clothing!"

"I'm eighteen, *grandfather*! And I've seen and done more than you have!"

"I imagine." Gull clucked at his mules. "They'll make good stories thirty years from now, when you're a fat grandmother."

"I hope so." She sighed suddenly. "But what decent man will wed a whore?"

"You'd be surprised."

"Would *you* marry a whore?"

Gull looked at her sidelong, thinking she teased again, but she was serious. "No, she'd have to give up whoring. And know how to cook. Mine's terrible."

Lily closed her hand around his on the reins. "The other dancing girls are jealous, you know, because I get you to myself."

"Well, tell them they're not missing much." He was suddenly angry with himself. Lily was so sweet, so considerate, yet he couldn't give her his full attention while his mind was still an emotional turmoil. Changing the subject, he asked, "So, we travel just so Towser can scribble in a book?"

Lily frowned at him, unsure what he thought, then shook her head. "No, we travel so he can gather *mana*. From what I understand, all lands have magic, some more than others. By crossing the country, Towser gathers its energy. He uses it to learn things, and to battle other wizards."

Gull tsked, "Why not to help people?"

A shrug. The girl peered at the sky. "It'll rain soon. Few men are like you, Gull. There's a city in the west called Estark, one of the places of power, I've heard, where the wizards have their own strange way of making magic. Once a year they joust in a tournament, sometimes to the death. The winner goes off with a supreme sorcerer, a Walker who descends like a god. The whole city exists to conjure magic, and make bets on who'll win the tournaments. Scouts canvass the countryside and find any potential magic users. As if the Domains were just a farm, with the wizards in control and the rest of us cattle."

Gull snorted. "This is one bull who won't go gently to slaughter."

Lily fixed him with aged eyes. "But you work for a wizard. As I do."

"True," sighed the woodcutter. The wagon jolted over a rock and he slapped the reins. "Easy, there! My father used to say the gods love nothing more than to make a man violate an oath."

"Oath? You swore an oath?"

"Aye. To kill any wizard I met. And look at me now."

Angry again, with himself and everything else, he said no more.

*   *   *

Later on, Oles, the quiet one on scout, waved him to walk ahead. Gull handed Lily the reins and hopped down.

The bodyguard stood at line with hemlocks. Through their lacy branches, Gull saw the forest floor turned to cedars and bog. He groaned.

"Like this all across the northwest," muttered Oles. He had shaggy hair and a brushy mustache, a sheep-skin vest and baggy pants. He swatted a fly from his ear. "I'd say impassable. Towser won't agree. He'll stay buttoned in his wagon while we get ate."

Gull swatted flies and midges that buzzed hungry from the bog. "What about due west?"

"Boggier. Sank to my knees." He pointed where mud had dried on his pants.

"North?" Talking to Oles shortened his speech too.

"Uphill. Dry, but you couldn't squeeze through. Big trees."

Gull swatted and swore. "What the hell—Oh. Greensleeves."

His sister materialized from the hemlocks, making no more rustle than a deer. She carried something long and saggy and gray. Another badger. Oles stared at the small girl clutching a wild animal to her bosom.

Gull caressed his sister's head. "You're lucky, you can't get lost. You're always lost. Or else never so."

Greensleeves burbled in her questioning tone. She looked at the wagons and the tree-choked bog, cooed like a dove.

"'Fraid so." Gull was just thinking aloud. "We'll be days dropping trees for a corduroy road—eh?"

Tugging at his hand, Greensleeves pointed north. Her brother said, "No, hon. The trees are too big."

Dangling by its fat belly, the badger kicked. The girl scooched and it slunk into the brush. But before it disappeared, Gull noticed its ear was notched, as if gnawed.

He jerked to a halt, almost pulling his sister over. "Hey! That badger—"

Wait now, thought Gull. She'd found a badger days ago, with a notched ear, but had let it go. Was this the same beast? Miles farther on? Badgers didn't walk miles: they stayed within their territory. Could it have followed them? For leagues? Nonsense. Then . . . had Greensleeves carried it all this way? No. Hidden it in the chuck wagon? Not possible. How then . . . ?

But Greensleeves tugged, and he had to follow. He was curious, too. She was rarely this insistent, unless there was a wounded animal she couldn't lift. She dragged him into the brush. A trail, only a foot wide, meandered through less-dense patches: a deer trail. Tufts of white belly hair, winter coats shedding, showed on snags. Greensleeves walked upright, but Gull had to hunch.

"Whatever it is, let's not go far, Greenie. I need to cut trees . . . "

Stepping between two forked oaks, they were suddenly in the clear.

They stood in a ravine like many they'd already passed, the sides lined with the scrub oak and bracken. But a sandy floor, rain-washed smooth, sloped gently upward. The only obstacles were rocks they could lever up. Gull pushed past his sister and climbed the slope, bad knee aching. Topping the ravine, he found big trees with open space between. He could see at least a half mile.

Rocks scrunched behind. Oles had followed, cradling his crossbow. "Hunh. Missed this gap. *She* should scout."

"Aye," said Gull. He stared at his sister, who'd pried up a rock to tickle a red salamander. "Perhaps she should."

Using Greensleeves's shortcut, they widened the deer trail and traversed the ravine in two days. On solid ground again, they made good progress for a half dozen days.

Though the others had no clue, Gull guessed they neared their goal. One day he was sure.

He smelled it.

A tang floated on the northern breeze, a wet reek like an old campfire. Only greater, and bitter, as if the earth had burned too.

As it had.

They saw the first marks far to their right. The scout, Chad, who hated to talk to Gull, simply pointed and walked away.

Gull only nodded. He'd been right.

A long dark triangle had marred the forest. The ground was blackened, the tree trunks scorched, the leaves withered and brown. The bottom of the triangle pointed northwest, whence the wind had lifted and tossed some fire. They trekked through more greenery, found another burned slash.

And finally came to where the forest fire had raged.

Even the fat cook got out of the wagon to look. Even Towser. The charred stink was strong in their nostrils, clung to their clothing and skin.

As if standing on a green shore, a black tide lapped away from their feet, stretching northwest out of eye-shot. The rolling country was scorched to black loam, though the fire had jumped some hollows and ledges. Big trees had survived, green high on their crowns, but smaller ones had perished like sagging candles. With a clear sky and weeks of spring, the earth sprang back, and green fingers infiltrated the black wastes. After days of marching through the shadowed forest, hot sunshine made the travelers squint.

Gull tested his theory on Towser. In his striped gown, the wizard glowed like a firework in the sunshine. "We saw a shooting star two moons ago. Could it have started a forest fire?"

"It might have . . . " said Towser absently, and Gull knew he'd guessed their destination. "Let's move on."

"Still northwest?" persisted Gull.

"Aye." Towser turned toward his wagon.

Felda objected. "We can't camp here. There'll be no water."

Towser waved the objection away. "There'll be *mana*. Get rolling. We'll figure how to camp once we find—" He stopped.

"Find what?" asked a dozen.

But the wizard climbed into his wagon and drew the curtain.

Wondering, the entourage climbed onto wagon seats and clucked to the stock.

The next day, they found it.

In the blackest, bleakest center of the burned area, devoid of trees or even rocks, the earth suddenly banked, a vast hollow circle. Again, the entire entourage came to peer over this earthen lip.

Perfectly circular, deep as a lake, but dry, was a hole two hundred feet across. Layers of earth showed black loam, yellow sand, gray clay, gray sand.

At the very bottom of the crater was a smaller hole they couldn't see into.

No one spoke. No birds sang, no butterflies fluttered. The soil was sterile, without even anthills. The forest held its breath, as if the shocking violence of the calamity still lingered.

"This is it!" Towser's gleeful chortle startled them. He pointed. "A star fell from the heavens and crashed right there! Fetch the tools!"

"What for?" asked Kem.

"To dig up the star!"

CHAPTER
9

They dug.

Each wagon carried a short-handled spade, and there were two picks and a crowbar. The men were ordered down the slope and into the small hole. They found it bell-shaped, two arm spans across, littered with rocks and branches and leaves damp from rain. Tossing out the debris, they dug.

To begin, all four bodyguards dug as one. When the hole grew too deep to hurl the dirt out, they tied buckets to ropes for hoisting and dumping. Slow work. In a feverish hurry, Towser ordered the dancing girls to help haul. When camp was established a half mile away, near a clear-running stream, the cook's helper and nurse were ordered to help too. Even Knoton the clerk had to dirty his hands and blow on his blisters.

"Whatever's down here," grumbled Gull, "he wants it bad."

Forced to work shoulder-to-shoulder with dangerous tools, Gull and Morven on one side and Kem and

Chad on the other formed an unspoken truce. They talked as needed and no more, but neither did they watch their backs for a pickaxe blow.

Gull pointed out, "Towser'd probably turn us into toads if we mucked around belting each other." No one disagreed.

Towser's entourage dug all day, with only breaks for meals and guard duty. Gull was glad of any excuse to stop shifting dirt, and when his turn came, grabbed his longbow and quiver and hurried off.

The new perimeter included both the camp and the crater, a circuit of a mile or more. The blasted forest—withered trees and leaning stumps and new greenery underfoot—let him see a good distance, though some rills and pockets still shut off sight. He crooked an arrow alongside his bow for a quick draw. Tracks showed deer and other beasts were attracted to the tender spring growth.

At one point he heard a sough behind him, and nocked as he whirled.

And almost shot Stiggur, the cook's helper.

"Don't shoot! Don't shoot! I'm sorry!" The boy raised trembling hands.

Despite regular meals, the boy was rail-thin and small. Starved at an early age, Gull assumed, never to grow tall. He wore a plain linen smock, very clean, and hair clipped short to keep lice and dirt out of the food. Felda was hellacious for washing hands, burying wastewater, scrubbing dishes, digging the privy far away. A bout of dysentery or camp fever could wipe out the entourage—and delay Towser's frantic schedule.

"What is it, lad?" Gull snapped. He'd never spoken to the boy much, only to request more food or bid good-morning.

"Uh, I just wanted to walk with you, sir." His voice

was warbly, about to break. Gull guessed he was twelve
or so—Sparrow Hawk's age, were he still alive.

Gull frowned, puzzled, and the boy backstepped.
Realizing it was a compliment, he said, "All right.
Stay on my right and behind, clear of the bow. And
walk soft. I'm hoping for fresh venison or pork."

"Yes, sir."

Gull resumed walking. "Save the 'sirs' for Towser.
I'll be plain Gull."

"Y-yes . . . Gull."

They walked, clogs and bare feet sinking into the
miry loam. Sometimes their passing shook burned
bark or branches from trees. Low bushes, recovering,
plucked at their ankles. Gull kept his eyes unfocused,
to better see movement, and carried his head cocked
to hear ahead.

He was startled when the boy spoke. "I admire the
way you snap that whip, sir—I mean, Gull."

Annoyed, Gull growled, "Do you?"

Encouraged, he jabbered, "Aye, sir, Gull. It's wonderful you can pop between the mule's ears without
hitting. And the way you split Kem's ear—" He
stopped, uncertain whether he should criticize another
adult.

"Poor Kem's ear must buzz, it gets talked about so."
Gull held up a finger for silence as they peered around
a tree bole. A brown bear cub underdug a log for
grubs.

Stiggur whispered, "You won't shoot it?"

"I could," Gull hissed. "Bear liver's fine eating,
especially a tender young one. But I'd have a mother
on my back before I could nock again. See there?"

He pointed. Down a slope, a she-bear still shaggy
with winter growth rocked an ash tree, trying to dis-
lodge a clinging possum. Gull led the boy in the

opposite direction. "Never shoot a brown bear, unless you've a pack of hounds and several lancers."

The boy stared, hanging on every word. Why was it, Gull thought, young boys followed him around? He couldn't walk through White Ridge without tripping over wide-eyed kids.

To stop the staring, he pulled his mulewhip from his back belt. It was oily and heavy and long, more than twelve feet, and always felt alive in his hand, like a snake. "Here. If we can't hunt—because someone's talking—we can practice this."

Sheathing his arrow, he took up the whip. "Hold it loose, then toss it back along the ground. Not alongside, mind, but behind. Straighter the better. Flick it forward, underhand to start. Light, like taking a girl's hand. Hit that bush."

Stiggur took the whip reverently, carefully trailed it out straight. Then he took a huge step, snapped with all his might.

The blacksnake humped, squirmed, slapped him smartly behind the knee. The boy yelped.

Gull nodded. "That's one advantage—if you don't listen, the punishment is automatic. Watch."

Accepting the whip, Gull flicked it easily behind, flicked underhand. Leather sizzled like a dragon's tongue and popped a four-inch branch off a pin oak.

"Wow!" bleated the boy.

Gull handed it back. "That's an easy pull. Your turn."

In four tries, Stiggur tagged his ankle, neck, and rump. But the flail shot pinked a bush. Bounding, the boy showed off the broken twig as if it were a prize swan. Gull laughed.

"A good start. Keep practicing, though. If we drop a deer, we can slice the rawhide and I'll show you how to braid your own whip."

"Really? That would be champion!"

"I said *if*. If it's ever quiet enough to hunt!" The woodcutter tousled the shorn head, but stopped. The boy reminded him of Sparrow Hawk so much his heart hurt. "Where's your family, Stiggur?"

"Never had one. Felda found me at a pasture gate one morning. That's what me name means: 'Gate.'"

"A foundling without a home, eh? That makes two of us, then." He shoved the boy good-naturedly toward camp. "Come on. My duty's almost over, if I read the sun aright. Digging for me and firewood for you."

Together, they kicked through the greenery.

Four days' digging found undisturbed soil.

Earlier had seen mixed sand, dirt, and clay churned by the impact of the shooting star. Now the hole showed clean, packed sand with only a dirty smudge in the center. Crowding shoulders, they dug with new vigor.

Towser wanted a large iron-and-nickel stone. It would be lumpy and rusty, melted and charred like cinder clinkers. That, he explained, was what stars were made of. It was news to the commoners. Morven speculated stars must be frightfully hot for iron and nickel to burn.

But it wasn't a round iron rock they struck.

Chad hit it first.

They all stopped at the sharp *chik,* an unfamiliar noise, not a rock. The bodyguard dropped to his knees, held the shovel blade in two hands to scrape gently. Towser had warned them not to chip the star.

A sharp square nose shed dirt.

The men bumped heads peering. Gull sent Stiggur to fetch Towser. Gently, two men scooped sand with their hands. When they had three sides uncovered, they quit.

The box was big as a skull and pink as sunburn. It was grooved, or etched, into regular furrows. Two faces had raised squares like belt buckles, and the other two round buckles. Ridges looked like straps holding the buckles on. Yet it was all of one piece, some porous pink rock.

"Coral," said Morven. "It looks like coral."

"What's that?" growled Chad.

"A stone that grows in shallow seas like trees. Under the waves. Fish swim through it like monkeys. It comes in all colors, but mostly pink. But coral's soft. You can carve it with a knife. This thing's tough, to fall from the heavens and blow open a crater like this, and stay intact."

"It looks like pig guts to me," muttered Kem. "Like you wrapped a box in pig guts like you'd make sausage with. Like something dead."

Gull tapped a fingernail against it. "Sounds solid. But it looks like it opens."

"Aye," said Knoton, the clerk. "Like a strongbox without a lock."

"Think Towser can open it?" asked Gull. "Dare he? It fell from the stars. Who knows what's inside?"

The clerk shrugged. "He brought us across half a forest to dig for days to find it. What do you think?"

Gull rocked back on his hams. "I hope we're elsewhere when he cracks it."

On that, everyone agreed.

*   *   *

The discovery so pleased Towser he gave them the day off.

With a grateful groan, the workers pitched tools out of the hole and trudged back to camp. They shucked their shoes and shirts and scrubbed in the stream. Felda sang as she prepared supper. Everyone was glad the thing was found, for now they could leave this ashy, smelly wasteland. Anywhere else had to be better.

In a rare jolly mood, Towser remained outside to plunk himself on a stump and sip honeyed tea. He toyed with the pink box, turning it, holding it to the sunlight, squinting for cracks or latches or any way to open it.

Gull accepted a plate of pickled herring and dried potatoes and the inevitable pickles, got a mug of ale from Stiggur, then sat against a wheel not far from Towser.

He chewed a while, then asked, casually, "So what is it, Towser?"

The wizard stopped his juggling to glare. "I don't ask you about mule tending. Kindly don't ask me about magicks."

"Fine." Gull shrugged. He watched the wizard play, waited.

Eventually Towser spoke, too thrilled not to chatter. "It's a *mana* vault!"

Gull looked interested, but stupid.

"It stores magical energy—*mana*! Magic is every-where, you know. In the air we breathe, the water, the land. But magic's spread thin. *This* thing *stores mana*, the way a purse holds gold! A whole *land's worth* ready for the magic user who needs it!"

"Really?"

The wizard practically bounced in place, like a

child with a new toy. "Yes, yes! If it's full as I think, I can conjure a hundred—a *thousand* spells using just this! It will speed up my studies tremendously! It's worth its weight in gold! Platinum! But it's worthless to any pawn, any non-magic user," he added hastily.

Gull played dumb. "Of course. No use to us. I'm just glad to stop digging."

Towser laughed at his hired simpleton. He slugged his cold tea, tucked the box under his arm to enter his wagon.

But Greensleeves blocked his path.

Towser frowned. He'd ignored the half-wit girl so far. He treated her like someone's cat, unable to work or take orders. He'd never spoken to her.

Now she barred his way. He made to shove her aside, and Gull rose.

Drawn to the box, like a bee to a daffodil, Greensleeves put out a grubby questing hand. Towser turned away, but she followed.

Gull found that curious. Nothing manufactured had ever interested her before. Bugs, birds, flowers, ferns, leaves, snowflakes: that was all she cared about.

But she wanted the stone box.

"Stop! You're not to touch it!" Towser raised a hand to bat her, but halted when Gull cleared his throat. No one would abuse his sister.

Gently, the brother caught her arm. "Come away, Greenie. It's not for you."

Towser mounted his wagon. Greensleeves strained against Gull's grip, mewing like a hungry kitten, even after the curtain was drawn. He dragged her to the firepit, asked Felda for some sweet, got a daub of honey on a spoon. But the half-wit just dropped it. Gull had to stop her climbing into Towser's wagon.

"Now ain't that curious," murmured the cook. "The little darlin' wants that box. Does she see somethin' we can't?"

Annoyed, Gull shook his head. "It's just the color, probably. It must look like a bunch of flowers, or . . . I don't know. A piglet . . . "

But the village elders used to say the "touched" had second sight, could sense things ordinary mortals couldn't. What had Greensleeves seen in that box?

Whatever, it didn't matter. It belonged to Towser, and Greensleeves would just cause trouble if she persisted.

"Come on, Greenie. I have to check hooves. *Come.* I'll let you pat the mules." He jerked her around. "Come *on!*"

Him dragging, her mewling, the two crossed the burned loam for the herd.

Tossing and turning, Lily elbowed and kneed Gull a dozen times.

Finally he sat up, ducking under the axles, and prodded her slim shoulder. "Will you sleep or dance?"

The dancing girl thrashed clear of the blankets, combed sweaty hair from her brow. Lily's face showed clearly, for the Mist Moon was up, bathing the night in white light. Skin ashine, she looked more a statue than living soul.

"I'm sorry. It's . . . bad dreams. There's . . . something in the air . . . "

Gull flopped on his back, groaning. "Not you too! First Greensleeves cries for a pink rock, now you ride the night mare."

The girl shivered, curled up against his bare

shoulder. "It's this place. It's full of whispers, talking in my head. I'm sorry I woke you, my love."

"Sounds like the Whispering Woods all over again," muttered Gull. "Greensleeves was sensitive to them . . . What did you call me?"

He got no answer, and propping on one elbow didn't help, because now he couldn't see her face in the dark. "Lily . . . "

"That slipped out." Lily suddenly wrapped perfumed arms around his neck and clung. Tears tickled his shoulder. "But it wasn't a mistake."

"Lily . . . " He didn't know how to begin.

A murmur. "You're so sweet. You treat me decently, speak as if I were a lady, not a—"

"Hush!" He clamped her mouth. "I don't like that word. It doesn't fit you."

A sniffle, a sigh. "It's what I am. A whore. I pleasure men for money. I've slept with all of them: Towser, Chad, Oles, Kem, even Morven."

Gull jolted. *"Morven?"*

"Aye. He was the kindest of the lot, lusty but gentle. He liked me to—"

"I don't want to hear about it!"

More sniffles. "You don't have to love me back."

"It's not that . . . " He raised his fists against the wagon bottom. He felt like punching the oak boards: words seemed useless. "Look, honey—"

A scream split the night.

Gull rolled from under the wagon, double-bitted axe in hand.

A man screamed. Oles.

In the black night beyond the banked campfire, Gull picked out the man's filthy sheepskin vest. It seemed to flap above the ground like a swan taking flight. The slowpoke ran faster than Gull had ever seen, even faster than at dinner call. He was armed with a sword at his belt and crossbow in hand, but seemed to have forgotten. Running flat out, he screamed all the way, one long keening note without breath.

"*What is it?*" Gull shouted. He took a fresh grip on his axe. Terror was contagious, especially in the depths of night. "*What's after you?*"

Then Gull saw.

Marching toward the wagons, in a wavering line, came a line of walking dead.

They looked like nothing less than walking birch stumps, so white and stiff were these creatures, these things long dead.

They shuffled over the uneven soil, bumped one another, bounced off, turned half round, stumbled on. Heads were mostly bald or lacked skin, so dull bone gleamed in the moonlight. Faces had dried to leather, puckered tight at their eyes. Mouths hung open as if decrying the injustice of being wrenched from the grave. They were wrapped in burial shrouds, or rat-torn rags, or nothing at all.

Slowly, clumsily, but resolutely, they staggered toward the circle of wagons, half a hundred or more in the dimness. Most horrible of all, they made no sound except the shuffle and rustle.

Sweating, wild-eyed, Gull tried to think. So slowly did the things move, they posed little threat. They could barely raise their arms. Yet neither could they be easily stopped, for they were already dead. One carried Oles's crossbow quarrel through its chest.

"Gods of Urza!" squeaked Lily. "Zombies of Scathe!"

The woodcutter had no time to wonder where a

dancing girl had learned of zombies and whence they came, if Scathe was a place. The camp was roused. People tumbled out of wagons. A dancing girl screamed so piercingly Gull's ears hurt.

"Here we go again!" growled Kem. He wound a crossbow held by a stirrup. "I need a new job!"

"Hide!" shrilled a girl. "Get under cover! Towser will protect us!"

"Towser got us into this!" snapped Chad as he yanked his checked shirt over his head.

"No, you don't, ya lubber!" sounded Morven. He dragged Oles from inside the men's wagon. "Ye're fightin' here with us!"

"Get up, Stiggur!" came the muffled voice of Felda inside the chuck wagon. "Get up, you clot! We're attacked!"

"Build up the fire!" shrieked Knoton from inside the wagon. "Towser orders it!"

Gull had found work. He grabbed chunks of cordwood, split the ends, cast about for some canvas or rags to make torches. Every living thing feared fire, maybe the dead did too.

There was more shrilling and shouting, but before sanity could be imposed, the scream of horses caused them to reel yet again.

As usual, the herd was not far off, hobbled so they could browse the night long. But something was amongst them. Gull heard growls like a wolf's, but deeper, and a coughing like nothing he knew.

Gull reached under the chuck wagon for his bow and quiver, found his hands full of weapons, thrust his axe at Lily, who promptly dropped it. The woodcutter nocked and drew, aiming toward the herd, still without knowing what attacked them.

Chad dashed across the circle, opposite from the

approaching zombies, swore, leveled his crossbow across a seat. The bow slammed *twangtunk* and a bolt sizzled through the air. Shoved by Morven, Oles fumbled into position and shot too. A mule shrilled.

Gull screamed, "Ease up, you fool! Watch where you shoot!" Cursing the gods, himself, and everything in between, he tracked along his arrow for a target.

The earth was black speckled with silver: moonlight on spring greenery. White and piebald horses showed as patchy ghosts, but the darker mules were almost invisible amidst burned black trunks. What was . . .

There. Something large as the horses, and tawny, leaped among the hobbled beasts. Gull couldn't see what for horseflesh. Then he glimpsed a yellow head with wild hair bob and dip. Then two more without manes. A brown cob broke his hobble and ran. Within three paces, twin tawny shapes flashed alongside, raking the horse's flanks with long claws. Blood flew and the horse sagged.

Big cats, Gull realized. Giant wildcats, all of a sand color. The males with shaggy manes.

Killing his livestock.

All this he glimpsed in seconds, and that a shaggy male was after a white mare, then he aimed behind the cat's shoulder and loosed. The arrow sped off with a slap of linen string against his wrist.

The big male shuddered and loosed its grip on the horse. Far off, the brown cob screamed, and frantically Gull tried to find it.

To trained ears came the pounding of hoofbeats. But from the other direction, out near the zombies.

Horses running in time.

Cavalry.

Throne of Bone, whence came these things?
Then he knew. He swore bitterly and hard.
"It's another damned wizards' duel!"

CHAPTER
10

Gull had two obligations in life: tend his sister and tend his livestock.

Slipping his bow over a naked shoulder, snatching his axe back from Lily, he vaulted onto the chuck wagon seat. He almost bashed heads with Greensleeves, sleepily fumbling past the curtain. Palming her crown, he mashed her back inside. "*Stay!*" The harsh tone penetrated even her befogged brain.

Then he hopped off the wagon and ran for his other charges.

The big cats—lions, Chad called them—had pulled down that brown cob. Though hard to see in shifting moonlight and shadows, Gull thought they'd hamstrung it or broken its back: the horse whinnied in terror while staying sprawled. One kill assured, the lionesses loped to the hunt again. Evidently they'd cripple half a dozen before feeding, as a fox would tear through a henhouse, then drag one home.

The cats fanned out in a three-quarter circle. The pincer movement forced the herd back against a granite shelf, a temporary pen. Gull took note. These lions were canny.

He remembered something else. Protecting the herd during a wizards' duel had gotten Towser's previous freighter killed.

There were eight or nine beasts spread out among the charred trunks. A big male with a black mane was out of the fight, for he spun in circles, snapping and pawing at the shaft lodged behind his shoulder. There were two more males, young and scrawny, and five or six lengthy females. From what he knew of cats, Gull guessed the lionesses were the more dangerous.

All were poised to tear into his animals like pigs through corn.

Don't rush. Shoot first, he told himself. Close only if necessary.

Huffing to a halt, he nocked a long arrow. A head shot would do little—they probably had skulls like oxen. Aiming in splintered moonlight, as if shooting through water, he lined on a female's belly and loosed. He heard a *tuk* as the arrow slapped into her. Startled, she hopped, then rolled, hissing and spitting. Gull heard the arrow shaft snap.

That made two heart shots on these lions, he thought grimly, and neither was dead yet. They were hard to kill.

And quick to anger.

The wounded male, old and wise, had fathomed the connection between the stings and the man with the weapon. Roaring, he whirled and charged the woodcutter.

Gull gawped. The beast came on faster than a horse, almost flying in great body-length bounds.

The woodcutter could never outrun him, or even duck behind a tree.

Dropping his bow, he snatched up his heavy axe, looped it back.

Just in time.

The golden lion filled his vision. Timing, cursing, Gull swung with all his might and prayed not to miss.

Or perhaps he should.

With a sickening *crunch*, the axe smacked the bony skull. Like rapping a rock. Gull got a glimpse of the long blade edge biting into the lion's brow, forehead, and eye, shearing skin and hair, then bouncing free. The shock of the blow rippled through Gull's arms, numbing them to the pits.

It didn't even slow the beast.

The lion hit like an avalanche—so many blows so fast Gull couldn't begin to count them, and all knocked him spinning.

A paw big as a dinner plate slammed him half around, raking his shoulder with a trio of razor-sharp claws. Only his full quiver of thick rawhide kept him from losing meat, and the bundle was ripped clean off his back. The huge bleeding head banged into his. Whiskery jaws rasped skin from his forehead. A chest big as a barrel bowled him over. Reek of cat sweat and ammonia gagged him.

Clutching his axe, his only hope, Gull curled into a ball as he bounced on turf five feet away. A back leg clipped his rump as as the lion sailed over him. Winded by twin blows, Gull gasped for air. Rubbing his chest, he found it sticky-slick.

Why the beast hadn't dug in claws and clamped down Gull couldn't guess, unless it was dazed by the head blow. He only knew he still lived.

For a few seconds, anyway.

Wheezing, he spun for the next attack.

Even on velvet paws, the lion shook the ground when it landed. Snarling, it wheeled. Gull got his bloodied axe up. Blood poured from the beast's brow, and a flap of skin hung over the split eye. Still, Gull knew, head wounds bled like mad but rarely killed anyone. So it must be with a lion.

Hobbling on his bad knee, which he'd wracked somehow, Gull sidled to the lion's blind side. The beast coughed as if spitting a hairball. Probably drawing wind for another lunge.

"Why not—forget it . . . " Gull panted.

The cat squatted. Gull knew what came next. He felt like a mouse trapped in a barn.

Springing from its back legs, the lion leaped, paws up to pin him.

Heaving so hard his gut felt to burst, Gull slashed upward to catch the lion under the chin, or in the throat. But a thick forepaw deflected the blow. Off-balance, the swipe and his own momentum pitched Gull to the ground.

Pain seared as he smacked on his lacerated shoulder. Dirt blew into his nose, stinging, itching. Loam and ash stuck to sweat and blood. Hot blood trickled into his eyes from his forehead scrape. His head rang.

Never mind! he thought wildly. Where was the damned lion?

A dozen feet away, limping, was where. Gull had broken or sprained its forepaw with his swing.

"Now we're even!" he growled. Both crippled and half-blind.

The wounded paw matched the blind side, so the cat stumbled at every step. Fighting for breath, it circled, as did the man.

Then, growling in menace, the lion hopped three-legged back to its pride.

Lions are smarter than people, Gull thought. *They don't fight to the death.*

Yet the shrill of horses and bray of mules whipped his head up.

The lionesses had ripped into the herd, raking, biting, batting the hobbled animals with sheer talons.

The battle wasn't over yet. It had barely begun.

Exhausted, outnumbered, and overwhelmed, Gull knew he couldn't fight them all.

Yet he had to drive the lions from the herd.

Maybe a bluff would work. Animals hated loud noises.

Hefting his axe in one hand, his longbow in the other, he waved both as he charged, shouting. He hoped he wasn't attacked by a half dozen hungry carnivores.

"*Yaaah! Hya-yaah! Git! Git! Git a move on! Hya-yaah!*"

It worked, at least for the moment.

Lions, male and female, shied as the crazy human rushed amongst them. Horses, front legs tethered by leather hobbles, hopped and reared frantically. Lions growled, butted heads, scuttled backward. Gull pushed his luck by swatting a slow cat on the rump. Then he shoved past a gray mule, ducked under a dappled mare's head, and hid amidst panicked horseflesh.

Instinctively, Gull consoled the stock, patted noses. The horses mashed together, noses in, nudging and banging his ribs. The lions milled just outside the herd. Knothead, the mule, brushed them back by kicking a lioness. Clopped in the jaw, she recoiled.

There was a moment of deadly calm. Lions growled

like distant thunder. Horses shivered and stamped like trees in a high wind.

For a few moments, Gull hoped the lions would retreat, be content to eat the brown cob: the young males already licked blood from its twitching flanks. He could use a rest: he bled in three places: forehead, shoulder, and tail. Yet the lions circled like vultures, tightening the noose. Startled horses banged one another and generated more panic.

The calm couldn't last.

If the lions did charge, they'd cripple or kill a dozen. Better to sacrifice a few. He guessed.

Cursing, Gull grasped his axe at the head. He hadn't room to stoop and untie the braided leather hobbles, and amidst skittish horses he'd only get brained by a hoof.

Knothead could fend for himself. He deserved to be eaten anyway, for as Gull bent, the ingrate nipped off a hank of hair.

The axe head dropped between the knobby knees and deadly hooves, cut through the hobble. Gull chopped more tethers. He'd be forever making new tack, he thought grimly, if he survived the night and had any stock left.

The axe thumped, horses and mules jumped, lions prowled, testing the herd's courage. Gull sweated and chopped and ate dirt and horse sweat as he fumbled in blackness amidst stamping feet. Somehow he managed not to cut his own feet, and skinned only a couple of fetlocks.

One by one, the animals discovered they were free. Snorting, they fought twin urges: to stay with the herd or to run.

Knothead decided them by suddenly wheeling and loping off, ungainly as a cow. Flossy followed, then one

horse, then another. Soon all were running free, and
Gull had to clutch bridles to cut the last four hobbles.
The stock thrummed south, the shortest distance to
unburned forest, and Gull swatted the last gelding to
fire it along.

Sweating, he mopped his face with a bloody hand.

And realized he was alone with hungry lions and
no cover.

But the lions dispersed. Four lionesses bounded
after the horses, seeing which would fall behind and
die. The young males had ripped open the brown cob's
side, strewn liver and lights and guts that glistened in
the moonlight. They squabbled over chunks of the
poor beast like piglets at the teat. The big lion Gull
had shot and axed had collapsed, flat on its side like a
rug.

Gull hunted his bow, found the string broken. He'd
lost his quiver anyway, so tossed the bow. Wasting no
time, he slipped around a ravaged birch copse, then
dashed for the wagons.

Where the noise had increased. Screams, shouts,
curses, the clash of steel on steel.

A troop of black-clad cavalry attacked the wagons.

Horses, tack, cloaks, visored helmets—all were
black. The visors were raised to reveal the invaders'
black-bearded faces. Only their shields sported color,
half-silver with a laughing demon's face at the center.

There were, Gull puffed and counted, ten or
twelve, ahorse, armored, and armed. Towser's four
fighters were children by comparison. Curved sabers
rattled at the black riders' sides. Yet what they wielded
were ropes tipped with steel grapnels.

The knights thundered in a tight circle around the

train—Gull was reminded of the lions' attack—black phantoms against a black sky, hooting orders or taunts or encouragement to fellows. They spun the lines overhead. The grapnels rattled and hissed, proving the last three feet to be chain, impervious to sword cuts.

Most of Towser's retinue must be cowering in the wagon, for only the four bodyguards braced for attack. Oles lined up his crossbow and shot, but the quarrel thudded into a shield. (The woodcutter surmised the shields were some very hard wood: hickory or rowan or ironwood.) A swinging grapnel either clipped Chad in the head, knocking him down, or he'd ducked violently. Kem scooted under a wagon, slashed with his short sword at a horse's leg, but the prime animal skipped aside without jostling its rider. Without losing a swing, that knight whipped out his saber and slashed for Kem's head. The bodyguard dived backward as the heavy blade chipped oak.

Only Morven was effective. Veteran of rolling battles on the high seas, the sailor calmly perched on a wagon seat, aimed his crossbow, timed his shot. The whirling marauders made confusing targets, but one suddenly whooped, bowled out of the saddle by a bolt slamming his face.

Helpless alongside a tree trunk, Gull fumed. He lacked his longbow, couldn't attack with his axe, couldn't get to the wagons. He scooted for a rock to heave, found none. Shivan Dragon, what to do?

And what were the horsemen after?

With a shout, three riders hooked their talons into the men's wagon. Cinching the lines to saddle pommels, they barked at their horses, who backpedaled neatly. One grapnel ripped loose of the canvas and skittered across the ground. But the other two bit deep.

The wagon jerked, creaked, rattled, tipped on two wheels.

The bodyguards shouted to get clear. Oles shot again, low, and a horse shrilled.

With a heave, the wagon crashed on its side.

It left a gap in the circle. Two invaders took it, charging in abreast.

Gull grabbed dirt, swiped grit up and down his slick axe handle.

Now came the killing. Of Towser's people, like fish in a barrel.

Two knights and chargers was a lot of man and horse. The riders found themselves in a tighter hole than they'd envisioned. Despite the heat of battle, Gull's flesh crawled. These strange-croaking men wheeled their animals like one flesh—like the centaurs Helki and Holleb.

Good thing, Gull thought, he was too busy to be scared.

For he charged the circle himself.

The two knights, brave, stupid, or glory-mad, spun their chargers, forcing back the bodyguards, chivying them to hide under the wagons. Flailing with long, curved sabers, they slashed canvas, wood, ropes, everything with their steely touch.

The outer riders, the woodcutter saw, resumed their circuit, grapnels whirling. So, he presumed, the centermost knights were to discourage crossbow shots as the others—what?—latched to another wagon further to destroy the train?

What did they want? Towser? And where was *he*, the cowardly bastard? This was *his* beknighted troupe!

Timing his rush, Gull dashed for a gap between a

horse's head and the end of the flopped wagon. He hoped his throbbing knee didn't kick out and flop him.

But, like magic, a black horse rushed, slid next to a wagon close enough to brush a feed bag, and cut him off. Gull gasped. These knights could almost make their horses fly!

With a slither, the man drew a saber. He shouted something: a challenge? taunt? Other riders sheared off, widening their circle.

Trapped between walls of horseflesh, Gull cursed. He had his dirty axe and nothing else.

The knight glared down, the whites of his eyes bright above a black beard, snapped the reins to halt the horse almost on top of Gull. Maybe the horses were trained to trample infantry, yet another killing method. Either way, the rider hoisted his saber to the sky. From that great height, he'd split Gull like a chicken.

Ducking instinctively, Gull jumped close by the horse's head. As he hoped, the knight was reluctant to swipe near his mount's ear, so slashed for Gull's exposed shoulder.

Gull threw up his axe, sideways, to catch the blow on the haft. Instead the saber clanged on the steel head, so loudly it was painful. Sparks flew, blinding in the blackness. The impact made Gull's fingers tingle. With a curse, the saber flashed up, silver in the moon-light, poised for another swipe.

Needing to do something, the muleskinner punched the horse in its big brown eye. It squealed and flinched. The rider jiggled in the saddle, lost his upthrust. Encouraged, Gull rapped the horse's sensi-tive mouth. The beast flipped its head aside. Again the rider was jostled.

Why not? Gull thought. He dropped his axe and lunged.

With a forked hand, he banged the rider's boot at the ankle, straight back, brushed it clear of the stirrup. The man shouted in surprise, and Gull jerked savagely on the ankle, his wounded shoulder burning like fury. The knight smashed down his saber guard at Gull's head, but he had to twist or dislocate his ankle. Stiff-legged, his rump left the seat—

—and Gull heaved.

With a squawk, then a rattly crash, the knight slammed the turf.

Gull could have crowed with battle lust and laughter, but a circling rider cut his humor short. The woodcutter ducked a sizzling stroke that would have decapitated him. He snatched up his axe. The fallen knight scrambled up on the far side of the horse.

What now? A saber-axe duel in the dark? With an expert?

"No, thank you!" Gull called.

Fumbling, he gathered the black horse's reins, clucked encouragingly, then backstepped through the gap in the wagon train.

With the horse as a shield, the black riders outside couldn't close. In black silhouette, Gull saw the felled man call, grab his comrade's hand, swing up behind the saddle. They were fine riders, Gull had to admit.

The woodcutter hauled the skittish horse into the middle space. He called, "It's Gull! Gull!" so he wouldn't get shot.

"Who needs ya?" came a surly growl. Kem, welcoming him home. Gull could have laughed. But there was a tremendous thrashing in the center of the wagon train. Images tumbled in Gull's mind: he tried to recall the danger.

Hurriedly, he lashed the dark reins to a chuck wagon wheel. Instinctively, he talked to the animal.

A cooing came to his ears. Hearing his voice, Greensleeves had shoved aside the wagon curtain. Gull shook his axe, hissed, "Get back inside! Inside! It's too—oh, my . . . "

Three more riders shouted, whirled and flung grapnels. Steel talons bit deep into painted wood, snugged tight.

The chuck wagon rocked. Inside, Felda screamed. Curious, Greensleeves craned out even farther.

Then she bleated like a lamb. The wagon tilted on two wheels.

"Nooooo!!!" howled Gull.

Gull snatched for his sister's arm and missed. The girl was bumped from behind as Felda, the fat cook, fought to jump out. Greensleeves tumbled into the footwell of the wagon seat.

The wagon tilted higher. The black horse lashed to the wheel snorted, then squealed in terror as its jaw was hoicked into the air. Gull grabbed the wheel to throw his weight on this side, but freed, the wheel spun and he fell.

At the end of the wagon, Morven caught canvas and hung on, stalling the tipover. A rider barked at his own mount, no doubt to pull harder. Hampered by his heavy axe, his shoulder burning as if lightning-struck, Gull caught hold of a side and clung desperately, dragging the wagon back down.

But a saber blade slammed wood near his head, and he had to drop.

He'd forgotten the two knights inside the circle.

It was too late to dodge, for the saber descended

again, a silver sliver like a new moon. Gull raised his axe.

Too late.

Instead of striking, the knight arched and twisted, flailed his arm wildly, pitched half out of the saddle. His blade slammed the canted wagon wheel, whacked an iron chip from the rim.

Supported by only a stirrup, the knight hung in the saddle. He seemed unable to grab anything, as if palsied. His head twitched from invisible slaps. The other knight in the cramped circle acted the same.

Gull stared. Whence came this affliction? And where had Gull seen it before?

Then he remembered. It had happened to him!

Quickly, he cast about. Towser's wagon. The magician was framed against the silver sky, stripes burning white and black. In one hand was the scepter he'd used on Gull, that which "turned attacks aside."

Gull knew how. It spasmed your muscles.

For a short time.

Even now, the knight jerkily dragged himself back into the saddle. But he'd lost his saber. The other marauder kept his seat. But neither man was attacked, and Gull wondered if Towser had also palsied his bodyguards.

No matter. He whirled to grab at the chuck wagon again.

Too late.

Despite the weight of Morven and the lashed horse, the wagon creaked, shuddered, then crashed onto its side.

Felda's scream ended as something crashed atop her. Greensleeves spun, light as thistledown, and rolled in the dirt. The three knights had dropped their lines, but the girl's sudden appearance underfoot spooked the black horses, who shied.

With the wagon flopped over, Towser had a clear line of sight. Waving his wand, he shot his spell.

A rider howled as muscles cramped. Even the horse threw its head, and the knight toppled from the saddle. Another's arm cramped so hard he dragged his horse half 'round, and the beast bolted as if from bee stings. The third man, seeing the silhouette of a wizard pointing a wand, reared his horse for partial protection, backed it expertly.

"Use the rock hydra!" shouted Gull. "It'd terrify the horses!"

"Hydras are day beasts! They need sun to fight!" Towser snarled, "Keep your advice, pawn!"

The backing knight let his horse drop to all fours. Out of the wand's range, he called some garbled phrase, an insult. The wizard shrilled back—the first time Gull had seen him angry. The knight laughed. Behind Towser, a vision in white poked out its head: a dancing girl, too curious for her own good.

Knights had scampered out of range to regain their saddles. With a mock salute, the laughing horseman, their captain perhaps, barked to his comrades. Kicking their heels, they made to ride off.

"We just let them go?" Gull asked the air.

Then he ducked.

Rather than circle the wagons, the boisterous knights charged the gap. Hooting, laughing, they thundered through the center as bodyguards scrambled. One snatched the reins of the lashed horse, but failed to jerk them loose and let go.

Towser jumped for the safety of his wagon interior. Gull heard the canvas curtain tear.

Someone was too slow.

The ghostly white figure stood abandoned on the wagon seat.

As the black captain's horse vaulted the wagon tongue, the man hooked the dancing girl.

With a squall, she slammed across the saddle, belly down. She kicked and squirmed, but a gloved fist bashed her neck and stunned her.

Laughing, the black captain rallied his troops. Like a murder of crows, they flocked together, he with a prize, the rest with bruises and wounds. Chopped loam dotted the air behind them.

By then Gull had realized.

"Lily!"

CHAPTER
11

Gull stooped for his axe, whipped loose the reins of the captive horse, jumped to the saddle, hissed as his rump wound stung. Yet he shrieked *"Hyah!"* and took off in hot pursuit.

Of armored, armed, and expert knights, while he was naked but for a kilt and axe.

Well, as his father used to say, "You can but try."

The well-trained horse shot the gap between wagons and thundered after its mates. Morven shouted, "Get 'em, Gull!" The woodcutter put his head down and tried to keep the saddle. He'd ridden plow horses before, bareback, for fun.

Still, he could but try.

Ahead, the company of knights split. The captain with Lily—her white-clad fanny and legs were bright in the dark—and two riders pounded right while the others sheared off. Why, Gull couldn't say. They must be ordered back to the other wizard—

"Hey!" He spoke aloud, surprising himself. Where

was the other wizard, the duelist? So far they'd sustained attacks by zombies, lions, and cavalry, but had yet to see who'd launched the attack. When would this mystery wizard appear?

And what sort of fiend ripped zombies from the grave?

For that matter, had this crowd made the wagon tracks Morven had found earlier? If so, where were the wagons? And why had Towser's entourage gotten here first?

"Never mind!" he chided himself. "Questions later!"

Squeezing with his knees, he spanked the black horse with the axe head. Surprised by the whap on its flanks, it spurted ahead until he neared the rearmost knight. Clear of Towser's wrecked camp, the trio had slowed.

The laggard paid for their laxity with his life.

With no finesse, only brute strength, Gull steered straight along his left side. Missing the hoofbeats in his muffling helmet, the man turned at the last moment, startled to see a half-naked wild-eyed monster upon him.

Gull swung his axe one-handed, the blow soft because his bad shoulder was weakening. Yet the sharp bit thudded into the knight's back. Spine severed, he flopped forward over the saddle pommel.

Wrenching his weapon free, Gull passed the dying knight, pounding, snorting as much as the horse.

The middle rider, sensing something wrong, turned, black against a black forest. No horseman, Gull had to approach the man's right, his saber side.

Thousands of hours of training showed, for the knight freed his weapon in a second. Out flashed the blade to shimmer in the moonlight. The man swung it flat, either to slash the horse's face or the rider's.

Gull had no protection, no idea what to do, so instinctively threw his axe high. The act saved his life.

The curved blade smacked the hickory handle, skidded, clanged off the axe head. Gull swore, glad he'd gripped low. He'd hate to lose fingers off his right hand, too.

He kicked his mount viciously, driving it into the knight, crowding, spoiling his aim. The knight spurred to gain elbow room, but Gull stayed close. Probably it was only the insanity of his attack that kept him alive.

In fact—

—he tossed his axe to his rein hand, stabbed with his left.

His arm bobbed to the pounding of the horse over the uneven terrain. (Where *were* these knights bound?) He snatched at the knight's cloak, missed, leaned from the saddle, shoved past his sword arm, caught an armor strap—

—and hauled.

Taken by surprise, used to battling saber to saber, not hand to hand, the knight yanked his reins to stay in the saddle. But that only pulled the horse's head around, stalling it. Gull strained like a block and tackle, shouting, screaming in the man's face, clinging like a leech.

The knight tried to bash Gull with his saber guard, but the woodcutter ducked, clutched tighter to his horse, leg muscles cramping, and yanked again, grunting with the effort.

A random bump, a space under the knight's seat, and he left the saddle.

As soon as he was airborne, Gull let go.

Riding on, laughing, he heard thumps and curses behind.

But only one rider concerned him. The captain ahead, with Lily across his saddle.

"Prepare yourself!" the woodcutter howled. Limbering up, he swung the axe to the end of the haft, slung it behind him. *"Remember White Ridge!"*

Despite riding hard and clutching the struggling dancing girl, the black rider had seen his comrades fall. He kicked his mount to stay ahead. Gull reckoned him a coward, or else too proud to give battle. Or maybe he wanted to escape with his prize.

Barking commands at his mount, the knight cut Gull's path, slid around a tree too big to die in the fire. The rider then slewed around another tree, making the mount dance. They approached the lip of the star crater. On more open ground, the captain would have the advantage. Pusuing a veteran horseman on a splendid horse, Gull would never catch him.

Unless he threw his only weapon.

He saw no alternative, for his own horse was foundering. The captain, on the better mount, would escape with Lily.

And if man and mount returned to whatever land they'd been summoned from (by this unknown wizard), Lily would go too, and Gull would lose her.

Suddenly Gull didn't want to lose Lily.

Rising in bare feet in the stirrups, bouncing wildly as the horse bounded and slewed, Gull hoisted the long, heavy axe over his shoulder and pitched it. He grunted with the effort, crashed in the saddle so as not to spill off. To lose the chase was to lose Lily.

The axe spun like ball lightning. Too low, haft first, it dinged the horse on the rump, bounced off the captain's back, ricocheted into the black-green undergrowth.

Nothing, thought Gull. His last shot gone.

But it was enough.

Touched in mid-stride, the horse crowhopped in the air. Burdened with a struggling Lily, the black captain tugged the reins, hollered to calm the animal, but confused by commands and the odd touch, it balked.

Or did it shy for some other reason? Gull couldn't see what.

No matter. For a second, the enemy was still.

Gull kept coming. And hit them.

With no weapon save his body, he steered his blowing horse alongside the captain's, plucked feet from the stirrups, hopped one foot to the saddle pad, and leaped.

An awkward leap in darkness from a surging platform toward a moving target. But again, enough.

Gull's right hand batted the captain's shoulder, slipped off, snagged his cloak. His bad shoulder banged the man's back, and Gull growled with pain, for the knights wore a backplate too. Slipping, his ribs slammed the saddle cantle, creaking and winding him. But his left found purchase on the captain's reins, and Gull hung on. He could smell the captain, smoke and manure and garlic and perfume. He heard guttural curses. Lily bleated as Gull's elbow rammed her lower back.

Thumped once more by a strange source, the horse sidestepped.

Thus Gull learned why the beast had balked.

They perched on the very lip of the star crater.

The horse lost its footing.

Three humans and one animal howled as they spilled over the edge in a tangle of arms, legs, horseflesh, black and white clothes.

*   *   *

The dark horizon whirled past Gull's vision. He was head up, then head down. The captain's cloak fluttered around him. Lily's white legs whapped his jaw. The woodcutter's stomach lurched, and he tasted vomit. He must be flying upside down.

And if he spilled after the captain, he might be crushed under a toppling horse. Gull let go.

Besides, he'd stopped the captain. He needed to recover first.

Slamming hard on bare feet, he skidded on his sore backside in loose soil churned by the horse's hooves. He banged a rock with his ankle, stabbed out a hand and missed the earth—he must be spinning frightfully—rapped hard enough to sprain his wrist.

Yelping, he tumbled after horse and rider. And Lily.

It was darker than ever, for the Mist Moon dropped behind shattered trees, splintering as if the moon itself cracked. But the yellow sand of the crater gave its own luminous light, as if the fallen star still glowed within the earth.

By this fitful light, Gull saw the captain and his mount part company.

The black rider kicked free of the saddle and tumbled backward over his mount's rump. Freed of the top-heavy weight, the horse didn't roll, but scrabbled legs madly, still sliding down the slope. Afraid to jump off, Lily clung to the cinch straps, jouncing like a white grain sack tied across the pommel.

The captain gained his feet, leaned on the steep slope, and snatched at his belt. Drawing his saber, Gull knew. He growled curses at the woodcutter above him.

Gull was angry enough to shout back at this seasoned soldier. "Have at you, then!" He charged down the shifting slope in a shower of dirt and gravel.

Running from higher up, he gained speed until he almost flew at each bound. He expected that silver sickle saber to swing his way, and no doubt he'd impale himself if the man raised it in time. Yet for some reason, the captain couldn't draw.

With a flash, Gull knew why. The tumble had bent the steel scabbard and trapped the blade.

Shrieking, the woodcutter leaped high and hit the struggling captain with both feet square in the breast-plate.

His impetus knocked them apart. Both rolled toward the bottom of the crater.

When Gull had stopped rolling and pushed upright, he found the captain charging. From a sheath on his right the knight whipped out a long white blade, croaked a strange command.

The knife caught fire in his hand.

More damned magic, thought the woodcutter. A blade that burned. Would it hurt more or less than a normal blade?

Scars of Scarzam! but he hated magic!

Yelling a shuddery battle cry, the captain halted, set his feet, and slashed toward Gull's gut.

The woodcutter responded with the only thing he had, a handful of dirt. The gritty shower hit the captain in the face, but he'd seen Gull stoop. He opened his eyes and jeered.

Gull backed as the knife sliced the air, back and forth. Blown flat by the wind, the blade's fire dimmed to nothing, then flared again. Gull found it hypnotic.

Missing a step, Gull lurched sideways, almost fell as his bad knee buckled. Behind him was the pit where they'd dug up the shooting star—the pink stone box.

He had no place left to go but into the hole—

Though unfamiliar with the ground, the captain saw the black hole yawning at his opponent's feet. Hollering, he rushed to knock Gull back bodily.

Instead, the woodcutter ducked low as a toadstool. But the captain stamped and stopped too. And swiped.

The white-hot blade kissed Gull's already-shredded shoulder. A crackling was his skin burning. He smelled charred flesh. The wound felt ice-cold and yet raging hot. Gull cried out, stabbed with his hands. He batted the captain in the knee, only brushing him aside.

If he spilled backward into the pit, he'd be trapped like a mouse in a flour barrel. If he tried to crawl or run, he'd take a blade through the back.

Groping for purchase, his knuckles cracked on hardwood. Smooth, shaped long, worn.

The handle of a pickaxe, left that afternoon by the tired diggers.

Grunting, grabbing, Gull hopped toward the captain to confuse him. The man leaned back, prepared to strike, then stabbed straight down—

—and yelped in surprise as Gull swung at his legs with a mysterious and heavy tool.

Awkward, Gull hit with the wooden haft, not the iron head. But the captain was bowled over. He rolled away quickly, half-entangled in his own riding cloak.

Gull leaped, aimed in a second, threw the weapon over his shoulder like an axe, and struck as hard as he could.

Pointed like a bird's beak, the heavy iron head punched through steel armor, skin, flesh, organs, bone, more armor, and finally dirt.

Panting, spent, Gull clutched the pickaxe haft.

Shudders from the dying man traveled up the wood, through Gull's arms, seemingly straight to his heart. But the woodcutter hung on relentlessly.

Gradually, the shudders quieted, then stopped.

The flames on the long knife, still clutched in a black gloved hand, flickered out.

A gasp made Gull whirl. A ghost charged him. Instinctively he jerked at the pickaxe handle, but it was stuck fast in armor.

Then the ghost leaped into his arms with a sob. Musk and perfume filled his nostrils.

"Lily," he crooned.

Hot body pressed against his, the dancing girl clung, shuddering. She cried like a little girl, begging to be held, but Gull had to pry her off. "We must get back. The others will need us."

"Kem? Chad?" she pouted. "Why risk your life to rescue them?"

"Greensleeves. Felda. Stiggur," he countered. "Come."

He had to keep moving anyway, he knew. If he stopped for a second, all his bruises and wounds would seize up and he'd be helpless.

Stumbling across the crater slope, he caught the captain's horse. It backed, but Gull crooned and snagged the reins and it obeyed. Too sore and tipsy to mount, Gull caught Lily's hand and smacked the horse so it towed them up the slope.

Atop the rim, Gull searched for the horse he'd jumped from, but didn't see it. With the moon gone, the night was black. Only ghostly birch stumps glowed, their scorched trunks gray stripes against blackness. He could barely see his hand by starlight. They'd have to creep back to camp.

Despite the dancing girl's protests—she didn't want to mount again—Gull climbed painfully into the saddle and hauled her in front of him. Upright, this time. Clucking, he set out west. Blown and carrying double, the horse would only walk. Blown himself, Gull let it.

Camp was perhaps a half mile off. Through twisted trunks and some brambly screen they glimpsed light. "The campfire!" Lily chirped.

Gull muttered, "Could be piled high as a signal for us."

"You think the battle's over?"

He shrugged. The moment's rest had recalled all his injuries, and each burned and twinged and itched and ached. Wherever his skin touched Lily's baggy soiled clothes, sweat and dirt and blood stuck. Yet she pressed close for comfort.

"Mayhaps," he said, "but that may be bad, too. If Towser gets himself outnumbered, he might flee, as that brown-and-yellow wizard fled the duel at White Ridge." The name of his lost village pained his heart. Angrily he shook his head. "That's why we must hurry back. If Towser disappears, he might take everyone with him, including my sister. She's the only one I care about."

"What about me?" Lily pouted.

Pained and worried, Gull was now irritated. He clucked and nudged the horse to a faster walk. "You too, of course. But we've got to—"

The horse whickered and stopped, as if it'd hit a wall. Gull swore, nudged, but then sensed something before them in the blackness. The slight breeze that had washed them stopped.

Carefully, he slid down and walked forward, hand out. And pricked his hand. He sniffed a familiar green-bitter smell.

"Balls! It's Towser's wall of thorns again. Now what?" He cast right and left, snagged his tangled hair in grasping thorns, swore. "Can you see a way around?"

Higher on the horse, the dancing girl craned. "Off to the right is something white. That wouldn't be thorns, would it?"

"Who knows?" Gull sighed. "Once they loose magic, there are no rules. Nothing makes sense."

He towed the horse toward the white whatevers, one hand up to shield his face in the pitchy darkness. The thorn wall meandered like a wild hedgerow, and he was tagged on the shoulders and hands by thorns, stepped barefoot on more, often banged into trunks and had to circle them.

As time dragged on, he fretted more and more. He had to get back to Greensleeves before some disaster struck the camp.

Nearing the white barriers, Gull found them to be—teeth?

At first the thorn wall intermingled with the white teeth, then gave way to them entirely. The teeth were all sizes, from finger height to taller than a man could reach. Gull felt a tooth, found it slippery-smooth, sharp enough at the tip to pierce skin. Testing, he snapped a slim one in his hand like an icicle. But any thick as his thumb were unbreakable.

"I've seen these," said Lily. "They grow in caves, from the ground and the ceiling. People call them stone spears. Smell? The earth is covered with bat guano."

Gull wrinkled his nose at the dry acrid smell. The earth was gray-white, and from the gunk came the chittering of a million insects living in the stuff. Another distant chunk of the Domains, thought Gull, ripped from the floor of some mammoth cave and dropped here, into the western reaches of the Whispering Woods. What wonders these wizards pissed away for their greedy ends!

White by starlight, the wall of swords waggled this way and that through the charred stump forest, as if sown by a drunkard. But it was no more two hundred feet wide anywhere.

There came another surprise.

With a clear line of sight, they could see the fire they'd glimpsed.

Not their own camp, but another wizard's.

It was not a pit for a cooking fire they saw, but a large heaped bonfire.

It was a few hundred feet off. *I've gotten turned around without the moon to guide us*, Gull thought. Between tree trunks like black bars he could make out little. Black knights encircled the fire, some mounted, some dismount. At the center walked a large figure—very big, he realized. Almost as tall as the mounted men. That figure stalked around and around, probably haranguing his troops, dangerous as the lions. Light gleamed from the man as if he were armored all over. Beyond the circle were curved ridges like distant hills: Gull finally decided they were covered wagons with the canvas painted dark.

So these were the wagons whose trail they'd cut weeks ago.

But where was Towser's camp? And the zombies? And what form would the next attack take? Something worse than undead?

Lily whispered his name, pointed. He followed the white curve of her sleeve.

Way over there was a glimmer of a sheltered fire. A suggestion of moving bodies and a hoop shape—the bow of a toppled wagon.

Hissing for silence, lest they draw down the black riders, Gull covered the horse's nose to prevent its snorting to its mates. Gingerly he towed the beast amidst the field of swords. In the murky nonlight, he shuffled his bare feet lest he step on a spike, and hoped the horse did the same. Bat manure squished between his toes. The crunching of insect shells was loud and sickening.

Soon they stepped clear of the cave floor to soft black loam. Gull wiped his feet, swung up behind Lily. With the tiny glimmer to guide them, they could ride to camp. They might have to flee if the riders came.

A thunder of hooves suddenly drummed on the ears, but not from the distant bonfire. From the direction of Towser's camp.

Gull reined alongside a thick trunk. Lily asked, "Who's—"

"Shush!"

Two riders, driving hard, swerving between trunks. A hallooing went up, a weird ululating war cry that split the night and sent shivers up spines.

Gull barked in surprise. He knew that cry.

"Helki! Holleb!"

Sweaty bronzed skin glistened by starlight. The centaurs were naked, without armor or helmets or warpaint, only their armbands and feathered lances. Ratty hair sailed behind them, grown almost long as their tails. *What had happened?* he wondered. Formerly they'd been so tidy and soldierly, with their gear painted and polished and stowed neatly on their harness. Why now so mangy and unkempt?

And why were they *here*? Why not home in their steppe country?

As they surged by, Gull called their names. Holleb only shouted his bloodcurdling cry. But Helki whinnied as if in fear or shame.

"Gull! We must attack! We are captives! We cannot—uh!" She interrupted herself to shout her cry, and the two leveled lances.

By the distant bonfire, black riders scrambled to mount. The big central figure waved gold-gleaming arms.

But Gull could only sit stunned at Helki's words. Captives? Again? The brown-and-yellow wizard had abandoned them. Towser had returned them home. So . . . had he summoned them himself, enslaved them for his own purposes? He must have, for they traveled from his camp toward the enemy.

Was Towser indeed as bad, as callous and cold-hearted, as any other wizard? Was Gull a gull to work for him?

"Oh!" cried Lily. "Look to the sky!"

A bright flash blinded Gull, made him blink.

Sizzling into the air, coming from the far wizard's camp, glowing like a rocket, soared a horse afire.

"Nightmare!"

CHAPTER

12

The magic horse blazed across the sky like a comet.

Body and face were gray as a slate tombstone. Feet were white hot and spilled yellow flame. Flaming mane and tail trailed out behind like a burning paper kite.

It had risen from the other wizard's bonfire as if launched from a catapult. Now it arced across the sky, painful to watch with eye-smarting brilliance, paddling its hooves above the treetops. They drummed on the ears and air, though they touched nothing. Nostrils snorted fire and snuffled gouts of black smoke.

Was it alive or dead? Gull wondered. Was it even a horse? "Riding the night mare" was what a mother called bad dreams, yet never had Gull imagined that a real demon haunted the dark hours.

Then there was no time for supposing, for the flaming monster dived straight at Towser's ruptured wagons.

"Greensleeves!" yelled the woodcutter.

He clutched Lily around the waist, kicked the horse

toward camp. But the flesh-and-blood animal balked, either at the fire or the brassy alien smell of the phantom horse. After three tries to force it forward, Gull gave up, slid from the saddle, and dragged Lily stumbling along.

"Come on!" But what he expected to do in camp he couldn't guess. He'd even tossed his axe away, was completely weaponless. The most he could hope was to grab Greensleeves and run like hell.

Whistling from the sky, like a hawk upon chickens, the nightmare swooped in a tight circle over the tumbled wagon train. The camp was clearly illuminated by its light. Gull saw women and bodyguards cringe. Even brash Kem and Chad curled into balls and covered their heads, like children afraid of a parent's wrath.

All of them, within the wagons and without, screamed for dear life.

Terror, Gull thought. *The thing spreads terror. It causes bad dreams you can't wake from.*

Without realizing it, he slowed, as if fear were a plunging tide to wade.

Concentrating, he almost fell as Lily suddenly gasped and yanked his hand. They were still hundreds of feet from camp. "What—"

Then he saw. By the flickering light of the nightmare, he discovered twisted shapes littering the forest floor at their feet.

The Zombies of Scathe, Lily had called them.

They lay like reaped corn stalks, every which way. Facedown, heads back, on top of one another. Threescore or more, unmoving except for fistfuls of writhing maggots.

Their rotten, bloated stink was almost palpable, like a fist in the face. Gull caught his nose and backed up. Gasping, gagging, he and the dancing girl stumbled wide around.

Despite the horror, Gull found the scene familiar. People sprawled like jackstraws. As in White Ridge.

Villagers, including his parents and siblings, had fallen near the end of the wizards' duel. A mysterious weakness, unseen, unheard, only felt, had leached the strength from their bodies. Gull himself had collapsed. Only the hale and hearty survived. Young, old, weak died. Many others had never recovered their strength, had lain unconscious until they expired, wilted like cut flowers.

And if that weakness spell—if this was it—felled zombies here, then the same wizard must have cast it in White Ridge.

Towser.

Gull stopped in shock. *Towser* had felled his family and neighbors?

Or did every wizard know such a spell?

If it were Towser, he grated, he'd pay with his life. Gull would kill him. Gull would break his bones one by one, all the while reciting the name of every White Ridger who'd fallen to his magic.

"*Damn* all wizards! And damn *me* for working for one!"

Screaming arose from the distant camp.

Gull waggled his head. Lily's red nails cut into his arm. "Let's get away from these dead!" Yet camp would be little sanctuary, beset by a flaming phantom—

"Look!" called Gull. "Something's stopped it—"

Dancing on air higher than anyone could reach, the nightmare stopped circling. Instead, it stamped the air skittishly, swished its fiery tail so globs of flame spun off like sparks from a grindstone. Where the blobs landed, they burned and winked out amidst new greenery, for nothing was left to burn in this twisted nightmare forest.

Yet it seemed the nightmare might dash off, for something held it at bay. By spitting crackling light, Gull saw Towser's lateral stripes standing on the wagon seat.

The wizard wasn't attacking much tonight, Gull thought savagely. He was hard put to defend the camp, keep his followers alive from the varied assaults.

Yet Towser held aloft a stone crock as for ale or moonshine. He gabbled some spell, honking lilting music.

Gull had seen this before, too.

From the mouth of the crock spewed a cloud that puffed and billowed, yet kept a shape like an inflated bladder. Gradually, it swelled like a soap bubble, snapped together to hover in the air.

And take the shape of a man.

A tall man, blue, so muscled he appeared fat, with a black topknot of hair and a tight vest and wide bloomers like the dancing girls'. Like a bubble in water, the blue man rose and faced the nightmare, which now stamped just outside the wagon circle.

The entourage stopped screaming. That alone, Gull noted, was a good reason to conjure the cloud-man. "A djinn," Lily breathed.

Like an animated cloud, the blue djinn wafted forward, slow as a fogbank. The nightmare swished its flaming tail, skipped on burning hooves—

—bared yellow teeth and charged.

Gull and the girl held their breath as the phantom leaped at the blue cloud.

And through it.

The results were nothing they could have predicted.

Fire met water, it seemed. A tremendous *whoomph!* shook the air, beat upon the ears as if boxed.

The djinn exploded into errant puffs of steam. They dribbled upward like smoke from a doused fire.

The nightmare skidded to a halt, shook itself like a dog from a pond. Its fire had dimmed until the night was almost black, but now it reignited.

High above, the dribs and drabs of smoke re-formed, coalesced, became a magic man again.

Snorting fire, the nightmare attacked. The very air sizzled from the fierce blaze. Where its hooves tipped burned trunks, the wood crackled and caught fire.

Its power increased as it attacked, the woodcutter saw. So did its flame. So far, only the fact the forest had already burned saved them from a conflagration. But if the flaming beast burned hot enough, the heat might scorch even these charred trunks of fire-resistant bark, ignite their heartwood.

"Come, Lily!" he tugged her. "We need to get inside the circle!"

She didn't resist, just hesitated. Over the noise of burning wind she asked, "But . . . what's happening over there?"

Gull gaped. He'd forgotten the other wizard's camp. Now the bonfire burned higher. He stepped past a trunk to see better. Silhouetted before the blaze, the siver-armored figure issued orders.

Only now it was bigger. Closer.

Striding great lengths, swinging gold-chased armored limbs, the wizard was so massive and heavy, it sank to its ankles in the soft forest loam.

And around its legs capered a horde of skeletons.

*   *   *

The skeletons were small, no taller than children, of slight build. Their jaws were long and lined with pointed teeth. The spiny silhouettes jiggered before the distant bonfire, impossibly thin and disjointed, yet alive.

Skeletons of goblins, Gull realized. Those vicious, conniving, skulking thieves. Alive, they were useless. Perhaps they served better dead. . . .

With a shrill neigh, the captured cavalry horse reared, jerked the reins from Gull's hand. He let it go. "We should run too! For the camp! And don't stop!"

They heard the skeleton army now. Piercing piping cries, like a colony of bats, carried on the thick night air. Overhead, the nightmare rushed the cloud-man again.

Of a sudden, Gull's mind couldn't encompass the strangeness. Phantom horses, armored titans, squeaking skeletons, cloud-people, dead and undead zombies, all haunting a blasted forest. If he dwelt on them, he'd panic or go mad. He forced them from his brain. *Get Greensleeves*, he told himself. Get his sister and run as if devils pursued. For probably they did, somewhere in this vast mad landscape.

Towing Lily, he lurched for the camp, until he could make out sweat-shiny faces that gaped up at the phantom battle and out at the armored wizard and his bony horde.

Overhead, the nightmare again plowed through the blue cloud-man. This time, however, the shredded blue mist dribbled away on the night air, faded to nothingness. It did not re-form.

Clearly, the nightmare ruled the night.

Triumphant above the treetops, the horse-thing snorted and stamped, stronger and brighter than ever. It was so hot that sparks spit from it like steel burning in a forge. They landed in the camp and winked out like fireflies.

But Gull couldn't see much of the camp now. A fog was rising, as mist issues from a swamp. Panting, running into it, his eyes stung. This was smoke. Ground-hugging smoke such as campfires spilled when the weather turned dirty.

No one had touched the cookfire, no trees burned much, yet the smoke thickened as if the night itself smoldered.

"More damned magic," Gull wheezed.

Squinting, half-blind, the woodcutter and dancing girl stumbled past the overturned men's wagon, tripped over the jutting tongue. Somehow, Gull realized, the wagon had been dumped over again, or slewed around: the top was toward the center. A good thing, for the bottom formed an outside wall.

Someone challenged them, and they gasped their names. Guided to Morven, they hunkered behind the tipped wagon seat. By now the smoke was so thick the campfire was an orange smudge. Gull couldn't see any more than Morven's gray-white hair.

"What happened to the wagon?" rasped Gull.

"We tried to hoist her, got spooked, and dumped it the other way," muttered the sailor. "It's a cock-up for certain. This smoke don't help none. One of Towser's less thoughty spells. Smoke's good for driving off animals and people, but it won't hamstring that armored bastard or his bony buckos. Might kill the fleas in me blanket, though."

"How can—" Gull hacked, sneezed. "How can you jest?"

He felt more than saw the sailor shrug. "Ye get used to it after a while. Tow waves his hands and shit falls from the sky. Just keep your chin down and mouth closed. None of us've been scuppered yet."

"The old freightmaster died."

"Oh, aye." Another shrug. "But he left the circle of protection. Poor Gorman was more for shovelin' dung than thinkin'. I just hope Towie can pull something out of his sleeve. That armored monster looks like he'd eat through a wagon in three bites."

"What would he do to us?" Gull snorked. Like the rest of the entourage, he breathed through his hands or clothing while watching the oncoming horde. Through billows of gray smoke, they saw it wasn't a hundred feet off.

At least the terror had abated among Towser's followers, for the nightmare hovered at treetop height to the south, opposite the armored wizard, as if marking a beacon in the sky. Towser had slipped into his wagon.

Morven rubbed watery eyes. "Oh, probably they wouldn't eat us or torture us to death. Steer clear and you don't run afoul, usually. We're just ants to wizards. We'd be scattered to the winds, like happened at your village there. Oh, sorry. But I'll bet this pirate's after that coral box. If it's brimful o' magic energy, like Towie said, it's a magnet for handwavers all 'round the compass."

"Maybe Towser will just give it up," murmured Gull.

Morven and Lily snorted.

Gull clasped and unclasped empty hands. Without a weapon he felt helpless, naked. He was, mostly, clad in a leather kilt and nothing else. He told Lily to stay put, then clambered past them to the toppled chuck wagon.

He didn't get far. The wagon was a tumbledown mess. Heaped together against one canvas wall were boxes, crocks, bowls, loaves of bread, cooking tools, bedrolls, spilled flour and beer and wine and butter. Perched atop the mess, with a shawl over her head, was a besmudged Felda clutching Greensleeves tight, with Stiggur huddling behind. Gull's sister slept. One advantage to being half-witted, he thought, was few worries. She clutched something gray, like a tassel of horsehair, and he wondered where she had found it.

The fat cook asked him what transpired, but he ignored her. He'd come to check on his sister and to fetch his small axe, stored with his saws and other tools behind some crates. But he'd have to unload the wagon to get it now. He asked Felda for a weapon and received a poker of heavy steel and a butcher's knife which he slid carefully into his belt.

He told them, "If there's any need to get out, I'll come fetch you. Otherwise, stay here." No one argued.

Gull climbed out in time to see the skeletal goblins disappear.

The smoke had lessened, settling, leaving a burned tang in their mouths and a rash like sunburn on their faces.

Capering around the armored wizard, like sparrows before a raven, the skeletal goblins had spun, shrilled, waved stick-arms—generally acted like useless idiots, as in life. Gull was unsure if they were a threat or not: what could they do but bite you? And one swift kick would knock them to skittles.

Now, one by one, each gave a queer sort of hop, spun around, shriveled into a twist like a beech leaf, and flickered toward the sky like chaff caught in a dust devil.

From Towser's wagon came a crow of delight and triumph. Sleeves shot to the elbows, the wizard dusted his palms as the last of the skeleton horde whisked away like ashes in a wind.

"One summons, one unsummons," Morven commented. "Doing and undoing to get the better of each other. Would I had a hundredth of the energy these wizards waste . . . "

Then even the laconic sailor shut up, for the armored wizard arrived. Towser could not unsummon him, it seemed.

The warrior wizard halted twenty feet from the wagons. Halting, he sank even deeper into the forest floor. *He must weigh as much as a stone barn*, thought the woodcutter. By the fitful light of the hovering nightmare and the campfire, Gull studied the enemy for weaknesses.

There seemed to be none. The wizard stood seven feet tall in spectacularly ornate silver armor. The breastplate, leg armor, and even sleeves were sculpted like the muscles underneath. Red piping or reinforcing straps crossed the armor at stress points. Where there wasn't plate armor there was chain mail, enwrapping the throat and groin and wrists. Wide wings lined with spikes jutted over the shoulders, and spikes jutted from the back of the gauntlets. Twin horns of silver tipped with red stuck outward from the bucket helmet, and the planes of the face were coated red around silver whorls. Nothing fleshy showed, not even the lower part of the wizard's face. It was a fantastic, unreal sight, something no nightmare could conjure. The armor looked solid and unmovable as a granite wall. Yet he carried no weapons that Gull could see, making him look unbalanced and unprepared.

Towser posed atop the wagon seat. Gull was surprised—no one could stand toe-to-toe in combat with this armored vision, but Towser calmly folded his arms into his sleeves. He showed no fear, in fact feigned boredom.

The warrior lifted a hand, clamped a fist, and the light above suddenly dimmed. The nightmare twisted into an ash leaf and wafted upward, away. Only the meager cookfire gave any light, for the smoke had dissipated. And in the east, Gull realized, glowed the gray of false dawn. The duel had stolen most of the night, and suddenly the weight of sleep loss and fighting and wounds settled on Gull like a yoke of stone. Despite his aches and pains, his eyelids drooped. He yawned so hard his jaw cracked.

But Towser's words jolted him. He called across the span, "You waste your time and effort, sir wizard. You'll not steal what you've come for, for it works for me."

"Magic works for no one, but we for it." Oddly, the warrior's voice was not a deep boom or harsh drawl, but the easy speech of a middle-aged man. Gull wondered if the being inside actually filled that giant suit of armor. "Until you learn that, you know aught." He added something in a strange cant of grunts and growls.

A snort came back. "I've no desire to discuss thaumaturgy before breakfast, certainly not with a lout who abuses my hospitality by sundering my wagons. You'll not get what you seek, so you may as well depart."

Again the warrior growled and grunted, but halted when Towser reached behind him into the wagon. He plucked out the pink stone box. By dim light it resembled, as Kem had said, pig guts strung tight. As if it would rot in the morning sun.

The warrior spoke again, but Towser lifted his free hand and pointed, then clenched his own fist.

The armored warrior staggered as his knees buckled. With an amazing display of strength, he propped himself upright and waved a clenched hand. Gradually,

he righted. Probably he'd blocked Towser's spell—
more weakness?—with a counterspell, Gull thought.
But who knew what wizards did: mortals could only
watch and wonder.

The woodcutter wondered what came next. If the
warrior couldn't stand up to Towser's *mana* vault, then
what?

Wood splintered and cracked. Towser's wagon
groaned, jiggled, and tilted, pushed from underneath.
Gull craned to see in the dim light. White swords,
from the cave floor, multiplied under the wagon.
Rising, they shoved the wagon off its wheels. And
continued to grow, and push.

Towser cursed, grabbed for a grip, struggled to hang
on to the *mana* vault.

Strength returned, the warrior dropped that attack,
began another.

With long strides, he stamped toward the chuck
wagon. Grabbing hold of the axle, he dragged it sideways. Inside, Felda screamed. Lily yelped, Morven
cursed, and Gull hefted his poker.

It wasn't much to battle an armored magician.

He heard his sister shriek. Finally, she'd discovered
terror.

Swinging his thin poker in his left hand, Gull
hopped around the tongue of the overturned wagon.

"Fight *me*, you fiend!" he shouted. And he charged.

Things happened too fast for Gull to follow. Part of
him said it didn't matter. He must protect his sister.
That was enough. So he attacked.

The warrior-wizard snapped wood like kindling,
ripped the wagon tongue and front axles from the
frame. A wooden wheel bounced off his silver helmet.

A metallic hand tore boards off the wagon's side. Canvas split, tangled. Splinters flew. Screams rang.

From the hole in the side of the wagon, like a woodchuck, popped up Stiggur. He flung a bottle at the warrior's helmet. It shattered, and Gull smelled vinegar. The wizard sliced with a metal hand that would have decapitated the boy, but he disappeared into his den.

By then Gull had dashed around to the wizard's back. He saw no chinks in the armor. And where the blazes was Towser with his bag of tricks?

The woodcutter wound up and slammed the poker at the back of the wizard's knee. Chain mail protected him, and the poker only bent.

The only sign the wizard gave was to slap backhanded, like swatting a fly.

Gull shot out his arm to protect his head, but the armored glove slammed his elbow, almost breaking it. Gull's own hand banged his rasped forehead, which bled anew. He felt he'd been crushed by a tree. Reeling, the woodcutter bounced on the turf.

Through a haze, he heard screams.

Vision whirling, he saw a spinning wizard drag his sister's gown, yank her from the wagon. The wizard pinned Greensleeves by one arm. She shrieked like a trapped rabbit at the cold touch.

Gull tried to sit up, but his muscles wouldn't respond. He couldn't find his arms or hands, as if they'd been wrenched off. Perhaps they had. He tried to kick, to sit up, but only twitched. Panic set in. Perhaps his back was broken, like his father's.

Another scream joined Greensleeves's. Kicking with an armored boot, the wizard knocked the wagon askew, reached behind, caught Lily by the waist— kidnapped for the second time this night. She tugged at the metal hand until her fingernails bled, but couldn't get free.

Morven the sailor leveled his crossbow and shot from ten feet away. The heavy steel-tipped bolt spanked off the wizard's helmet, ricocheted away. Chad ran up, racked the bow on his crossbow, but stopped: if one bolt had failed, surely another would. But it was all they had. Kem and Oles waved swords feebly. They saw no place to attack. Jonquil, one of the dancing girls, ran up with a torch, but halted too.

Gull shook his head, grew dizzy. Through a fog he saw the warrior turn toward his camp with two captives, heard Towser bellow some magical command.

About time, the woodcutter thought.

The command got results. The warrior-wizard paused, half turned, and—

—his helmet exploded.

One second it was there, the next his head sundered as if struck by lightning. Hot jagged metal flew in all directions. A piece nicked Greensleeves in the forehead and made her bleed. Lily yelped as a fragment pinked her bosom. Gull heard a piece flicker into dirt nearby.

All that remained was a fragment of molten collar. As the warrior took another step, this charred twisted strip sloughed off and crunched underfoot. Chain mail from the coif hung in tatters on the red-and-silver breast.

But the armored wizard kept walking.

With no head at all.

"An *avatar!*" shrieked Towser. "You *cheat!*"

Vaguely, Gull wondered what an avatar was. But not for long.

The titan—phantom or ghost or whatever it was— strode toward the distant bonfire with his captives.

Paralyzed, Gull lay in his path. But the armored giant couldn't see him.

A huge foot reared over the woodcutter. Eyes bulging, Gull remembered that the giant had sunk into the loam, heavy as a yoke of oxen.

He was about to step on Gull, crush him like a cockroach.

Then the world went white.

CHAPTER
13

One second Gull stared helpless at a hobnailed armored boot poised to crush him—

—the next the sky filled with white, and the dank moldy smell of mushrooms washed over him.

Something huge loomed over Gull, something that made the armored avatar seem a mouse in comparison, as if the moon had come to earth.

The thing cast its own cold sickly light, like the foxfire of swamps or the glitter of lightning bugs. The woodcutter saw a head the size of a cottage, goggling glowing yellow eyes, and teeth like the stone spears of a cave. The beast was white all over, with that dank glow, speckled with rows of brownish-gray lumps.

Mushrooms, Gull realized. The beast was one giant mushroom speckled with a thousand more. The rank musty smell was overwhelming. Flakes big as plates fell from the beast's shoulders and broke on the ground, the way oyster mushrooms sloughed from birch trees in fall.

But the teeth were what touched the armored wizard.

The headless warrior balked as if hitting a wall. The mushroom monster's maw swung toward it and bit down. With a sickening crunch, stone teeth shattered on red-silver armor.

The women dropped to the ground as the avatar struggled, grabbed for anything to prevent disappearing into the maw. The mouth, big as a well, opened farther, swallowed half the armored carcass. Metal gloves plucked at the lumpy lips. White chunks crumbled, rained on Gull and the dancing girls. With a sudden surge of strength and terror, Gull crawled out of the way, bumping his sister and Lily with his head.

Then the armored wizard was gone.

Gull blinked. Swallowed? Or . . . ?

No. There went the avatar, a wisp like ashes, flickering into the sky.

The giant mushroom monster growled deep in its throat. Goggle eyes like a fish's rolled, hunted. The thing was huge, tall as the dead trees, long as a barn. It picked up a bloated pulpy foot, lurched toward the wagons. People howled.

Then the beast changed color.

Waves of brown welled upward from the ground, flushed green near the middle, flooded blue at the top. Gull was reminded of Towser's gown, with its ascending stripes. For a few seconds, the mushroom-monster stood bathed in multicolored light. Then it collapsed onto itself, withered, and sank into the ground.

Leaving no trace.

Gull sat up, propped by one hand. The distant bonfire had died, unattended. The black riders were gone, as were the dark wagons, the lions, the avatar, the smoke, the skeletal goblins, the nightmare. Only a jumble of zombies and a meandering wall of swords, pitifully thin, remained.

The battle was over.

From his perch on the wagon seat, Towser peered around the horizon. The sun leaked through shattered trees in the east. The warm light was encouraging, for it revealed the brave greenery, the renewal of hope.

"We beat him!" the wizard crowed. "Let's pack up and git!"

But the sunrise, and the return to sanity and normalcy, also revealed the aftermath of battle: wreckage, wounds, and ruin.

Most of the entourage had only slept a few hours after a day of digging, then suffered a night of fighting. They were baggy-eyed, bruised, dirty, half-naked, crow-voiced. Gull couldn't count his wounds: a triple rake on the shoulder that needed the nurse's stitching, a pinked ham, scabby forehead, sore ribs, mashed fingers, and more.

Yet they must move on. Though Towser wouldn't confirm their suspicions, the *mana* vault might attract magicians from miles around, as Morven speculated.

As Felda spiced ale and sliced bacon for breakfast, the bodyguards and Gull inspected the chuck wagon. It was a loss. Axles and wheels were broken, the side smashed, the tongue snapped off. They righted the men's wagon, which was intact, and pushed it alongside. They hauled out the bodyguard's rucksacks and bedrolls—soldiers of fortune, they owned little—and hung them outside the wagon. The bodyguards would have to sleep outdoors in cold and wet and mosquitoes.

Silently they transferred the chuck supplies to the

new wagon. Most cooking goods were intact, being of iron, but plates and crocks and bottle had smashed, barrels had leaked, some dry goods had spoiled. There was room enough in the new wagon, though things were heaped on the floor instead of nesting in cupboards, and everyone feared short rations later.

All went smoothly until Gull, exhausted, stumbled and banged shoulders with Kem. Instantly, every man dropped his goods and reached for a knife, Gull for his drover's whip.

Kem the Scarfaced growled, "You're too clumsy for this work, shit shoveler! Let men finish the job!"

"I didn't see you slay any dragons last night!" Gull grated. "Were you guarding the women from the rear?"

"Gut him, Kem!" shouted pretty-boy Chad, too loud. Their dulled nerves were rasped raw. "I can handle the horses! Let him feed beetles!"

Morven shifted his feet. "You're fast with your mouth, Chad, urging others to brawl. Mayhap you'd dance a hornpipe with me—"

Actually, Gull thought, if anyone swung a fist, he'd probably fall down and stay down. Then a high-pitched shout from Towser interrupted them. "I don't pay you to stand and talk! You're all docked a day's wages! Knoton, take note! And next time'll be a week!"

None answered back. It was only the generous pay that kept them here. With snorts and muttered threats, they picked up tools and victuals. Kem hissed, "We'll settle later, Gullshit!"

"You'll talk me to death, eh, Kem-pletely Helpless?" Gull threw his load inside and stalked off to count livestock.

Only a half dozen animals had returned to camp. The rest were scattered through the forest. Gull needed help, and said so to the clerk. Sorting his own papers and supplies, Knoton nodded. "Take Jonquil. She came from a ranch and knows how to ride. And Chad. He worked with horses on the plains. And the bard. She can do everything."

So Gull got the yellow-bedecked Jonquil, a big woman with solid arms and legs and large hands and feet, freckles and red-gold hair, as well as the beribboned bard, Ranon Spiritsinger. Civil enough under Towser's eye, Chad agreed to hunt south in the woods for the animals, while Gull and Jonquil would hunt north near the crater. Everyone rode bareback, for there were no saddles. They used the long wagon traces as reins, which meant a lot of leather draped over the withers. For the pain in his rump and the burn in his shoulder, Gull had to hold the animal's mane too.

With the forest so open, it didn't take Gull long to locate two stray mules, a pair of horses normally yoked together, two black cavalry horses with shiny black saddles and tack, as well as his axe, which lay near the rim of the pit where he'd hurled it at the black captain. He frowned at the dew rust on the blade.

"Is that him down there?" asked Jonquil. Her voice was plain and uncultured, not trained for singing. She reminded Gull of the farm girls of White Ridge, and—a pang—the lost Cowslip. A sturdy finger pointed into the crater where sprawled a black corpse.

"Aye." Gull picketed the black horses to a lead. "Something will eat him soon enough."

Jonquil swung from the saddle with easy, if chunky, grace. "He won't need whatever's in his purse, then."

As Gull worked, she slid down the crater and looted the body. Upon her return, he asked, "Find anything?"

"Not much." She brushed back her hair, but her casual air was forced. Idly Gull wondered how much the captain had carried. He should have looked himself. But warfare—and scavenging—were still new.

"Here. You can have this." She handed Gull a sheathed knife. Curious, he took it, then remembered. It had caught fire last night. The handle was jet, black leather wrapped with black wire. The pommel was diamond-shaped: a skullpopper. He drew the long white blade gingerly, expecting it to flare up, but nothing happened. Had the enchantment been linked to the man's life force? Shrugging, he tucked it in his belt, thanked her. Though he guessed she'd never have surrendered it, had she known it was magic.

"Do you love Lily?" Jonquil's sudden question jarred him.

"Eh?" Gull stalled as he remounted. "Love? Oh, I don't know . . . I . . . like her very much. . . ."

Gull frowned. In truth, he didn't know how he felt. Lily was pleasant company, comforting. Starved for simple affection, she'd latched onto him. Was that love? He had panicked when he'd thought to lose Lily. Was that love?

Jonquil shrugged big shoulders, grabbed the mare's mane, hoisted her broad butt. "She loves you."

Gull flapped the reins, suddenly unsure what to do with them. "If you say so."

Jonquil rolled red-rimmed eyes and clucked to her horse. Expertly, she wheeled her mount to circle the crater.

On the way back, Gull dismounted, secured the string of horses to a tree, and inspected the wavering line of stone spears that jutted incongruously from the forest floor. By day, they were not white, but shimmering rainbows of pale earth colors: white, tan, brown, red, blue-gray. What part of the Domains grew these, he wondered? Shaking his head, he snapped a spear off, a present for his sister. She liked pretty oddments.

Back in camp, Gull gave the stone spear to Greensleeves, was rewarded by a happy cooing.

He found himself fairly happy when he counted the livestock. They'd lost four animals to lions or flight, had found two cavalry horses with saddles, so were down two, but less one wagon, were actually two ahead. The bodyguards were pleased, for they could ride the saddled blacks. Towser decided to put one bodyguard on scout, but also one in the rear to see they weren't followed.

Gull was less pleased, for the new chuck wagon had a mixed team, two horses and two mules, always trouble. Different heights, different gaits, and who was ahead got their tails bitten. But his mulewhip would break those bad habits.

Eager to be away, Towser pushed, berated, insulted, threatened to fire the lot—an empty threat out here, Gull thought. Still, everyone picked up, dumped stuff in the wagons, looked around for anything left—only the dead knight Morven had shot—then rolled off through the blasted forest. Within two hours they were out of the burn zone, back in natural forest. By noon the wagons slowed as the drivers fell asleep at the traces. Towser relented, allowed them to camp the night. Everyone dropped where they sat and slept the afternoon away.

They were not attacked, which Gull thought just as well. One and all would have surrendered just to rest.

But even in his logy afternoon dreams, Gull framed questions to Towser. Dozens of questions that robbed his mind of rest.

* * *

Supper was quiet. Felda groused she couldn't find anything, and what she did find was bent or broken. Stiggur wore a path to the new wagon fetching things and shifting loads.

Gull folded his salt pork and pickles into a half loaf of bread and worked as he ate. Hobbling, bent as an old man, he checked hooves, smeared salve on lion scratches and branch scrapes and strap chafes—smeared some on his own scrapes and wounds—checked the wagons for large damage. He skipped many items, for he wanted spare time before bed.

It was still late when he approached Towser.

The wizard sat in the back of his wagon. The flap was up, the first time Gull had ever seen the interior. It was gaily painted inside as out. There were, as Lily said, boxes and boxes, of books and stinkpots and little clockwork engines, all framed along the walls, and glassed-in lamps that let him work at night, though one had cracked in the battle. In addition, an ornate bed that folded against the wall lay wide enough for three people: the wizard and two dancing girls.

Gull recognized a few things Towser had evidently picked up. A grimy bone, perhaps plucked from a zombie. A hunk of mushroom from the beast. A long gray hair, perhaps from the nightmare.

But Gull wasn't interested in Towser's habits or work. Only—

"Towser, I would have some answers." Gull knew he sounded surly, for he was angry. Further, having grown up in a village of equals, he knew not how to defer to "betters."

The wizard didn't look up. By yellow lamplight, he sketched with a quill in his little book of magic, the grimoire chained to his belt of pouches. He averted the page lest Gull see. "And why need I give you answers? Do you work for me or the other way around? And do you realize that princes give whole fortunes to wizards for answers to their questions?"

His tone was lofty, aloof. Gull suspected he'd practiced these words—indeed, had anticipated his coming.

Stubborn, the woodcutter was not put off. "There are things I do not understand, things you do, or I suspect you do. Things—"

Towser blew on the page to dry ink. "Can you understand this? I mind the answers, you mind the stock and wagons—"

"—I need to know to continue in your employ. Otherwise, I take my sister and my pay and go. We can find our own way out of these woods."

Towser rolled his eyes and sighed, as an adult will at the prattling of children. "Very well. I need a freight-master. Ask and be quick about it."

Gull was surprised he acceded so quickly, but again it felt rehearsed. Was this wizard that much smarter, and dumb as the horses? Whatever, he asked.

"Last night, I saw the centaurs from the battle at White Ridge. Helki and Holleb. She cried they were captives, forced to fight. You sent them home to their steppes. But have you enslaved them to fight for you, now?"

Shaking his head, the wizard flipped through his book, stopped at a different page. He rubbed his stomach as if it hurt, and Gull remembered he had troublsome bowels, or imagined he did. "The centaur-folk of Broken Toe Mountain in the Green Lands are mercenaries. Parceled all over the Domains. Every wizard uses them: they are superlative fighters. But if I conjured them, 'twas accidental. Probably they've sold their allegiance to some other wizard and become part of another army."

Gull shook his head back. "I don't understand. Why claim they were captives?"

"Perhaps they are." Towser stopped fidgeting and stared Gull in the eyes. The woodcutter couldn't look away, as if he were a chicken hypnotized by a hawk. "Mayhaps the party they *joined* was captured. They prosper by ransom. My bringing them here and then returning them to their home in the steppes would have freed them. No doubt they'd thank me."

Frowning, Gull pondered that magic was beyond him. He tried another question. "Did you fell those zombies with a weakness spell? And was it the same spell that felled so many villagers—and my family—in White—"

"I have no weakness charm, for it's too cruel a spell. I used an unlife spell on the zombies. It doesn't steal life, just returns it whence it belongs, leaving them inanimate corpses again. It has the advantage of not driving *mana* from any human or beast in the area—you'll notice there were no dead birds near the zombies."

Dead birds? wondered Gull. What had that to do with anything? He was mixed up. Towser continued to stare. With the light behind him, his eyes glowed like an owl's even as his finger drew queer circles on a page.

"Well, never mind," the woodcutter acceded. He shifted his feet. "Uh . . . what's an avatar? You used that word—"

"A projection of your persona at a distance. I thought we fought an actual wizard in that armor. Turns out the wizard stayed at some distance and worked the armor from there. And gave voice. Like a simulacrum. A handy spell I wish I knew."

Me too, thought Gull inanely. Then he could be

elsewhere, out from under this burning stare. "Uh . . . what was that mushroom-monster?"

A small shrug, and the first sign of reticence from the wizard. "A . . . fungusaur. As you say, a mushroom-monster. They live underground."

Gull could have sworn. Of course. He was so tired he was stupid. "Why did that wizard—or avatar—try to kidnap my sister? What is she to him?"

Another shrug. "Why did the black knight carry off Lily? Men have needs only women can satisfy. The wizard could not know your sister is simple. Not that it would matter, for his purposes."

Before that insult could penetrate Gull's fogged mind, Towser said, "It's late, Gull. We must get an early start. Why not retire?"

Suddenly, Gull felt a weight descend on him, almost press him to the ground. He gasped. He'd barely crawl to his bedroll, he was so exhausted. "Y-yes. Good idea . . . Good . . . night . . . "

"Good-night, son," smiled the wizard, as the wood-cutter trudged away yawning.

Gull peeked in on his sister, asleep curled in her shawl like a cat, and then crawled under the wagon. Lily waited in his bedroll. "Did you get any answers from Towser?"

She scooted aside as Gull crashed down and yawned. "Yes . . . I found out . . . everything . . . "

"I doubt that. Towser's got questions himself. I know he wonders about that mushroom beast."

"Eh? What . . . about it?"

"You didn't notice how it vanished? No? It was strange. When Towser conjures a thing, it twinkles like stars on a summer night. True?"

Gull groaned, "Whatever, dear . . . "

"And when that armored wizard conjured and banished, his pawns withered to ashy things and blew away. Yet when the *mushroom-beast* appeared and disappeared, it flooded with colors from the ground up, like a big plant growing! That's neither Towser's magic, nor the other wizard's, else the monster wouldn't have attacked him. So you know what *that* means!"

"No." It ached just to say that much. Gull hurt all over, so tired he couldn't lift his head. His lion wounds burned and itched.

"It *means* some *other* wizard conjured it, someone close by!"

"The astrologer, perhaps. Or the bard. Don't they do magic, little bits? She can even ride a horse . . . And that reminds me . . . " Despite his fatigue, Gull propped on his elbows. "Lily, why did Towser hire me as freighter? Chad's a bastard, but he's a better wrangler than I. Jonquil's the same. I saw that today. Why did Towser need me?"

The girl frowned in the dark. "Jonquil told me she told you I love you. Is that true?"

"What? Hunh?" Gull's mind reeled. What had happened to his question? "Um, yes, she mentioned it."

"And what do you think of it?" She leaned over him in the dark. He could smell perfume in her hair, mint on her breath.

"I'm glad you—like me," he mumbled.

"Love you," she whispered, her breath warm in his ear.

"Yes," was all he could answer. "I—like you very much, Lily."

"That's not what a woman wants to hear."

"I know, and I'm sorry. I don't know . . . what I know anymore. Every day I know less, it seems."

The dancing girl laid her head on his shoulder. Her hair tickled his nose, but he was too tired to brush it away. "You and me both."

"Hm? How's that?"

She murmured, her breath warm on his skin. "Something's happening to me, Gull. Strange . . . ideas and feelings I've never had before. The whispering in my head. And sometimes a tingling in my hands and feet, as when the armored wizard came near. I don't know what it means . . . I do know I love you, though."

Gull patted her head awkwardly, fought to stay awake. "You deserve better than me, Lily. Someone to love you and care for you, give you a decent home. I don't own but my clothes and some worn-out tools and a handful of silver."

"I don't care about that. You saved my life. Rescued me from that rapist knight. I won't forget that." She rolled onto him, pressed her lips and body against his.

Half-asleep, Gull never was sure what happened next.

A few days later, they left the Whispering Woods.

The break was clean. They came to a drop-off where the black forest loam and big trees ended. Thirty feet below the land turned sandy, clothed with stiff grass and evergreen trees no taller than a man.

"A pine barrens," Morven told them. "Easy enough to cross, if you didn't mind stickers in your britches, but water's scarcer'n rum. It sinks into the sand and disappears. These pines and cedars have taproots a mile long, I've heard."

From this lip, they saw that beyond the barrens lay some lower pocket where vultures circled, then gray-green hills rolled out of sight. Towser unfurled a parchment map, pronounced them the Ice-Rime Hills, and noted a swamp before them: the hidden pocket.

"Should be lots of black lotuses there, children. I'll give a gold crown to the first person who shows me one. Alive. Don't pluck them."

They backtracked to a stream, filled every empty vessel and stoppered them. Then Gull began the heartbreaking task of easing the wagons down the drop-off. After thought and argument and experiment, they worked out a way of emptying a wagon, warping it to trees as a brake, then using a doubled team of mules to lower while some plied levers to prevent it flipping. It took three days before they could march across the pine barrens.

The land was sandy and crisscrossed with foot-tripping roots and grass sharp enough to pierce a girl's slipper. With the air trapped between forest and hills, flies and mosquitoes plagued them, until Gull and the nurse Haley mixed up pennyroyal extract and paraffin in mineral oil as a repellent. The mules walked slowly, careful of their footing, but the wagons rolled lightly over the corduroy roots. They made good time.

Within four days, they reached a swamp. A road of sorts, much bogged, skirted along the south. The insects were worse, but the hills looked rounded and surmountable, Gull was glad to see.

The bodyguards argued about first watch. Each was eager to hunt black lotuses. Lily explained Towser often offered bonuses for certain prizes as they traveled. Black lotuses were full of *mana*, it was said.

Drawing the short straw, Kem got first watch.

But around midnight, at changeover, Chad paced so much he woke Gull. The woodcutter growled,

"Take it out there, will you? Some of us want to sleep!"

Chad suggested an obscenity, but added fitfully, "Kem hasn't returned yet. He's late."

"Late?" Gull eased Lily's head off his shoulder, rolled out of his bedroll. Quickly he reached for the pennyroyal oil and slathered it on. "He's never been late before."

"I know that!" Chad sneered. But clearly he was worried. "Once the fire died down, I saw lights out there. I've been wondering—"

Gull grabbed his arm. "Lights? Where? Show me!"

Fretful, Chad didn't argue. He led down to the edge of the swamp. "Somewhere out—there!"

Gull gaped. At a stone's throw, winking off and on, floating and sinking, of all sizes, bobbled soft glowing balls of green-white light.

"Knees of Gnerdel," the woodcutter gasped. "Don't you know what those *are?*"

"No," Chad muttered. "What?"

"Turn around or you're lost! Don't look at them!" Spinning, his back to the swamp, Gull explained. "They would appear sometimes in the bog below White Ridge! Those are will-o'-the-wisps! They lure folk into the wetlands to die, and the swamp feeds off their bodies!"

"Then Kem's out there!"

CHAPTER
14

Gull rapped his axe handle against the chuck wagon, the women's wagon, the astrologer's, even Towser's, chipping the paint.

"Rouse! Rouse! We've lost someone! Stiggur, build up the fire! High! We'll need a beacon to get back!"

People spilled from wagons and instantly cursed the hordes of insects. Gull shrugged on his leather tunic, slathered on more pennyroyal, grabbed his whip and axe, lit a torch of folded birch bark shoved into a hickory handle. After a hurried explanation, he dashed to the swamp's edge. Torch high, he hunted along the shoreline.

He recalled the muddy bottom with its reeds and grasses extended a way, then pools of open water took over. Past them started weird twisted trees, cypresses, Morven called them, with knobby upthrust roots like knees, and branches festooned with vines and grapes. Those curtains cut off any more sights.

But clear were the will-o'-the-wisps, bobbing and

weaving, teasing like children playing hide-and-seek.

Seek, he thought, surely. For he found Kem's foot-prints, deep holes in the mud where his boots had stuck. Fifty feet into the grass, he found a boot. Gull swore: leaving something vital proved Kem was mesmerized.

The woodcutter took care not to look directly at the lights. It was dangerous as looking at the sun.

When the black mud became too plocky, Gull shucked his wooden clogs and hurled them toward shore. Cold mud oozed between his toes, but at least he could walk. He thrashed through saw grass that cut his legs. Dripping water and mud, hoisting his legs high—they'd ache soon—he heard splashing behind.

Chad followed with another torch. He carried a crossbow and short sword.

Beyond his flickering light, Gull glimpsed Greensleeves. "Go back, damn it!"

Chad shouted, "He's my friend and I'll rescue him! What the hell do you care about Kem anyway?"

"Not you!" Gull tried to turn, but was stuck fast. In fact, standing still, he began to sink. "I meant my sister, damn it! And Kem might be a prick, but he doesn't deserve to wander in a swamp till he dies! No one does! *Greenie, go back!*"

His sister ignored him. She had enough sense to tuck up her tattered skirts and walk parallel to the men's footprints so she didn't sink. Her legs were black to the thigh. Gull gave up yelling. Short of tying her to a tree, he couldn't stop her. He'd just have to watch front and back.

He tried to recall the legends of will-o'-the-wisps. Back in White Ridge, they sometimes appeared in summer three years in a row, then disappeared for three years or more. No one knew what they looked like up close. Folk who watched too long became mesmerized, walking toward the lights. If restrained, they fought like wildcats to go on, had to be tied in a closed barn until dawn, then watched each night else they pursued anew. What the lights wanted, no one understood. It was whispered they lured victims to wander until they died, where their corpses would feed the swamp itself. But no one knew for certain.

Queerest of all, only people became entranced. Animals ignored the lights. What did that mean? Again, no one knew. It was just something to speculate on through long winter nights.

Perhaps tonight, thought Gull, he'd learn. Whether he'd survive was another matter . . .

Oddly, the woodcutter found the pools easy to traverse. The bottoms were solid but slick claypans. He welcomed the chance to walk more easily and wash off rotted-green mud.

Until he discovered his legs peppered with leeches.

He bit his tongue to keep from screaming, fought the urge to run ashore. He ripped at the slimy bumps, but they stuck fast, greedily sucking his blood. Gull gave up, shut them from his mind. Maybe they'd make his sister turn back. As for Chad, let him get eaten.

Slogging, lurching over treacherous ground, juggling the torch so it wouldn't fall—extinguish and leave him in blackness—he reached the first cypress. With his axe he slashed to part the tough vines and grab the bole, but the woody knees were slippery.

Nothing was easy in this godsforsaken swamp, he thought. No place for mortals. Further, he couldn't track Kem. He might have gone anywhere.

Which meant Gull could only steer for the dancing wisps. Tempting death.

Growling, swearing, he glanced quickly at the wisps, looked away, then turned that way. Chad came behind.

Greensleeves, he was astounded to learn, was ahead of him.

The girl had flipped her soggy skirts over her shoulders. Her bare bony behind glowed like a small moon. She, too, was dotted with leeches, but fewer than Gull bore. And when she scratched, they dropped off. More of her strange power, he thought. Even insects respected her link to nature, plagued her less than clear-headed folk.

Somehow she'd circled a hundred feet beyond, almost out of the torchlight.

Gull shouted for her to slow down. She cruised on, light as a deer. He was forced to steer after her now.

But who knew? Maybe she tracked Kem. Maybe with her otherworldly vision, she could see what he couldn't.

Checking that Chad followed, Gull cursed and hopped and floundered after her. Maybe idiocy was its own queer blessing—

—or maybe not.

Greensleeves shrilled like a rabbit caught in a trap.

Gull bellowed.

Green-slimy skinny man-shapes swarmed over his sister.

Some dropped from trees, some skipped across roots, and two erupted from the water like bass leaping after dragonflies. Three grabbed Greensleeves's arms, one her legs, and they pulled.

In different directions, squabbling the while like a catfight.

Gull had seen this before. The tiny goblins had argued like this. Maybe these creatures were cousins.

Howling, wishing for his longbow, Gull scrambled onto a root, slipped, jumped for another. But he raced like a snail after spiders, him plodding while the big goblins flitted across water and roots and vines.

For despite their haggling, they dashed off with their prize. The horde melted into the night, away from Gull and his wavering torch.

As Gull clutched at vines, Chad came level, raised his crossbow. It twanged and thunked. Gull batted his bow up. "You'll hit my sister!"

"Ha! Not likely! Look!"

Indeed, one shrieking goblin was pinned through the guts to a cypress trunk. Splashing in water, slipping on roots, clawing aside vines, the men bulled up to it.

By torchlight, the thing was so ugly it hurt to look at it. Gray-green skin, pointed ears, lank black hair. So skinny its ribs and hipbones showed, it was naked, covered with warts and leech scars. The crossbow quarrel had pierced its hip, and it screeched as it tried to pull free, slimy hands slipping on the shaft.

"Sedge trolls," Chad muttered. "Halfway between goblins and orcs."

Vaguely, Gull wondered if these trolls were in league with the will-o'-the-wisps. Or were actually the wisps, using some light trick. Or simply followed the wisps, waiting for a mesmerized victim. Then he pushed that aside.

"Where have they taken my sister?" he demanded of the monster.

Clutching a tree bole to keep his footing, Chad growled, "You won't get answers. They're animals. No minds."

And before Gull could act, the mercenary smashed

the thing's head against the tree with the stock of his crossbow.

The troll was tough. One dirty ear dribbled blood, but it shook its head, only dazed. Chad hauled off and smashed again, crushing its skull. The troll slumped to hang on the bolt.

Shocked, Gull demanded, "Why do that?"

"To save another arrow," Chad tsked. "Come on, we've got to find Kem."

"And my sister."

Together they waved torches and cast about. Gull pointed out a gap in grapevines. They shoved through, Gull in the lead, axe held close to bat at foliage, and make a quick strike.

Blundering through vines, duck walking on aching knees and ankles, slapping at insects, cursing as the torches fetched up, the men pressed on. At one point they heard a faint scream—a man's—quickly cut off.

Mincing around tree stumps into ever-thicker bracken, they touched solid ground. An island. Gull discovered a path no wider than a deer's, and they slid along it. Another scream split the air. Chad grunted when they smelled a cooking fire like burning garbage.

There were no troll guards, and soon whiskers of fire showed through the vine curtains. They extinguished the torches in a puddle, crept over chaff and trampled bracken.

It was no village, just a clearing two arm spans' wide. The firepit was a circle of rocks. Bones and waste littered the ground along with heaps of rotted grass for beds.

Gull burst onto the scene first, Chad squeezing behind.

Greensleeves was mashed facedown in a pile of grass. On her back sat four trolls pinning her hands.

Close by the fire, five more, male and female, sat on Kem's back. One gray-haired hag plied a rusty knife blade to saw through the bodyguard's elbow. Blood spurted as far as the fire, making it smoke with a brassy stink.

The two rescuers couldn't believe the trolls' surprise. Green faces turned up, crooked jaws dropped, eyes popped. Gull realized they were dumb as dumb dogs.

Then he swung his axe, and trolls died.

Yelling for Chad to keep clear, the woodcutter whipped the double-bitted axe behind, fetched up slightly in vines, then swung with a grunt and heave.

The axe blade sheared through the troll with the knife. Like a punky stump, his skull flew apart, spewing blood and brains. The blade carved through two more trolls and thudded into a fourth. The others were already scampering away.

They didn't get far. Something burst into the clearing from the opposite side. Long, low, wide, gray-furred and striped. Gull saw a flat partistriped head, then white teeth flashed and snapped shut on a troll's leg, severing it.

It was a badger big as a mule.

Chad ducked to Gull's off side, circled the fire, ran straight at the trolls atop Greensleeves. But he balked as the giant badger spit out a leg to scurry after another victim.

It wasn't hungry, Gull realized. It attacked to kill, the same way it pursued chickens. Like a thick-bodied snake, it raced on short legs after a troll that shrilled like a mouse.

Trolls boiled everywhere. Chad stabbed a female through the chest, kicked her jaw to free his blade. He stamped for footing, jabbed at others that squirmed and dived and clawed to get clear like maggots off meat. He skewered one more troll through the back before the clearing emptied but for the dead.

And dying. The badger clamped jaws on a troll, snarled and snapped and shook its head till blood gushed around its whiskers.

The bodyguard aimed his sword at the beast as a precaution. "Where did *that* come from? Urza's Udders, that's a *big* badger!"

"This island must verge on high ground, all the way across the swamp," suggested Gull.

Stepping to the firepit, the woodcutter jiggled brands with his axe to brighten the flames, to see if they scared off the badger. The beast just fed, growling the while. Squatting, careful of jaws and claws, Gull grabbed his sister's foot and towed her clear.

Muzzily, she sat up, then clawed into his arms. Gull pried her loose for an inspection, found nothing wrong except fright. He patted and soothed her, asked about Kem.

The scar-faced man could sit up. The trolls had almost smothered him, and he wheezed for air. His arm leaked blood. Chad sliced his shirttail, made a bandage to stanch the bleeding. Still holding Greensleeves tight, Gull helped Chad get Kem on his feet.

Still groggy, Kem croaked in Gull's face, "Don't expect me to thank you."

Gull thought of many replies, picked the most insulting. "You're welcome."

Days later, Gull still mulled aloud. "Damned funny the way that badger showed up all of a sudden."

Rocking beside him on the wagon seat, Lily

shrugged. "It was just a big animal. The trolls were bigger than goblins, maybe things grow larger in that swamp."

"But this badger—oh, it was *big!*—was clean! It even had yellow sand stuck to its fur, not mud! No leeches, and we were covered with 'em! It must have—"

"You told Chad the island rose to higher ground. It just came out of its burrow after trolls. What's so strange?"

"But it—" Gull paused to shout his mules around a rockslide.

They'd left the swamp behind. Along its southern edge, Towser had located his black lotuses. He spent the morning touching them and sketching in his grimoire, while the entourage swatted bugs.

The track grew firmer as they approached the hills, and they'd found a pass in an old riverbed. They had to circumvent large rocks, or lever them aside, but they made good time. The hills at either hand were grassy, with pockets of hardwood trees that sheltered mule deer and goats and stunted bison that made the horses snort in fright. From the crest of each hill they saw more hills, but then they ended abruptly. White birds wheeled there, and Towser said they approached the ocean.

The white birds, he told his freighter, were sea gulls—his namesake. Gull was eager then. He'd never seen the sea or a sea gull.

Someone else was eager, too. For the first time ever, Greensleeves took interest in her surroundings. A hundred times a day she stuck her head between Gull and Lily to peek at the countryside. Then she'd clamber over the cookware and cook and cook's boy to look out the back. She'd climb out, run 'round the wagon, pick up a rock or stalk of grass, show it to her brother, point to the distant deer and bison, chatter, climb back aboard, peek past his shoulder again.

"What's she looking at?" asked Lily.

"It beats me," Gull shrugged. "She's got her eye on something. Maybe those deer with the big ears, maybe something we can't see."

Greensleeves shoved a bunch of wildflowers into Lily's hand. Tiny buds formed a cloud of white. Baby's breath, Gull knew from his mother's garden. He told Greensleeves the name and saw her brow knit.

"She looks like she's thinking," Lily murmured.

"So does a mule just before he kicks," said Gull. But he had to agree. Greensleeves acted strange, even for someone "blessed with the second sight."

The next day, they crested a rise and saw the ocean.

Gull hauled on the reins in shock. It was so blue, and wide, and vast! Islands dotted the horizon and, to the south, formed a long yellow line. Ships, the first he'd ever seen, ghosted across the water like great wooden swans.

Lily laughed. "It's deep, too. Over your head."

"Don't tease," Gull chided. "It's just *so* much to look at!"

Again the dancing girl laughed, and adjusted the hood of her jacket, dug from a chest in her wagon, for a stiff breeze with a tang of salt blew in their faces. "I'm sorry. I'm just used to it. I was born in a seaport. My mother was a whore, like me."

"Stop," said Gull, and took her hand.

Greensleeves popped between them. She burbled like a badger as she stared at the blue. Lily laughed at her astonishment, told her, "Sea. *Seeeeea.*"

"Seeeea!" said the simpleton.

Gull jumped so he almost fell off the wagon seat. *"What did you say?"*

"Saaaay!" said his sister.

Gull's mouth gaped, and Lily laughed at both of them. Flustered, the woodcutter snarled, "Stop it! This is serious! She's never repeated anything before!"

"Never? Really?" Now Lily was flustered. Greensleeves studied the two of them like a patient dog awaiting orders.

Orders came, but from the wagon two back. Knoton, the clerk shrilled, "What's keeping us? Get moving! Tow-ser's wait-ing!"

Slumping back on the seat, Gull flapped the reins, plucked at the brake to slow the wagon as it rolled downhill. A track ran along the cliff's edge: the first road they'd struck since leaving White Ridge.

Greensleeves bobbed with the jouncing wagon, staring. Sea breeze spun her hair into a brown halo. She cooed, *"Seeeea!"*

After passing fields freshly plowed and seeded, a fortress farmhouse, scrubby ridges, then more farms and more fields, they struck the town of a few hundred houses. Again, Gull was awed. "So many people in one place!"

Lily laughed. "And this just a small town. You should see a real city. It's walled, yet 'twould take you a full day to walk across it. Or two days." Gull found that impossible to imagine. Yet despite her teasing, he was glad to see her laugh so easily.

Towser ordered the wagons halted at the first ale bar, for they had run out of beer weeks ago. From his own pouch the wizard produced coin to buy a round.

Dusty and weary and jangly-legged from the long haul, his entourage quaffed greedily. Towser had them all topped off, then raised his foaming jack for a toast.

"To you, my proud followers! I respect your hard work and diligence that got us here safely! Know you there will be ale aplenty, and fresh food, and days to wander at your will with fat purses!"

United for the first time, the party cheered and drank. When they'd fathomed the cask, Towser gave final orders. They were to set up camp outside town, secure firewood, post a guard, and then the rest could depart for sightseeing. Muzzily, they complied as the sun set.

Before he knew it, Gull had money in a purse, a black dagger on his belt, Greensleeves on one arm, Lily on the other, and Stiggur trailing behind like a puppy. Together, the four marched into town. Lily had promised them a good time, though Gull had no idea what that entailed. He was happy just to stare at the sights.

Over the next few days, they explored the town. Gull couldn't believe the diversity, the industry, the color. He loved everything. The streets were wide and fairly clean, though pigs and chickens and dogs ran hither and thither. The buildings were one or two stories, covered with salt-streaked shingles and clapboards, with painted doors and icons dotting the walls. The shops bore painted signs. The ale bars were crammed with sailors and pirates and farmers and artisans. The docks were heaped with goods unloaded from long graceful galleys and boxy cogs. Workshops lay open, so they watched horses being shod, ships being straked, fish being gutted, candles being dipped, cloth being dyed.

Lily bought them foods they'd never tasted. Fresh

ocean fish and potatoes fried in olive oil. Lamb roasted with onions. Honeyed squash. Beaver tails baked in beer. She bought Greensleeves and Stiggur huge chunks of rock crystal that proved to be cane sugar dipped on string. She saw Gull try beers from all over, brewed from barley and hops, but also pumpkins, potatoes, mushrooms, even birch bark.

With a purse full of money and some place to spend it, Gull had a seamstress cobble up a new dress for his sister, pale green with darker sleeves, as his mother had sewn long ago, though with a quilted bodice, as the weather was cooler by the sea. He bought Lily a white shawl embroidered with bright flowers along the edges, and she squealed with delight. But for himself, he could think of nothing to buy save a plain gray sweater.

Every afternoon, all four stripped and waded in the ocean, diving and surfing and blubbering and splashing each other like children.

One day, Gull tried to befriend his namesakes, offering scraps, tidbits of bread, but the birds flew off every time, never letting him get within petting distance. When he asked why, Lily told him, "They're scavengers, Gull. They live by their wits and are wary. They eat what they can, sometimes fighting with dogs and cats and other birds. And they're not really welcome anywhere, though the sailors refuse to kill any seabird. It brings bad luck."

"Unwelcome touchy scavengers . . . " mused Gull. "I'm more like my namesakes than I knew."

The dancing girl laughed and hugged his arm. "You're welcome. And hardly touchy. And you're just surviving, as are we all. Look at them this way. Gulls are tough, reliable, smart, quick, and lucky. Does that suit you?"

"Does it suit *you?*" the woodcutter laughed, and he hugged her waist.

Gull laughed again when he gave Greensleeves the bread. The girl had only to hold out a tidbit and gulls mobbed her, flapping around her skirts, hovering to eat from her hand, even standing on her head.

"What are they called, Greenie?" hollered her brother.

"Birrrdddsss!" giggled his sister.

Throughout their sightseeing, they patiently taught Greensleeves new words, until she pointed and named things like a bright baby. Soon she strung them together: "Want candy!" "See fish!" "Me hungry!" Gull shook his head at the wonder of it, and wished his family were alive to see her mind grow.

But on their fourth night, when most of the town was abed, they got the biggest—and rudest—surprise.

With Stiggur back in camp on watch, Lily, Gull, and Greensleeves walked out together. As Lily always insisted, they passed down the middle of the street to avoid alleys and footpads.

Yet feet came pattering, rapid.

Gull whirled, dragging the women behind.

And grunted in shock.

Chad rushed him with a long club.

Before he could even shout, Gull heard a dull thud. Lily slumped against him, knocked cold by another assassin. Over his shoulder, Gull glimpsed the stolid silent Oles.

Along with outrage at the sneak attack, came questions.

What the hell was going on, that members of his own party attacked him? Who was behind it?

Then came the biggest surprise of all.

A girl's voice called, *"Gull!"*
He whirled toward the speaker.
"Greensleeves???"

CHAPTER
15

Questions paralyzed Gull.

Greensleeves had called his name? Chad and Oles wanted to kill them? Or capture them? Bells of Kormus, *why?*

Something whistled at his head and he ducked, shot up an arm to deflect it. Oles, swinging his club. The shock on his biceps jolted him to the spine.

Then Chad charged, club in the air.

Rather than leave his head exposed to another shot from Oles, Gull charged too. Low down.

Scooching, he ducked under two sizzling blows. Stabbing, he grabbed Chad's booted leg and hauled. Chad swore and toppled onto the woodcutter. Gull rolled sideways, yanking, to keep Chad atop and block Oles.

The two men grappled in the dust and trash of the nighttime street. Chad was strong, but no match for Gull. The woodcutter heaved, grabbed Chad's throat. The bodyguard's surprised bleat was cut off. He gulped but couldn't swallow. Without air, panic set in.

Unable to cry for help, Chad drummed his heels. From above, Gull heard Greensleeves mewling. He yelled, "Run, Greenie!"

Because he was busy. Squeezing the life from a traitor.

Chad kicked, thrashed, gurgled as his air ran out. He beat at Gull's head, but the woodcutter was too close for a solid blow. He scrabbled at Gull's face, clawed at his eyes, but Gull bit a thumb until salty blood stained his mouth.

Strangling, Chad found manic strength. Arching his back, he dragged his short sword from its sheath. He swiped—

—as Gull tossed him away and bounded to his feet.

Wheezing, Chad clutched his throat, but remembered his danger. On all fours, he tried to raise the sword—

—and Gull hit him like an avalanche.

Kicking with wooden clogs, the woodcutter cracked the man's collarbone, smacked his shoulder, grazed his handsome head. Gull stooped and hoicked Chad into the air, rending his shirt. Spinning to keep from where he supposed Oles to be, Gull hustled the dancing Chad a fast five steps.

Both gasped as they struck the corner of a building.

Gull crowded Chad, mashing him against the corner with his hip. The bodyguard flailed his sword, slashed at Gull's back, slit leather tunic and skin, but his arm was trapped.

Like a blade, the woodcutter's hand chopped down on Chad's arm. The sword clunked in the dust.

Gull grabbed a fistful of Chad's hair. Lifting the bodyguard on his tiptoes, he pulled to his shoulder—

—then slammed the handsome man's head against the corner hard as he could.

Like stunning the sedge troll, the first blow dazed
Chad, took the fight out of him. Dark hair and skin
stuck to rough building shingles.

The second blow was harder, better aimed, and
knocked him out.

The fifth killed him.

Gull dropped Chad's maimed body, wiped blood
from his hands onto the building.

"Feed the rats, rat."

Battle-fury abating, he remembered the rest of the
attack. Oles. Greensleeves. Lily.

But he was alone in the dark street. He shouted the
women's names, got no answer. Where the hell had
they gone?

Frantic, he searched up and down the wide street. If
Oles were returning to camp—why?—he'd go west,
away from the docks.

Gull took a chance. Snatching Chad's sword,
running on his aching knee, peering through the
darkness, he hunted his sister.

Hundreds of feet on, Gull spied a wide man toting a
struggling girl on his shoulder.

Greensleeves squirmed, twisted, hammered with
bony fists, kicked, all while mewling like a starved cat.
Oles lurched onward, shifting his burden, peering
around for the town watch.

Kicking off his clogs, Gull pattered full tilt.
Greensleeves's noise drowned out his approach.
Leveling the borrowed sword, Gull aimed for Oles's
back, low so the blade wouldn't bind in his ribs.

The sword bit clean as a snake's fang, slithered a

cold path through Oles's gut. The sword point jutted from his belly, then withdrew, the rasping steel making him shiver.

Oles's strength failed as blood gushed from the wound. He stumbled, tried to hold the girl captive, but she was plucked from his shoulder.

He landed facedown in the dirt without a sound.

Gull towed his sister along the strand. The sand was firmest between the high tide line, marked by seaweed, and the waves. From what Lily had told him of tides, incoming water would cover their tracks.

Because most of all, Gull needed time to think.

Waves crashed and collapsed on the shore, streaming toward their feet as creamy white foam. The beach became rocks farther on, and he ducked between them, hopped from one salty boulder to the next, squished over heaps of seaweed that popped underfoot. The Mist Moon and starlight and the glow of the ocean itself lit their way. Wakened sea gulls squawked and took flight. Gull hoped his namesakes didn't betray him.

Past the rocks was a headland of sea grass and scrub oaks. He boosted Greensleeves up, climbed after her, and dragged her to the deepest patch of cover he could find. Grass and brambles tugged at her skirts and his bare legs. Kissed by the breeze through his slit shirt, his sword slice burned and itched.

Once past the first barrier of brambles, he used Chad's sword to hack through mulberry bushes. Cuttings gave a sweet resinous scent. A large flat rock stippled with lichens formed a clearing big enough for them to sit. The rock was warm from the day's sun, and they were below the chill sea breeze. Surf sound was muted.

Gasping, Gull collapsed, careful he didn't nick his sister with the sword. He took quick stock of their situation. He had his black dagger and mulewhip, Chad's sword, a purse full of coins, and nothing else. Greensleeves had less, a gown and shawl.

The question was, how much trouble were they in?

Had Chad and Oles worked alone? Had they planned to . . . what? Kill Gull for revenge, over a few insults? Not likely, since they'd used clubs and not swords. Sell Greensleeves to prostitution? Slavery? Sell both of them? Lily had warned merchants sometimes kidnapped landsmen, "crimped" them to be sailors, since seafaring was a harsh and miserable life. Was Greensleeves bound for a harem? Whom had they been after, exactly?

And more importantly, and darkly—

Had Towser sent them?

Gull disliked Towser as a man, considering him foppish and superior and snotty and fussy, but perhaps all people of education or position were that way. Still, he hadn't minded working for him, as the wizard was a fair and undemanding master. Mostly Towser was distracted and aloof, his head full of mystical plans and problems. Gull didn't trust him, but had no reason to distrust him.

Until now.

So what to do? Approach Towser and demand the truth? Would anyone in the entourage help if treachery were afoot? Morven, maybe, Stiggur, perhaps. Lily, of course, but where was she? He'd felt her slump, but then she'd disappeared. Crawled off? Hauled off?

A thousand questions and no answers. Nothing made sense.

As always, he spoke to his sister, as to his mules, to clarify his thoughts. "Any ideas, Greenie?"

He got his biggest shock of the night.
She answered.
"N-no."

Gull rubbed his brow. Maybe he'd been thumped on the head without knowing it. Quietly, he asked, "What did you say?"

"No . . . "

"You can understand me?"

"Y-yes . . . " Her voice was hesitant. Also pleasant, he noted, like birdsong, or his mother's singing. But very slow, as if she had to fathom each word. In the shadowed glen, he couldn't see her eyes, but sensed she watched him.

For the first time in her life, she showed intelligence. "A-always c-could."

"Could what?"

"Under-stand . . . I kn-knowed you were th-there, but h-hard to—to—I c-couldn't—" She flapped small hands in exasperation. "I—heared you. B-but there was—was so much el-se. Birds. Flow-ers . . . Sk-sky . . . "

Her brother strove to understand. "You always knew my words, but other things distracted you?"

"Yes . . . yes!" Her voice became animated, like a child's.

Gull pondered. When he was young, a father in the village had fallen from a roof. He'd landed on his head and almost died. Forever after, he'd be some days foggy-minded, some days clear-headed. Brain-damaged, in short, like his sister at birth.

Or so they'd thought. Now she was lucid. Had she been hit on the head too?

"Why can you suddenly talk so well? Do you know?"

"T-trees," she intoned.

"Trees?"

"Too much trees. All around." Gesturing, she formed a canopy over her head. "W-words of trees—talked in my head. Told me . . . stories."

"Whispers? The Whispering Woods? You heard *stories?*"

She nodded, her face a pale blob in the semidarkness.

Gull scratched his head, found a crusty scab that stung. So . . . the mystery of the Whispering Woods was solved, partly. The trees *did* talk. Except normal folk couldn't understand them, as if they spoke a foreign tongue. But his poor benighted sister heard their songs and secrets, so many they overwhelmed her poor brain.

So that meant . . .

"Oh! We left the Whispering Woods *behind* when we struck the pine barrens . . . Then a few days of travel . . . and you started to talk. Oh! Once clear of the forest, your mind cleared!"

"Yes. T-talk on my own, now. To you. Br-brother Gull."

Gull was surprised at the sob that choked him. His name, so sweet coming from his sister—who'd lost her mind and found it.

Grabbing, he squeezed her till she squeaked. "Sq-squash me . . . Gull."

"Yes," was all he could say.

Then it struck him. He held his sister at arm's length. "Oh, my. All this time I took you to the forest because you loved it so, and to keep you out of trouble, and here the *forest* clouded your mind! It's *my fault* you were—stricken."

"No," her smile was gentle, "I—I love the w-woods. I—"

She stopped. Hunting the right word, Gull assumed. But her glance went over his head, into the moonlit sky.

Within bowshot, hovering against the canopy of stars, a man flew.

A dozen thoughts crashed upon Gull.

They'd been found! By Towser!

And the bastard could fly! So it had been *he* and not the brown-robed wizard who'd flown over White Ridge and unleashed the weakness!

And now he hunted Gull and Greensleeves. Probably not to succor his lost lambs.

"Get down!" Gull hissed. He mashed his sister flat, leaned over her. But it was probably too late. Between the hush of surf and hum of sea breeze, and excitement over their fantastic discoveries, they'd talked normally. Anyone nearby could have heard them, especially in the air. Gull knew that from climbing trees.

He looked again, but the wizard was gone. Was that good or bad? Either, they must get away.

A barbarian shout shook the night, issuing from a score of throats. Gull had heard that before, far away—

Brush rattled, thrashed, split. A blue-painted warrior, white-haired and tusked, armed with a curved sword and leather shield, charged. Gull shoved Greensleeves, ordering her to flee, then lifted his sword—knowing full well he was no swordsman. But even if the barbarian killed him . . . But there were a score or more: he'd heard them shout . . . How many could he battle before he was killed? One? Who'd guard Greensleeves then . . . ?

Another blue barbarian burst into the clearing,

and a third and fourth, men and women. Gull didn't
know which way to point. The invaders smelled
oddly sweet: their blue color must be berry juice.
They panted from their shout, growled with battle
lust.

Gull stood ready to kill or be killed. But
Greensleeves—

A shadow like an eagle's swooped overhead, and
Gull swooned. So weak he couldn't stand, his knees
buckled. His sword arm drooped.

He landed on his sister, who'd also sunk. A blue-
painted man collapsed too, tusks striking rock with a
sickening crunch. Another. But more barbarians
thrashed into the clearing.

With the flat of their swords, they whipped Gull as
if threshing grain. A blade hammered his arm, his
thigh, his shoulder, his head—

Lights twitched, faded, came back into focus.
Someone called outside the circle. The beating
stopped as the barbarians grunted in a guttural tone.
As a half dozen pinned Gull's arms, a woman raised
her club high, took aim.

The heavens crashed down on Gull's head, stunning him. Stars whirled around the compass.

And winked out.

Voices woke him. Towser's. Kem's. Felda's.

For a moment he imagined he woke beneath the
chuck wagon, as always, while people talked around
the morning fire and waited for Felda to serve breakfast. Suddenly he felt a great and surprising pang of
homesickness for those simple times.

But he couldn't move, and when he tried, ached all
over. He could only open one eye, for the other was

swollen shut. Biting down a groan, he pried open his good eye.

It was still full night. His arms trailed over his head, swollen and dead from lack of circulation, bound to a wagon wheel. The four wagons were circled, and he was lashed to the chuck wagon.

By campfire light, the scene was almost normal. Knoton the clerk sat on his wagon seat, looking ill at ease. Dancing girls peeked from various wagons. Lily was there, looking fatigued and anxious, and Gull wondered if she too had betrayed him, deliberately led him into a trap on that street. But the brawny Jonquil hovered close behind, and when Lily would have spoken, yanked her head back sharply by the hair. Felda sat dumpy on a box to one side, next to the old astrologer. Stiggur leaned from the chuck wagon over Gull's head, looking as if he'd cry. The nurse and bard were nowhere in sight. Kem with his scars and missing ear, Morven the sailor, and the partistriped wizard Towser stood with jacks of ale by the fire.

Greensleeves sat next to the clerk on Towser's wagon, hands tied behind her back, head throbbing.

Gull wondered where the bodies of Chad and Oles lay.

Fully awake, the woodcutter cleared his raspy throat. Licking his lips, he found them so swollen he drooled. But he could still speak.

"Towser!" he bellowed. "You treacherous black dog! You yellow cur! You lousy dirt-grubbing shit-eating muck-wallowing son of a poxied whore! You slit-eyed bastard . . ." He went on and on, using every filthy phrase a muleskinner knows, for a long time, until he began to repeat himself and his voice gave out.

Towser took no notice. He pointed to the hills north of town, along the coast. Quietly, he gave Kem

orders about laying in supplies, hiring more bodyguards, replenishing the livestock, finding a new
freighter, moving out soon. The scarred man nodded
at his mental list. Idly he scratched the bandage
around his elbow.

Having caught his breath, Gull shouted, "Kem! You
one-eared son of a *bitch*! You owe me your *life*! I went
into a stinking swamp and fought off *trolls* who
planned to *eat* you, you prick! I carried you on my
shoulder when you blacked out and Chad gave up! Do
you remember that, you miserable *dog*? Or are you *less*
than a lousy garbage-eating *mongrel*, for even the ugliest
ass-licking *dog* knows gratitude!"

Kem showed no concern, but did walk around the fire.
Standing over Gull, he pitched ale into the woodcutter's
face, followed with heavy slaps, across, back, across. He
only stopped because his arm ached at the elbow.

Towser nodded. "He's become tiresome. We've got
his sister, we don't need him anymore. Bury him in the
scrub before the sun comes up. Deep, so the dogs don't
dig him up."

Gull wanted to scream with rage. Towser's casual
indifference to his death, as if Gull were a hog for
slaughter, was the greatest evil he'd ever seen. Kem
and Chad might be thugs, but they were honest men
compared to this wizardly viper.

And for the first time, Kem showed emotion. Gull
saw his brow cloud. Maybe the mercenary did feel
gratitude after all, Gull thought wearily: *he might make
my death a quick one—*

Something tugged at Gull's wrist. His hand flopped
into his lap.

Kem growled, "Hey there! *Stop!*" He reached past
Gull, whose other hand plopped in his lap. The woodcutter hissed at pins and needles.

Snarling, Kem dragged out Stiggur by the wrist. The boy had slipped under the wagon and cut Gull free with a kitchen knife. He yelped as Kem cuffed him.

His hands useless, Gull raised a clog and kicked Kem in the ankle. The bodyguard flipped forward and smashed face first into the iron rim of the wheel.

Things happened very fast.

Morven tossed his jack and grabbed Towser by his stiffened collar, hauled him to tiptoes, swung him broadside into his own wagon. Knoton, the soft-handed clerk, slapped at the sailor with the trace reins. With long red fingernails, Lily jabbed Jonquil's eyes, blinding her, and leaped from the wagon, bound for Greensleeves. But the old astrologer hooked a skinny foot and tripped her so the dancing girl crashed in the dust.

Gull rolled to his feet. He'd learned who was friend and foe, and there were no surprises. A shout turned him. Stiggur.

The boy swung both arms, lobbed something at the woodcutter. His mulewhip and axe. Hands unable to clasp, Gull let them thump his chest, bounce to the dirt. Kneeling, he cursed as he tried to pick them up, clumsy as a child. Finally he fumbled the whip in his belt, clasped the axe against his hip.

He turned for Towser. Morven struggled to hold him as Knoton slapped his face with the traces.

Up beside the clerk, Greensleeves was safe for the moment. Tingle-fingered, Gull leaped and bit the reins, jerked his neck to tug them from Knoton's grasp. He kneaded his fingers, felt them respond slowly—

Someone hit him from the side, and he banged against the wagon. Kem, angry froth on his lips. He slammed a forearm across Gull's throat to pin him.

Gull kicked but couldn't connect. He didn't dare move his numb hands lest he drop his axe.

Rasping, the woodcutter croaked into the scarred face, "Less than a dog, is it?"

Kem spit back, "A dog obeys its master." Then he pulled back a fist and slugged Gull in the breadbasket, hard, three times.

But Gull was too furious to notice more pain. Bracing his back, he waited for the man to swing again, then lowered his head and rammed.

The crown of Gull's head smashed into Kem's mouth, making both bark, for Gull had been bashed unconscious earlier. Grappling, the groggy men stumbled toward the fire.

The camp was a riot. Gull shoved Kem so he tripped over the campfire. Sparks glittered, scattered light. Lily wrestled with the old astrologer, strong as rawhide. Felda flapped her fat hands, unsure what to do. Unnoticed, Stiggur latched onto Kem's ankle and made him stumble again. Morven gripped Towser's collar in two hands and banged his head against the wagon. Greensleeves was gone, down on her back behind the wagon. Gull saw slippered feet, red-nailed hands plucking her up. He wanted to hoist the wagon into the air, send it flying to the moon to rescue his sister, and felt he had the strength. He flexed his hands, found he could carry his axe.

Grabbing Towser was the key. He wouldn't kill him outright—not yet. But he'd break his arms and legs with an axe handle, then slowly twist out the truth . . .

Morven suddenly flopped backward, out cold. Slumped against the wagon, Towser poised both hands as if still pushing.

Spells. Magic. He had to be stopped.

Gull rushed the striped man, but suddenly his feet were floating above the ground. Or so it felt.

What was—

Ghostlike, Gull saw his legs twinkle blue, like early morning stars. His arms twinkled too. He could see the bright paints of Towser's wagon through his wrist.

His vision went twinkly, growing brighter as if stars exploded before his eyes.

Then everything went black.

Then bright, white, hot.

CHAPTER

16

Surf surged around Gull's ankles, slapped his knees.
For a second he thought he'd been cast over the town
into the ocean.

But the sky was white, the sun straight overhead.
Seconds ago had been midnight: now it was noon.

He was somewhere far, far away.

Before him lay a shoreline so green and verdant it
hurt the eyes. White sand sprouted tall fleshy plants
adorned with flowers like rainbows. Long-tailed birds in
all colors squawked in tufted trees hung with strange
fruits. Beyond rose a dull gray cone a hundred feet high.

Something twinkled beside him, lost its balance,
and fell in the water, spluttering. Shifting his axe, Gull
reached into the gushing surf and plucked out Stiggur.
Another splash revealed Morven, facedown, unmoving, drowning. Shifting his axe again, Gull towed the
sailor to the beach.

"Wh-where—are we?" gasped the boy. Skinny and
streaming wet, he looked like a muskrat.

Gull knelt, hoicked Morven over his knee, jounced him. Dully, the sailor vomited seawater, waved his arms like a crab, growled to lay off. Gull dropped him.

Stiggur shucked his tunic to stand naked. He wrung it out, then donned it. "Where *are* we, Gull?"

"Hush. We're safe." The woodcutter scanned the horizon, empty but for heaving swells and dots of islands. He sighed. "Towser's safe too. We're as far away as he can send us, I'd guess."

Then he howled, a drawn-out scream of pain, and slammed his axe against the sand so hard it buried half its length. Screaming, shouting, cursing, Gull pounded his fists until they were raw and bloody. "All my fault! My fault! So thick and trusting! This—is—all—my—fault!"

A hand touched his shoulder and he froze.

Morven's forehead bled, his face was white from vomiting, his hands shook. But his eyes were steady. "It's not your fault, matie. The wizard gulled ye. They lie, cheat, and steal. It's their nature, like vipers bite babies."

Gull's anger returned with a rush. Hopping up, he banged both fists against Morven's breast, rocking him. "Then *why*, you know-it-all *bastard*, did you *work* for him? Why didn't you tell *me* he was rotten?"

The sailor's tone was mild. He'd faced bigger threats than berserkers in his day. "I only signed on a little afore ye. Towser seemed different. Honest. Should'a known 'twas a spell on me mind. So if you blame anyone for this mess, blame me and not yerself."

Fists swinging by his side, Gull panted, spent. The mild words extinguished his anger as water damps fire. "But—what can we *do*?"

Morven looked at the sky, turned to listen to a birdcall like water gurgling from a jug. He only sighed.

Stiggur pointed. "Look!"

Coming down the beach, lurching CLUMP CLUMP CLUMP crunchgrindgrowlsnap CLUMP CLUMP . . . lurched the clockwork beast on three good legs and one bad one.

A shout from a break in the foliage turned them. Naked and shaggy, the centaur Helki cried, "Oh, no! Not you too!"

Lo and behold, they were all there.

Helki led them between fleshy green plants, up a mild slope, to a clearing with a firepit and huts of different sizes.

The centaurs went naked except for their armbands, Helki distracting with her tight breasts and brown, thumb-sized nipples. Their manes and tails were shaggy and matted.

Liko, with slant eyes and two bald heads, still wore his patchwork suit of ships' sails. His severed arm, Gull noted, had healed to a clean white stump, but had not regenerated. So Towser had lied about that, too.

On a log sat three tough-looking bronzed men with black beards. They looked at Gull's scars and bruises with professional curiosity, but kept quiet. Gull recognized their red kilts from the battle of White Ridge: the scale-mailed mercenaries summoned by the brown-and-yellow wizard. Evidently this trio had been left behind, like the centaurs, and Towser had sent them here. These hard men may have threatened Gull's family, tried to rape Cowslip. But he couldn't deal with that now.

Also present was a tall man in chain mail who kept sword and shield handy. Gull guessed him a paladin from the northern lands: only one of those would go armored in this heat.

While Helki gave everyone's name, the woodcutter glanced around. "Is everyone Towser ever touched stuck here?"

Helki's four feet danced. Tears spilled down her face, the same as Holleb. "No, not everyone. Some pawns he must return to homelands. This place, this island, is midden—dumping ground."

Tearfully, she explained, "We all tell same story. Summoned to fight by Dacian, she in brown and yellow, abandoned in chaos, Towser offers send us home. But he not know where our home, so sends us here to use when needed. We can never escape," she added miserably.

Gull nodded. That explained what Helki meant by "We are captives!" that black night in the burned forest. Suddenly weary, he collapsed on the sand, propped his axe across his knees. It was already tinged with rust from the seawater.

"A wizard's greatest skill must be lying. I should have guessed. How could a wizard know your homeland? He even claimed to know the origin of the clockwork beast, a thing without a brain."

Bardo, the tall paladin, nodded. "It's partly our fault. Ve hear fabulous stories about vizards until ve believe they can do anything, like gods. Thus ve believe their lies." His accent clattered on the ear like a raven's croak.

"How did Towser know Broken Toe Mountain," Holleb growled, "if he was never there?"

A black-bearded, balding soldier named Tomas waved both hands as he spoke. "I think one wizardly power is to read your thoughts. They ask of your homeland, and a picture comes to your head. They read that and pretend to know it. They bewitch you, too. I've had it happen."

"True," muttered Gull. He rubbed his aching head. "I've felt it. While they talk, the lies seem believable." Others nodded, and Gull felt less stupid and gullible. "I never even objected when he called me 'pawn': a tool to be used and discarded."

Since Helki was crying, Holleb spoke in his harsh voice. "More are stranded here. Goblins who fly by balloon are here, but we banished to other side of island, they steal and lie so. Some orcs there. Big ant-folk on mountaintop."

"Banished, we all are," said Helki. "Forever."

Stiggur began to cry.

Gull stood up. "No, we're not."

People looked up. Stiggur rubbed streaming eyes, "Not what?"

"Not banished forever." Yet Gull wavered. Lack of sleep, battle fatigue, mental exhaustion, worry over his sister—all conspired to crush his will and sap his energy. He brushed them aside. "Think, everyone. We come from all over the Domains. There must be a way out of this—cage. Who knows something?"

No one spoke. Stiggur dried his face with sandy hands.

Sighing at impetuous youth, Morven the sailor touched the corrugated bark of a palm tree. "I've sailed these waters, I think. We're way t'south, where the islands lie far apart. Most're too small to hold fresh water: we're lucky we got that. But we can't build a boat with these junk trees: they fall to pulp and string. So we can't sail away."

"Nor can we make goblin balloons," said Gull

bitterly. "So the only escape is by magic. And only wizards possess that."

The leader of the red soldiers, bald, bearded Tomas, sketched in the air. "Our best bet is on the battlefield. Once we're summoned, we must attack—such is the geas placed on us. But if we defeat our immediate foe, we're free to act on our own, usually. That's the time to get away."

"But you are not home," growled Holleb. "You are with wizard elsewhere in Domains."

Powerful round shoulders shrugged. Arms and neck were laced with scars from a lifetime of war. "True. But we're somewhere civilized. We can walk to the sea and take passage for our homeland."

"*If* we can find it," objected one of his men. "*If* anyone knows where it lies."

"Has anyone ever known?" asked Gull.

Tomas shook his shiny head. "No. If we've learned one thing, it's the Domains stretch on forever. Under Dacian, she of the glossy black hair, we've seen a hundred lands. Some were pleasant, some were hellholes. But all were different and far from one another. Never have I met anyone who knew the way to our homeland. Of course, I'm usually stabbing them . . ."

"Dacian," muttered Gull. "The name of the one who killed my family. Though now I know Towser lies, so he must have had a hand in it too . . ."

Morven crossed his arms, leaned against the palm tree. "In my travels, I've seen a *thousand* lands. The Domains are all islands, some hundreds of leagues long, some small as a kerchief. But the seas run on forever. Some navigators think the world is round, like a ball, and if ye keep sailing, ye'll circle and find yer home port. But how long? Years? Decades? No one's ever done it, or even lied about doing it. It's impossible."

"It vill get vorse for us," intoned Bardo the paladin. "Truly powerful vizards move beyond humanity. They learn to valk the planes between vorlds, lands ve can't imagine, vhere the sky is green with five moons, and men turn inside out, or breathe smoke, or . . ." His imagination failed. "For now, the vizards Dacian and this Towser valk lands ve can understand. Vun day, vhen they're powerful, ve'll be summoned to places even the gods shun . . ."

Silence followed this prophecy.

"I don't understand," Gull groused. "If wizards can pop from one place to another, the way a rabbit can dive in a hole and surface a bowshot away, then why does Towser travel in a wagon train? Why not wave his hands and move the whole kit and caboodle to the next spot leagues on?"

"Ye need someplace to store yer food and loot," put in Morven. "Even wizards have to eat."

Holleb frowned in thought, swished his tail. "There are places to more easy jump off—magic places where music sings in the ears. Your rabbit has many tunnels underground, yes, but only two–three holes. He cannot dive through earth—he must run to opening."

Gull fingered the edge of his axe. "Yes, that's wise. I learned from my sister—gods, just this past night—that the Whispering Woods are such a place, a magic jumping-off place. Towser came there and destroyed our village, but then needed to drive his wagon train cross-country to get to the next jump-off, wherever that is. Chatzuk's Curse! What does he *want* with my sister?"

At the confused faces, he explained his sister's words, how she could suddenly talk, how Towser had betrayed them. "But where is he bound? And why?"

It fell silent in the clearing. Trade winds soughed in

the treetops. The clumping of the clockwork beast came closer, then receded. A green lizard skittered from under a leaf, and Stiggur, a boy, caught it instinctively.

"We may never know," Morven sighed. "Holleb, have you figured how to brew beer from coconuts?"

"*No!*" Gull's shout startled them all. Fear for Greensleeves had renewed his anger. "We're *not* going to settle in here! We're *not* going to get comfortable in this cage! We're *going* to find a way out!"

Everyone just stared. Stiggur showed a glimmer of hope, knowing his hero could accomplish anything. But the rest were sober. And resigned.

Gull couldn't stand their helpless air. "Stiggur, get up! Morven, you too!"

Sitting, the sailor just shook his gray head. "Me days o' taking orders are done, bucko."

For answer, the woodcutter grabbed his shoulder, hoicked him to his feet.

The sailor rubbed his arm. "Belay, belay! I'm with ye! Where are we bound?"

Gull didn't know. But they mustn't sit idle: that was slow death. "Around the island. We'll see what there is to see."

"Not much," droned Tomas.

Ignoring that, the three walked off, Gull setting the pace.

With every step, Gull's resolve to escape increased. This island might be paradise, but it was still a prison. He strode down the beach while Morven and Stiggur struggled to keep up.

Surprisingly, there was much to see.

At the center of the island they found Holleb's "ant-folk." Upright, five feet tall, brown as tree trunks, made of articulated segments covered with stiff black hair, they looked as if some wizard had kicked an anthill and conjured its denizens into soldiers. Their only decorations were palm fronds cemented with some gum—ant spit, Morven suggested—to their helmetlike heads. They carried crude iron blades, a cross between a shovel and a spear. In the crater of the dead volcano, they dug tunnels, ridges, trenches. Some fetched leaves and fruit while others stood guard. They worked in an eerie silence, waggling antennae as if talking.

The travelers did not test the guards, but watched from a low tor. As best they could count the identical bug-beasts, there were at least a hundred, though there could be scores more underground.

"Let's hope they don't develop a taste for meat," Morven hissed.

Moving to the island's far side, they found the goblins, including the skunk-striped thief Egg Sucker. With them lived some large gray orcs, the first Gull had ever seen. Orcs of the Ironclaw Clan, they shouted that they ruled the island—until Gull flattened one with his axe handle. After that, they were all whining politeness, but knew nothing.

The explorers passed on, slept the night curled in the warm sand.

Birds sprang away at their steps, wild pigs scurried through brush, even a sea turtle was sighted beyond the reef, swimming slow as a barrel. They came across a primitive clay statue a dozen feet high. It had obviously been dropped there, for it lay on its side in a thicket of fronds. Along a spit they found an old shipwreck, a caravel, Morven explained, with high forecastles and aftercastles like a wooden shoe. Much of the ship was intact, but her bottom had been torn out by the reef in a storm. Other than scrap iron and some broken masts, there was nothing the ship could offer.

That second day, they passed the clockwork beast, stumping, stumping along.

When the sun was high on the third day, they found their landing spot.

Morven and Stiggur trudged into the rude camp and plunked down on the sand. But Gull's quick tread made the sleepy giant and red soldiers and centaurs look up.

"Gather 'round!" the woodcutter ordered.

Curious, ready for any diversion, the motley crew rubbed their eyes and prepared to listen.

The woodcutter did not sit, but paced the small circle. As he talked, he tapped the axe haft in his hand. Bobbing in the air, the big steel head almost hypnotized them.

"We're stuck here," Gull began. "We feel helpless, as if we must sit and wait for salvation."

He paused. Everyone listened, rapt.

"We might be stuck, but we're *not* helpless. We got sent here, we can be drawn back."

A murmur ran through the small crowd. Morven said, "But that—"

Gull cut him off. "We're fighters, all of us. We've been thrust into a war: the common folk against wizards. Yet just to *sit*, and *slack off*, and *despair*, and *wait* for someone to help us—is to lose the battle without raising a hand! We're *not* sheep awaiting slaughter! Are we?"

A negative mumble. But mostly the listeners looked at each other.

"*What?*" Gull hollered. "All I hear is the mutter of surf. Are we, or are we not, *sheep?*"

"No!" said the black-bearded Tomas.

"No, we're not," said Morven mildly. "But what can we—"

"We can prepare to *fight*!" Gull bellowed. "Fight! But we're *not* ready! Where's your weapon, Morven?"

The sailor waved vaguely at the air. "Last I saw, in the men's wagon."

"Then we'll get you a new one! Where's yours, Stiggur?"

The boy piped, "I ain't got a weapon."

Gull plucked his whip from his belt, tossed it into Stiggur's hands. "You do now. I want to see you plucking gray hairs out of Morven's beard by the end of the week."

The boy looked stunned, held the whip like a dead snake. Morven nudged him, thumbed his chin. "Aim for black ones. Fewer targets, more of a challenge."

For the first time, folks laughed.

The woodcutter kept up the pressure. "There's one volunteer armed and ready to practice! Helki, Holleb, where are your weapons? When I first met you, you were festooned with weapons and tack, all neat as a pin! Now . . ."

The centaurs looked shamefaced at their slovenliness. Their breastplates rusted in their hut, their lances had been used to broil fish. Without a word, they turned with swishing tails, plucked up their armor, scrubbed at the rust with sand.

Tomas nodded to his comrades. They fetched short swords and hunted whetstones. Gull followed his own advice and honed his axe blade. He continued to talk. "We're agreed then. We'll be ready for the call when it comes."

With empty hands, Morven could only scratch his armpit. "Ain't ye forgettin' somethin'? Towser picks who he needs for a battle. Same as ye and me can pluck up a chessman and move him thither on a board. He might conjure the centaurs, or these blokes, but why conjure ye and me? They might twinkle away anytime and we're left to build sand castles—"

"Morven," Gull interrupted, "while there's life, there's a way. *All of us* will work together and *all of us* will get off this island. And when we do, *we'll kill Towser and every other wizard we find!*"

At that, Tomas gave a glorious war cry from deep within his soul. People started, then laughed. Helki reared onto her back legs and whinnied her battle call, and Holleb joined in. Morven laughed and hollered a snatch of sea chantey.

Then all were whooping and hollering and shouting and dancing around the clearing.

Gull called the loudest of all. "Remember White Ridge! Remember White Ridge!"

Long into the night, they made plans.

They worked out a watch, everyone standing three hours around the clock. They worked out warning signals in case anyone was suddenly "summoned," compared notes and the little knowledge they possessed. Could someone disappearing drag a companion along? Was it better to run, or return to the island with news? Was that possible?

At dawn, Morven groaned and stretched his back. "But still, just hangin' around waitin' . . ."

"We don't wait," said Gull. "We work."

The sailor was caught in mid-stretch. "At what?"

"We work with what we have, fix what needs fixing. We'll start with the clockwork beast."

"Eh?" asked several. "What good is that?"

Gull shrugged. "Some wizard created it, other wizards summon and banish it, so it must have a use. Howsoever, we'll knock it down and replace that missing leg with a mast cut from the shipwreck. Morven, that's your job: tell us what you need. And tear that wreck apart, see what else you find. Liko, can you help? Good man. We'd best carve you a club so you can whomp Towser's bullyboys. Stiggur, I want you snapping that whip until you can flick the eyelash off a gnat. You're a bright lad and quick, so I know you can do it."

Beaming with pride, the boy nodded. One of the red soldiers, a thin man named Varrius said, "I can help with that repair. I was apprenticed to a blacksmith before I ran off soldiering."

"Fine, good," said Gull. He was discovering powers of diplomacy he never knew. "Helki, Holleb, will you go up to that ant colony? You've got patience and sense, see if they've got brains and can help. They might want to go home too. Tomas, Neith, you've led soldiers, commanded their respect. Will you organize those goblins and orcs? Tell 'em we're planning to leave and they must help. Kick their arses if they grumble. Make spears with fire-hardened points, or whatever you think practical, and drill 'em as shock troops." The soldiers rubbed their hands, glad for the compliments and the hard work ahead. "Bardo, you've traveled, seen much of the Domains. Hunt up that clay statue, hew down the grass and get it upright, see if it can help us. Does everyone have a task?

"Right then. To work!"

It was marvelous to see the troop hurl themselves into their tasks, proving old Brown Bear's saying, "To be happy you must be busy." They were busy, and more.

Armor and weapons polished, kept close at hand, people dispersed over the island.

Within a day, they fell to their first big task.

Having impressed the goblins and orcs, Morven directed the piling of rocks and slash into a barricade, the digging of a long trench. Then the crew waited, each poised with a long pole lever.

As the clockwork beast clumped down the shore, hitting on three legs and missing the fourth, Gull reflected what a strange contraption it was. Was it even alive? It showed no wear, as a millworks would, even bore spots where wood and iron had seemed to scab and heal. Further, it never walked blindly, but steered around large obstacles. More and more, he wondered what lay inside that wood-and-iron head. But short of breaking it open, there was no way to tell.

As the beast approached their barricade, it steered for open sand. Shouting for courage, men and centaurs and orcs stabbed levers at its great iron feet, while Liko put out one huge arm and shoved, ramming the thing sideways. The crash it made shook them off their feet.

Wedged sideways in the trench, the beast mindlessly churned powerful legs.

Then suddenly stopped, the first time anyone had seen it still. Up by the massive head, Stiggur shouted for joy. "Look what I found!"

Behind the beast's ears were four iron rods with polished hardwood heads. The boy pushed one lever forward, and the legs churned. Another, and they churned backward. Then right, then left. Hauling all the levers back stopped it.

"Stiggur," Gull laughed as he tickled the boy's ribs, "you'll be general of this army before long."

*   *   *

For days, they worked from dawn to dusk.

Helki and Holleb struggled to learn the ant soldiers' language. In the meantime, the centaurs drilled, charging and galloping and wheeling in tandem, shouting battle commands, then racing flat out, laughing like young lovers to crash into the surf to kiss. Every morning, Tomas and Neith rousted the goblins and orcs and drilled them in spear work. The trashy fodder whined, ran off when they could, but fear and raps on their bony heads sank in, and the gray-green villains learned. Stiggur not only split leaves with his new mulewhip, he did it while riding the clockwork beast up and down the beach. Morven sharpened a rusty cutlass he'd scrounged from the shipwreck, killed a pig, and fashioned a scabbard from its hide.

Everyone maintained his or her watch without complaint, and slept with armor and weapons close at hand.

And a good idea that proved to be.

Gull dreamed of Lily.

He shared a hut with Morven and Stiggur, lying under palm leaves to stave off the morning chill. Yet many nights he tossed and turned, groping for Lily's sweet soft form, waking when he didn't find her.

Did he love her, he wondered? Did he know what love was? He'd always liked her, enjoyed her company, her chaste yielding body pressed against his. Gull missed her the same as he did his sister. Or more? What was love, really . . . ?

"Gull, wake up!" came a voice. "For pity's sake, *wake up!*"

Morven swore, "Lord of Atlantis!"

Muzzy-headed, Gull croaked, "What? Get that light out of my face . . . "

No light. He was shining.

Bolt upright, Gull grabbed his axe, looked at his hands. Outlined ghostly white, they glowed like fox-fire on a swamp log. The light grew brighter, spread to his whole body, making him squint and the others fall back.

Neith, the red soldier on watch, had awakened him. "You're being summoned! Through the void, to battle!"

"*Me?*" gasped the woodcutter, blinded by his own illumination. "*Why me?*"

Then the earth moved.

CHAPTER
17

Thrown through space, pitched through a void, from one spot to another hundreds of leagues off, from nighttime to day, Gull could only grab his head as images crashed upon him.

In a heartbeat, he saw:

A wide bluff arced out over the sea. There were no towns or farms, no ships on the water, only yellow grass stretching to forest half a mile away. Dozens of feet below the bluff, the ocean roared and churned and thrashed against seaweedy rocks, throwing spume that speckled . . .

A black basalt monolith, a shiny jet-dark cone tall as a church, rearing above the bluff and ocean, at the bottom of which . . .

Greensleeves was trussed hand and foot on a low black altar carved into the foot of the monolith, where . . .

Towser, with a silly-looking pink box tied atop his head by a blue scarf, poised a knife like a sickle above Gull's sister. He was ringed by . . .

Kem and three new bullies armed with short swords. They guarded the wizard, facing out, staring gape-mouthed at Gull, while . . .

Far behind him, inland, was Towser's circled wagon train, where his clerk and cook and dancing girls and bard and astrologer and nurse carefully tended their handiwork, so they might not see their master's work at the monolith altar, or . . .

Standing beside Gull . . .

Lily, her face white as her dancing togs. She chirped like a baby bird. "Gull?"

"Lily!" Visions and ideas swirled around Gull, stunning him. The sea breeze soothed his sweating brow: it was cooler here than on the tropical island. Then one thought soared like a skyrocket. "You're a wizard!"

"What?" She gaped at her shaking hands. "No, it can't be!"

But Gull caught one hand, forced it open. Faint in the seaside glare, her palms still glowed with the white light that summoned Gull.

"It's true! You brought me here! You've got magic inside!"

"Love of the gods!" The girl was thunderstruck. "That explains . . . my feelings, those voices! Oh, Mishra! I just missed you so badly! And wished you were here! To stop that!"

She pointed to Towser, who stood with sickle knife poised. He didn't look surprised, and suddenly—more thoughts, like waves sweeping him off his feet—Gull knew why.

Towser knew all along that Lily had wizard potential! He'd canvassed the women of the bawdy house, had each don the silver medallion Lily spoke of: a thing that could detect magic within, even if the wearer were unrealized. Towser had bought her contract, ostensibly as a whore, but in fact, to keep her close, for study or . . .

Sacrifice.

As if struck by lightning, Gull cast off thoughts and confusion, and moved.

Too late.

Kem and the bodyguards rushed. Gull barely hefted his axe before they jumped him. They swung fists, kicked to trip him, body-slammed him to the dirt, mashed him under a half ton of flesh.

Past Kem's scar-laced head, Gull saw the sacrificial knife rise.

And fall.

"Noooo!!!!"

Gull bucked against sweaty bodies, bit, thrashed, jerked his arms and legs, but stayed pinned as if by a landslide. A fist smashed Gull's mouth, bloodied his lips. Yet the bodyguards didn't kill him: they must think Towser wanted him alive.

Through a haze of pain and madness, Kem's face loomed. Scars overlaid veins that throbbed with exertion, and the mangled side that lacked an ear was glossy with sweat.

"Kem, you bastard! You murdering fiend! You whore!" Unable to move, Gull spit filthy oaths into the man's face. "I went into a leech-infested swamp after you! I battled trolls to save your miserable life, you worthless cur! You *owe* me! That man's out to *murder my sister*!"

"You went after your sister, not me, you liar!" Kem growled from inches away. "You didn't care about me!"

"I went in after *you*, damn it! No one deserves to be eaten by cannibals! My sister went after you, too!

Because she's got heart!" All this time, Gull pleaded inside that his sister wasn't already dead. "*You* never showed the gratitude of a cockroach! *But you owe us!* And now's the time to pay back! Or will you be a dog forever?"

For the first time, Gull saw the scarred brow pucker. Deep pockets lined Kem's eyes, and creases tightened his mouth. He was a haunted man.

Kem suddenly rolled off him. He whapped the other bodyguards. "Let him up!"

Confused, the thugs dropped away. They worked for Towser, but Kem had hired them. Whom to obey?

As they deliberated, Gull shot up like a catapult and brushed them aside. Scrambling on hands and knees, he snatched up his axe.

If his sister was dead, a bloody wreck gutted like a fish, he'd chop Towser into a thousand pieces.

Gaining his feet, he raced across the yellow grass for the monolith. The setting sun just topped the tall cone, casting a halo, and Gull could not see its darkened base clearly.

But he could hear. A savage growling and snarling and snapping welled up. And a man's shriek's.

Squinting, Gull sprinted into the shadow.

A giant badger savaged Towser.

Atop Greensleeves, who was unharmed, stood a small badger with a notched ear.

Half-mad, Gull stumbled.

And thought.

The notch-eared badger had come from the Whispering Woods, leagues away. It hadn't been carried here, couldn't have followed them, wasn't hidden in the wagons.

And only Greensleeves had touched that badger.

So Greensleeves must have conjured it.

So Greensleeves, too, was an unrealized wizard!

Like pebbles falling into slots, a dozen clues clicked and questions were answered. Greensleeves could summon animals she'd touched in the past. That was why the notch-eared badger seemed to follow them. Why the mushroom-beast, the fungusaur, attacked the armored wizard before he stomped Gull. Why it glowed green, brown, and blue, not twinkling from Towser's conjuring nor glowing white from Lily's. Why the giant badger appeared in the troll's lair when Greensleeves was endangered. Why it savaged Towser now.

His sister had nature magic: he'd always known that. Her "second sight." Her ability to tame wild animals, to find strays. How animals never harmed her, not even flies and leeches.

Recently he'd learned there was more: that the magic of the Whispering Woods had flooded her mind, made her a simpleton. Clear of the forest, she learned to think clearly.

But now she could conjure whatever she'd touched.

Greensleeves was a full-blooded wizard!

And Towser had known all along!

As with Lily, Towser sensed Greensleeves's wizardness. So he'd hired Gull as freightmaster, (though Chad could do the job), just to get Greensleeves. (And Gull had thought himself clever in bargaining her passage, while Towser feigned indifference. What a dunce!)

Towser had plotted all along to sacrifice Greensleeves, to steal her *mana* on this black altar. But his scheme had backfired.

Unrealized or not, his sister had conjured two badgers to protect her.

Yet two badgers wouldn't protect her from an enraged wizard and his bodyguards.

Unless . . .

Big as a bull, wide and flat and gray-backed, face a riot of white and black stripes, the giant badger crouched low to the ground and shredded Towser's fancy striped gown.

The ridiculous box, tied with a scarf, tumbled from atop Towser's head and bounced across the trampled grass. Gull recognized the pink block from the crater, the *mana* vault. Towser must have planned to store his sister's mystic energy in it.

Except her badger had interrupted the sacrifice.

The skirts of Towser's gown were slashed, and the badger pulled on more cloth clamped in its fearsome jaws. Yet the wizard seemed unharmed, only discombobulated.

And sure enough, Towser spit out a spell and thrust up a hand, and the badger bowled over backward with a snort. Gull had seen that before, in the burned forest. A personal protection spell, an impenetrable aura.

Which Gull longed to test.

"Towser!" he screamed. "Fend off this!"

Gull slung his axe over his shoulder and pegged it like a thunderbolt straight at the wizard's chest.

Wood and steel whirled, end over end. But the heavy sharp head simply bounced off an invisible wall inches from the wizard's nose. Towser never even staggered from the blow. The axe thudded into the shadowed grass around the monolith.

The wizard held up a hand, fingers crooked, and backed away. He shouted over his shoulder, "Kill him!

A hundred gold crowns to the one who beheads him!"

Like hounds to the scent, the bodyguards, who'd stood stunned by the strange turn of events, rushed Gull. All except Kem, who was rooted, face twisted by conflicting loyalties.

That left only three tough fighters with swords seeking Gull's head.

If they killed him—and they would—Greensleeves would be next.

The word returned.

Unless . . .

Whirling, Gull plucked his sister from the altar, sending the smaller badger tumbling. Plunking her down, he snatched up his axe—thank the gods he'd sharpened it—and parted the rope on her wrists.

"G-Gull," she bleated. "What do we d-do?"

Running was out. There was no place to go but over the cliff edge onto rocks.

"Conjure something!" He took a new heft on his axe, ready to swing on the three killers.

"W-what? I don't kn-know—"

"*Anything! And hurry!*"

Behind him came a small sigh of despair. This wouldn't work, he thought savagely. His sister was unpracticed in magic. Conjuring was an accident, an act of desperation. She couldn't just reach across the void and . . .

The air before him shimmered. Colors flickered like a rainbow touching the earth. Brown near the ground, green in the middle, blue at head height, yellow above . . .

Gull was bucked off his feet as the ground erupted.

Brambles, trees, and stone spears shot into the air.

*   *   *

Walls exploded everywhere across the bluff, random, rambling, haphazard.

The tall curly green-brown briars, from the battle of White Ridge, intermixed with the cave swords of the burned forest, as well as curiously stunted trees that twisted back on themselves to make an impassable barrier. The last, Gull knew, were from dismal reaches of the Whispering Woods.

Red earth supported the briars, white muck marked the stone swords, and carpets of dead leaves gave birth to the wall of wood. Smells rolled over Gull. Iron from the red earth, ammonia from bat guano, rot from churned leaves, all mixed with the salt tang of the sea breeze.

Yet the walls made no sense.

A jumble of trees, briars, and stone swords ran from the bluff's edge at his right hand, twenty feet or more thick, then ended suddenly, leaving virgin grass. Another mixed wall curled on the left, no wider than a privet fence, then spun in a spiral like a maze. Way past the wagon circle stood a stand so thick it looked like forest, dense and black with white stripes. Another patch at a stone's throw was square as a kitchen garden.

The thick wall on the right rose fifteen feet, and tendrils of vines hung down and snagged Gull's hair. He backed and snapped stone spears with his clogs.

And swore. Defensively, the right wall was fine, but the leftmost wall wouldn't delay a child. And between was a gap twenty feet across. Towser's bullies could rush the breach easily.

Within seconds. Gull saw the ragged Towser jog past a wall for a better view, then point and shrill orders. Having recovered from the surprise of the green explosion, the three bodyguards raised swords and shot the gap. Yet their feet dragged when they beheld another wizard with her hands in the air.

"More!" Gull shouted. "You've slowed them! Now conjure more!"

"I—I c-can't!" the girl wailed. No higher than his shoulder, tousled hair around her face, tattered shawl drooping off one shoulder, she gripped her brother's elbow. "T-that's all I h-have!"

Gull stifled a groan. He took a fresh grip on his axe. "Try something else! Conjure Morven!"

"W-who?"

She knew no names. "The sailor, damn it, with the gray hair! And the cook's boy, Stiggur! And the centaurs—the horse folk! Hurry!"

Earth tones rippled alongside the woodcutter, and Morven stood there holding his breeches. He cast about wildly. "Ahoy, we're back!"

Gull took one look, roared, *"Where's your cutlass?"*

"One second I laid it down to hit the bushes! *Right* beside me—"

"What's the good making plans—"

Behind his bodyguards, Towser set a finger in his grimoire, pointed another, barked in an arcane tongue, then smiled smugly at Gull.

Before the woodcutter's eyes, in the shadow of the monolith, a twinkling filled the air. He reared back.

Whatever Towser conjured, it was big. Like fog issuing from the ground, a body big as a house took form. Slate gray. Above it writhed a half dozen misty gray necks. A fearsome hissing made him flinch.

We'll be eaten, he thought. *Like minnows by a bass. Six bass.*

Frantically the woodcutter backed, banged into Morven, who cursed as he buttoned his breeches. "Watch where you're—Lance of the Sea! A rock hydra?" The twinkling deepened, solidified, until Gull could bearly see the bramble wall through it.

Better to jump to the rocks, Gull thought. *Some of us might survive. None will up here.*

Yet Greensleeves hummed, and earth colors rippled not a dozen feet from Towser. With a flurry of brown, green, blue, and yellow, the cook's boy stood coiling his whip, blinking.

"Stiggur!" shouted Gull, and the boy jumped. "Hit him!"

Confused, but heeding his hero's voice, the boy flicked the whip backward along the ground, not straight, and whisked it forward, too hard and fast.

But the tip of the mulewhip cut the air, popped almost in Towser's eye. Startled, the wizard grabbed his bloodied cheek.

The conjuring spoiled, the twinkles before Gull's eyes faded. The fierce hissing gasped out. Like the last smoke of a campfire, the rock hydra dwindled and disappeared. Gull saw dents in the grass where its feet had begun to form.

He heaved a great sigh. That had been too close.

But their luck couldn't last. They needed to organize a defense.

Or die.

Towser had ducked behind a bramble wall. Stiggur stood, whip lying limp on the ground, and regarded the bodyguards, who cast about for orders.

"Stiggur! To me!" Gull bellowed. The boy zipped past the confused thugs before they could stop him. But Stiggur looked up, over the monolith.

A steel spike flashed from the heavens and thudded into the ground at Gull's feet. Another few inches and it would have buried in his skull.

Overhead lofted four balloons, their baskets filled

with shrieking goblins. The onshore breeze pushed them rapidly over the bluff. Dangling from rigging, tussling with awkward loads, squabbling with one another, the first crew of leering gray-green goblins dropped spears at the company trapped in the pocket.

Spears clattered off the monolith, ricocheted off the black altar, bounced off the earth. Grabbing Morven and his sister, Gull hauled them into partial shelter against the shadowed monolith. Goblins cackled with glee.

Gull's head throbbed as he tried to track the confusion. They still needed a solid defense. The bodyguards hung back, guarding the gap, but Towser must be conjuring something dreadful. He barked, "Greenie! Fetch the rest! Anything you've touched! The clockwork beast! The centaurs! Our own stinking goblins, even!"

Frowning with concentration, Greensleeves shot her green sleeves to her elbows, raised her hands, murmured. Gull didn't know what she whispered. Prayers? Rhymes? Nonsense?

Close above, the second crew of goblins upended another basket of spears. A steel spike chipped wood off the toe of Gull's clog. Morven stabbed out a hand, deflected a spear. "Quickly, darling!" Two more balloons had yet to assault them.

From behind the twisted wall, a barbarian shout shook the sky.

"Oh, no!" Gull groaned.

Then suddenly they stood in shade deeper than approaching dusk.

Four tree trunks appeared around them. Jointed trees, like a horse's legs. Gull recognized a lower back leg—hand-hewed by himself from a ship's mast.

Stiggur whooped with delight. The clockwork beast stood stationary above them. Gull could have reached up and touched its beamy belly. Above, goblins squawked as their spikes thudded into seasoned wood or clanged off sheet iron flanks. The deadly pointed rain missed the humans.

The cook's boy looped the whip over his shoulder, grabbed a knee joint, and scampered up the clockwork beast's leg and withers like a monkey.

Gull barked for him to stop, but the boy crowed, "They're past!"

Indeed, the stiff wind had pushed the sausagelike balloons out of range, over the wagon circle now. Goblins howled with rage, fistfought in blaming each other. One old bald goblin, in stupid rage, stabbed upward and pierced the balloon, which wheezed like a teakettle as the crew screamed. When the bag split, they hurtled into the densest patch of brambles and stone swords.

Stiggur yelped, laughed like Gull, and yanked a lever. Instantly, the articulated cone eyes of the clockwork beast blinked. A huge iron-shod hoof came off the ground. Towser's bodyguards took a step back, mouths gaping. The boy crowed, "I'll get 'em, Gull! I'll squish 'em!"

But square in the path of the stamping beast, colors gushed like a fountain. Armored and armed, appeared Helki and Holleb.

Stiggur shrilled, yanked, turned the wooden beast and promptly crashed into the bramble wall. The centaurs had already skipped nimbly aside. They saluted Gull with their feathered lances. Spotting the boggled bodyguards, they trumpeted their war cry, leveled their weapons, and charged.

The woodcutter felt a stab of satisfaction that

choked him. It'd been his nagging that made them gird for war again . . .

But they *still* needed to organize a defense! They had plenty of help, but had to get out of this pocket! If those blue barbarians trapped them here, they'd be slaughtered.

Morven plucked a steel spike from the ground. "I can stave someone's hull with this! Who's for hitting?"

Gull cast about. Clashing and thrashing, Stiggur fought with his levers to free the clockwork beast from the bramble wall. Unable to back out, the boy elected to drive forward. Huge wood-and-iron limbs shredded brambles and snapped stone spears. As the construct and its rider disappeared through the rambling wall, Gull couldn't help. Stiggur had opened yet another gap.

"You'll have a snootful in a moment!" Gull shouted over the noise. "That shout was—Greenie! Hold up!"

But lost in her own world of newfangled magic, his sister went on whispering and waggling her fingers.

A roar answered her.

A pair of humpbacked grizzly bears big as hayricks winked into being thirty feet away. One of the shaggy brown animals roared, snapped slavering jaws full of long white teeth, looked around for something to bite.

And spotted Gull and company against the monolith.

The woodcutter gulped. He never knew his sister had touched grizzly bears!

But why did they turn this way . . . ?

Then he realized.

Greensleeves couldn't control any of these creatures.

They'd attack whatever they liked. Including him and his sister.

*   *   *

In a flash, Gull saw the problem.

Towser, with years of training and experience, had learned to control whatever he summoned. Laid on each being, magical or not, was a geas, a compulsion to serve the wizard. Thus Towser could summon the darkest monster and point it at an enemy, himself immune from attack.

But Greensleeves had neither training nor years. Whatever she conjured did as it pleased. The badgers, befriended, had chosen to defend her.

But these grizzlies . . .

Suddenly they had too much "help."

The bigger bear, the male, kicked its back legs to gather speed, rolled at them like a boulder from a mountaintop.

"Greensleeves!" shouted Gull. "Something to stop it!"

His sister saw the charging bear, threw up her hands, bleated.

An upwelling flare of multicolored light, a rapid barking and woofing, and suddenly nine husky gray timber wolves, thoroughly fuddled, spilled across the altar.

They thumped at Greensleeves's feet, tumbled against the monolith and bounded away, dumped on their rumps in the path of the grizzly bear.

Instinctively protecting his pack, one huge wolf leaped at the grizzly's face. With gleaming fangs it latched onto the bear's muzzle. The bruin half reared to bat it away. The wolf kicked scrabbled for footing in the grass, yanked to tear flesh and pull its opponent off-balance. Other wolves nipped at the bear's flanks, but the rampaging female smashed amidst them, bowling them right and left.

"Rabid wolves to stop hungry bears?" rasped Morven. "That's an improvement?"

Gull only shook his head. "Badgers, I'd seen her play with! Deer! Wolverines, even! But I never imagined she'd touched—"

He turned at a snarl. Atop the monolith perched a tawny mountain lion. It clung with razor claws. White whiskers bristling, ears laid back, it screeched a challenge to this indignity.

A louder roar distracted the fighters. Yelping, howling, leaping, screaming, a horde of blue-painted, white-haired, tusked barbarians gathered at the gap in the crazy bramble walls.

And charged.

CHAPTER
18

"Fall back!" shouted the woodcutter over barbarian screams. He caught Greensleeves's arm, plucked at Morven's, all while juggling his axe. "We need cover!"

"There ain't no cover!" Morven yelled. He turned the air blue shouting sailors' oaths at the oncoming barbarians.

Gull didn't argue. They couldn't fight an army. Dragging his companions on tiptoes, he backpedaled around the monolith till it rose like a wall on their left.

Near the altar, the bear-wolf fight sent fur pluming into the air. Five wolves tumbled and snapped at the grizzly bears, more snarling than fighting. The male grizzly batted a wolf, rushed and trampled over him, then whirled. Gull could have touched the bear's tail.

But at the barbarians' rush and shout, the dogfight split apart. Yelping wolves shot across the warriors' front line and vaulted through the thin brambles. The grizzlies bowled after them and bashed straight through stone spears and vines.

Nothing protected them now, thought Gull.

Threescore blue barbarians ran five abreast. They cheered, lusty and proud, some garbled the name of a war god, loudly enough to hurt ears. They laughed as if going to a holiday instead of slaughter. Gull and his companions would be mincemeat.

Dashing all the way into the pocket behind the monolith, a second's glance showed they were trapped.

The bramble-sword-wood wall was still a solid barrier, thirty feet thick here, that halted abruptly at the cliff's edge. Roots and branches stuck into space. Gull had vaguely hoped they might run around the monolith, since it didn't sit on the very lip of the bluff. But rocks higher than his reach were piled against the back of the dark cone, possibly to prop it, a jumbled line of them some twenty feet long. Given time, they could boost and climb over: but they had no time. Squinting into the setting sun, Gull found the cliff edge dropped sheer thirty feet to surf-swept boulders.

There was only twelve feet of space between the monolith and bramble wall, yet they had nothing to plug the gap, for Stiggur's clockwork beast was still fetched up in the brambles. The boy yanked at the controls. Levers clicked, pulleys raced, gears clashed, but the construct was mired in vines. Gull wasn't sure it would make a barrier anyway.

This pocket would prove the last stand for Gull, Greensleeves, and Morven. They would fight and then die. In dying, choose blades or a fall.

Gull shoved his sister behind him, against the rocks, and hefted his axe. Morven lifted his pathetic steel spike.

The barbarians struck.

*   *   *

The same people who had captured Gull and Greensleeves in that copse at the beach, the barbarians were normal humans except for tusks and white hair. Tattooed and berry-stained blue, they dressed in skins and war harness, carried painted rawhide shields, and either curved bronze swords or obsidian-headed clubs like small pickaxes. Gull noted the few women among them were equally tusked and tattooed. They rushed blindly forward, weapons raised, howling like demons.

Gull's vision filled blue, and he had no more time to think, or even call to his sister. This was the fight of his life.

A screaming barbarian swung his sword overhand. The woodcutter shoved his axe haft in the air so the blade gouged hickory. Wheeling, Gull slammed the butt end into the man's temple, dropping him.

A woman rushed, jabbed with her burnished sword for his groin. Gull dropped his axe handle to block, but her thrust was a feint. Quick as a snake's tongue, the sword flicked back, aimed for his belly. He flinched and ducked, caught the point in the ribs. It hurt like fury. Swearing, he batted the sword up, smashed the handle into the woman's jaw. Teeth broke, then her jaw. She collapsed, and Gull was glad. She was too dangerous to fight.

Gull cursed steadily as he swung and dodged. He hated to fight them. These people were as much slaves to Towser as Gull had been. But under the wizard's control, they'd kill him if they could.

And undoubtedly would. They were warriors bred to the sword, and Gull was a woodcutter. He'd been lucky so far, but it couldn't last. Someone would gut him before long.

From the corner of his eye, he saw Morven had

gained a bronze sword and shield, flailed about as if
threshing grain. He dinged heads and hands and kept
a half dozen warriors at bay.

A pair of barbarians, male and female, sized Gull up
and attacked from two directions. From the right, the
man swung his war club, and Gull shifted. But that
was the plan. The woman stabbed from his left,
chipped his elbow so blood spattered his side. Gull
could see the advantage of fighting with a shield.
One-handed, the woodcutter slapped his axe at the
man, but he'd jumped back. The duo called to each
other, closed to set up the same attack.

It had worked once, it would work again. Gull
would be nibbled to death.

Then sounded a crashing of breaking wood and
stone spears.

With a snapping of vines and clumping of great
wood-and-iron feet, Stiggur broke the clockwork beast
free of the bramble wall.

The beast's articulated-cone eyes trained on the
woodcutter. Atop, like a child on its father's shoulders,
the boy looked frantically at the barbarians about to
engulf his hero. Hanging on to the lurching beast's
neck, hauling levers, the boy steered for the wave of
barbarians, trailing vines by the bushelful. Threatened
by the fearsome feet and legs, the blue men and women
backed from Gull's pitiful line, retreated around the
beast toward the clearing by the altar. One barbarian,
ducking the wrong way, was pinned between a back leg
and the monolith, crushed so blood spurted from his
mouth.

As the beast loomed overhead, Gull fell back
against Greensleeves to keep from being crushed

himself. Stiggur brought the monster to a thunderous halt on the very lip of the bluff.

Morven and Stiggur shouted hoorays, but Gull shushed them. "They'll regroup and come at us again! They must, the geas compels them! Stiggur, get the beast to lie down! We need a barricade!"

Leaning out and down, biting his lip, the boy frowned, ready to cry. "But, Gull, it can't lie down! There ain't no lever for that!"

"What?" The woodcutter cursed. Of course there wasn't. The beast remained upright like a sleeping horse. Liko and levers had shoved it over. So what to do? "Well . . . blast! Turn it, then!"

Gears whirring and protesting, Stiggur inched the monster in a tight circle, all the while Gull feared it would sunder the cliff and pitch them all to the rocks below. They ended with their gap shrunk to nine feet or so, the width of the beast's underbelly. The stout legs, thick as wharf pilings, offered shelter like four tree trunks.

But barbarians hooted, chanted to taunt their enemies and egg each other on. They elbowed and shoved and argued, shuffling into rough ranks for the next attack. Gull guessed they used some hierarchy for who attacked first and who second, a function of caste or family or past deeds. It made for much arguing.

In the momentary lull, Gull tried to think what to do. Could they survive a drop to the rocks below? Not without breaking limbs. Was it worthwhile to scale this rock jumble? What lay on the other side? He clutched his bleeding elbow, rubbed slashed ribs, and despaired. They'd all die here, and soon. Could he put Greensleeves up with Stiggur, have him bash through the brambles and get away . . . ?

Greensleeves grabbed his arm, pointing up.

Taking advantage of the pause, the mountain lion gathered its haunches and leaped from the peak of the monolith to the heaped rocks. Though it dropped twenty feet or more, the big cat landed without a sound. Hissing at them, it bounded over the rocks and out of sight. Yet a great snapping and snarling welled up, another scrap, and Gull recognized the snattering of an angry badger. So that was where the giant badger had gone.

"We get more catfights," muttered Morven. He plucked and yanked at a boulder, trying to free it, roll it down for protection, but it stayed put. "Handy. Why not fire-spitting dragons?"

Gull rubbed his brow, pressed his bleeding ribs. He could have screamed in frustration. If only Greensleeves could control the damned animals, turn them against the barbarians, compel them to fight. Or conjure something that could think . . .

He barked so suddenly his sister jumped. "The giant, Liko! Remember him, Greenie? Call him! And the centaurs! No, wait . . . " She'd already conjured them, but they'd galloped off, cut off by the blue army. He searched a mental list as jumbled as the rocks. "What about Tomas, the red soldiers—" No, Greensleeves never met them. Who else? The paladin? No. The ant soldiers? No good either. "Get the goblins, even! Remember that little thief, Egg Sucker?"

From atop the clockwork beast, Stiggur called, "They're getting ready to charge, Gull!"

"I want to know, where's Towser?" said the sailor. "I don't like him running loose, thinking up more things to hurl at us!"

But a shout from Stiggur made him pause. The boy behind them.

Burned gold by the setting sun, a lone man stood atop the stone pile. In black leather and plain helmet, he carried a short sword and shield, was scarred down one side of his face.

"Kem!"

The bodyguard scuffed across the rocks, hopped and thumped down alongside Gull.

The woodcutter griped, "What do you want? Come to beg our surrender for Towser?"

Puckered skin sneered high on one side. "I knew it'd be a mistake helping you."

The two men argued calmly as if standing before an ale bar in town, rather than awaiting slaughter. Gull said, "We don't need your help."

"Well, you got it, like it or not."

"Don't expect any thanks."

"I'll thank you!" Morven called, still yanking at rocks. "Thank you! Now kiss and make up and fight the enemy, you codfish peckers!"

Gull gripped his aching elbow. Blood trickled down his forearm and made his axe handle slick. "Sister, can you think of anything to help us?"

But Greensleeves listened to silent sound. One hand against the monolith, she curled the other, raised it . . .

"Here we go!" shouted Kem. He pushed to Gull's left, his wounded side, and lifted his sword. Gull wiped blood on his tunic, hefted his axe. Morven clanged his stolen sword against his shield, sang a snatch of some sailor's ditty.

The barbarians finally had managed ranks of six. Chanting together, banging weapons, they advanced in step.

This charge was different. After a dozen paces, the main body halted and kept chanting, while the front six launched themselves at the line. Gull guessed they were either a suicide squad, or else young warriors out for their first kill. Or else the barbarians pitied Gull's small force and only sent in their clumsiest warriors.

These proved unblooded warriors, for the defenders killed them outright.

Restricted on either side by Morven and Kem, restricted by the low ceiling of the beast's belly, Gull hoisted his axe, cocked his arms tight, and struck. It was a woman before him, young under her tattoos and berry stain, even pretty despite the tusks. Gull hated to kill her.

But he must. He swung the huge axe at an angle, smashed through her leather shield, and cleaved her shoulder. Blood spurted and she toppled leaking at his feet. Wrenching the axe free, he found the shield tangled around the handle. He lost precious seconds sliding it off—

—A barbarian whipped in close, stabbed with his sword—

—and died on Kem's blade.

Having dispatched his two assailants, the trained fighter had spare time to kill Gull's.

"Don't thank me!" grunted Kem. "Again!"

"I won't!" Gull panted. "But we're drawing even!"

"Even? Ha! You owe me—"

Another shout welled from the barbarians. The first line dead, the second peeled off to rush them.

Hopeless, Gull thought. It was hopeless.

Then a green-brown blur rippled in the sunset red air, and another monolith reared into the sky.

*   *   *

Backed against the black monolith, Liko scratched one head with his one arm, tried to fathom the scene around his knees. Fortunately, Gull saw, he'd brought his newly carved club. Slowly, the giant pieced together the picture.

"Hit someone blue, Liko!" shouted the woodcutter.

"Ahhhh . . . " Both heads nodded.

The giant stumped forward, tangled his feet in the twisted briars strewn by the clockwork beast, and toppled full length.

His crash shook the ground, stunning everyone. Yet he shot out his only hand and caught a barbarian by the leg, as a child might catch a frog. The blue man stabbed his fingers and the giant let go.

The second wave of barbarians struck the line, paired this time. A chunky blue woman pinked Gull's knee. Her partner, probably mate, flicked at Gull's opposite side, flashed a tusked grin to frighten. The woodcutter couldn't slash either with his axe without driving his guts onto a sword. Crowding, hiding behind their swords and shields, they'd crowd and drop and dress him like a deer.

But the barbarians stalled their attack, withdrew from striking range, as more earth colors rippled just behind them, cutting them off from their comrades. From the size of the shimmers, Gull hoped for something formidable, some potent force, though he thought Greensleeves's cupboard empty.

Squalling, a handful of goblins burst into being.

Only three of the gray-green goomers carried their char-hardened spears. The rest came empty-handed, except for one with a drumstick fresh from the cooking spit.

The goblins blinked around dazedly. Then all screamed together as they spotted the barbarians.

Three spears flew in the air like jackstraws. Goblins ran every which way, welcome as a porcupine in a hammock.

A warrior knocked a goblin aside, only to trip over him as he clutched the man's ankle. Another jumped into a barbarian's arms, latching onto the woman's head so she couldn't see. A goblin scrambled past Kem, scampered over the rocks and, by the noise, plunged straight into the cougar-badger fight. Another ran smack into the monolith, stunning himself; then on fingernails alone, scaled halfway up the monolith. Watching over its shoulder, a fool ran clear off the cliff edge, still milling his legs. Gull saw a black-streaked goblin, Egg Sucker the thief, flit by and slither under Greensleeves's skirt to hide.

The woodcutter booted another goblin into the legs of the male barbarian, so both went tumbling. The woman erred in watching her lover fall, and Gull swatted her alongside the head. As the male reared, rising and stabbing, Gull split his skull as if chopping wood.

"*Damn you!*" he shouted, so angry he was almost hysterical. "*Stay down!*"

Beside him, Kem used the woman's white hair to swipe blood from his blade. "You should stick to tending horses, woodchopper! This is man's work!"

Morven snorted, "You boys'll never grow to be men!"

Gull clawed sweat off his face. A short distance away, Liko had found his feet, but a half dozen barbarians menaced him with swords and he shuffled backward, awkward still with his single heavy arm.

Faintly, Gull heard a halloo from the centaurs. Damn it, they were needed *here*! Beside him, Greensleeves cooed. What was *she* gabbling up? More useless goblins? Couldn't she conjure any *fighters*?

Then he had no time to think, for the third wave of barbarians began their charge. How many had they killed or felled? A dozen? Leaving what? More than twoscore? Gull huffed as he hoisted his axe once more, waited for the rush to overtake him. And perhaps drown him.

Yet a tall male barbarian, charging, grunted as an arrow struck his chest. He crashed on his face and the black shaft split his back. A woman warrior raised her shield, but an arrow punched through it like paper and lodged in her heart. Another barbarian died from an arrow in his throat. Then the rear ranks, the chanters, began to fall under the black rain.

The woodcutter risked a glance backward for the source of the arrows. What people did Greensleeves know that shot deadly black arrows?

He got his answer.

Not people.

Lining the rock heap, from teetery cliff edge to monolith, were two ranks of folk Gull had only imagined existed.

Male and female, they were five and a half feet high, slim and knotty-muscled, pale as corpses. Black hair rippled and twisted in the breeze. They wore only short green tunics like snakeskin for clothing, but were decorated with red arcane tattoos, feathers, foxtails, woven arm bracers. One and all, they carried carved and twisted bows taller than themselves, and quivers of long black-fletched arrows.

"Elves," breathed the woodcutter. "Real . . . live . . . elves . . . "

The elves perched easily on the rocks with sandaled feet, easy as eagles, and nocked more arrows. Just above Kem's head, a woman with a red-plumed helmet and embroidered eye patch barked a command, and the nocked bows raised as one. The archers needed to aim around and past the clockwork beast, but that did not hamper them.

Another bark, and arrows flew like a flock of birds taking wing.

Why would they help us? Gull wondered. Humans are enemies to elves—yet Greensleeves must have met them in the past.

His sister was an elf-friend? Elves lived in the depths of the Whispering Woods?

The flight of arrows struck blue skin. Ranks decimated, the tusked barbarians took flight themselves, dashing around the monolith for cover. Their attack was over.

Morven whooped, Kem looked disappointed, and Gull only sighed, glad to rest.

Then goblins died.

Greensleeves didn't control the elves. For the sake of friendship, Gull guessed, they had driven the barbarians away from her and her party. But that accomplished, they followed natural instincts.

Goblins were cousins to orcs, someone had said, the deadliest enemies of elves. So the elves killed goblins as a farmer would kill rats in a grain bin.

Black arrows sought Egg Sucker's companions. A goblin pinned by brambles was lanced three times. One clinging to the face of the monolith was swatted off like a fly. Screams issuing from behind the rock jumble told another died.

Gull sucked wind, tried to sort the madness and think, but a shrill howling split the air. Prodded by the spears of Towser's three loyal bodyguards, more goblins attacked down the body-littered alley between monolith and bramble wall. They were the balloonists, either crashed or landed, forced to attack by Towser's compulsion and three swords.

But their attack balked when they spied the elves and the dead. Then they died. Arrows whistled amongst them, spitting screaming mouths, splitting guts, lancing two at once so they died thrashing together. The balloonists turned and ran, around and over the bodyguards. The elves called to one another in fluting song, and Gull believed they made bets on striking fleeing targets. They were beautiful to look at, Gull thought, but cold as snakes and murderous to suffer.

There were no living enemies in sight.

Stiggur whooped atop the clockwork beast, which had not stirred even as war raged around its feet. Liko peered over the bramble wall at something below. The elves warbled to one another, and the red-plumed captain sang at Greensleeves. Morven squeezed a bleeding thumb, Kem nursed a chipped knee.

Gull noted Greensleeves still carried a bulge under her skirts.

Shifting his bloody axe, he snagged Egg Sucker by one skinny leg. Dangling, the goblin thief squawked, beat bony fists on Gull's shin. A mistake. Elven ears pricked, fingers flew to bowstrings. Seeing his danger, Egg Sucker whimpered.

Then, before the goblin was shot full of feathers, Gull flipped him over the cliff. He was tough: he'd probably survive the tumble. Better than being spitted like a turkey.

"Lord of Atlantis!" muttered Morven. "I'm dry!

Wish I had some of that coconut beer we was brewing!" Kem hawked and spit, but he was dry too. A professional, he pulled a whetstone and honed his sword.

Gull nodded abstractedly. He felt he could sleep standing up. He struggled to assess their position. What now?

Towser was still out there, the real danger. What else might he throw at them? The blue djinn? The rock hydra again? Gull had seen so many wonders and horrors since that fateful day in White Ridge, he couldn't recall them all, or who'd conjured what. Anything might pop up.

Should they continue to battle here? Or take the fight to the wizard? Or retreat over country? The forest he'd seen earlier was no more than a half mile inland. Could they count on the elves? Were Helki and Holleb all right? What was happening he didn't know about . . . ?

As if in answer, the bright ocean sunset was eclipsed. A rumble stirred the air. Clouds coalesced from inland, thickening faster than clouds should.

Then he recalled one conjuring from White Ridge as a pattering sounded around him.

Raindrops stung his face, cold and hard. In seconds he was plastered head to toe, leather tunic and kilt glued flat like a second skin. Morven's salt-and-pepper curls lay flat on his head. Kem flicked water from his helmet rim. Elves glanced upward, fluted to one another, and minded their arrow fletching. The elvish captain sang at Greensleeves, the only one ignoring the rain. The girl only shook her head. As a simpleton, she'd established some rapport with the elves; now she couldn't communicate with them.

With the onslaught of rain and failing light, Gull couldn't see beyond thirty feet. The rain roared as it spattered and pattered off the monolith, but aside from that it was quiet.

Had Towser conjured the rain? Maybe to cover a retreat? Leaving them victors on the field of honor, as the old legends said? Gull could have laughed. How he'd loved the glorious stories of honor and valor, yet now that his day had come, he was hungry and tired and cold, with icy rain running from his hair down his back.

His thoughts—wandering, he knew—were interrupted. Liko suddenly roared a double battle cry and hefted his club. Through a curtain of rain, a gray dragon's head reared past a bramble wall, then another, and another.

Towser's six-headed rock hydra, finally conjured in whole. The beast that had chewed off Liko's arm.

So Towser wasn't quitting yet.

Morven whapped his shoulder, pointed up.

Rain spattering his eyes, Gull squinted. In semi-darkness, a striped form flitted across the sky.

Towser could fly?

If so, then *he* must be the one who'd—

A flash blinded Gull. Forked lightning split the stormy sky and shattered against the monolith.

CHAPTER
19

When the lightning struck, Gull felt a shock like a slap on the soles of his feet, a burning as if his clogs had caught fire.

The sensation faded, leaving him tingly, cold, and drenched. He couldn't focus his eyes, and put out a questing hand. A craggy claw grabbed it and dragged him stumbling from the monolith. A crash of thunder almost threw him to his knees.

Someone pushed him down. Wet leaves curled around his ears. Blinking hot tears that mingled with cold raindrops, he gradually made out Greensleeves and Kem and Stiggur, all tucked close to the bramble wall. Morven chivied them deeper into cover.

The sky split again. Jagged spears of white light smashed the storm darkness. Splintered streaks of rain glowed on the monolith. Another crash of thunder rocked them.

"Lance of the Sea!" gasped the sailor. He sounded exhausted. "Look there!"

Gull squinted. Against a gray sky floated a blue cloud, like the smoke of a soggy campfire. The cloud lengthened, took the vague shape of a man with a pointed tail. When it balled two hand-shapes together, light crackled between them. The hands clapped and shook, like a dog shaking off water, and lightning streaked down, too fast to follow.

The bolt struck the clockwork beast with a dull shudder. Gull smelled burned rust and charred wood on the wet air. Dimly, he heard Morven lecturing Stiggur, " . . . why! Because iron attracts lightning! Iron on a ship will fair burn out'a the wood! If you hadn't come down—" A peal of thunder wiped out his words. "—monolith must have iron in it, 'cause it's sucking up the lightning and keeping us safe! Towser never considered that, the daft bugger!"

"But where *is* Towser?" Gull interrupted. "He can *fly*! You never told me that!"

Stiggur answered. Streaming-wet, he was blue-lipped and chatter-toothed. Greensleeves wrapped her dripping shawl around his shoulders. "He d-don't do it much. He can't f-fly like a proper bird, flapping his wings—arms. He j-just soars, like a—a g-gull."

But Gull wasn't listening. "If he can fly, that means . . . " People waited, and Gull's thoughts tumbled. "It must have been *he* who flew above our village, not Dacian, that black-haired female wizard. *He* felled our family, my mother, with that weakness spell that stilled her heart . . . "

Only hissing rain answered.

Sorrow choked Gull, stung like a knife wound. Along with a raging thirst for revenge, for Towser's blood.

But caution ruled too. And fear, for himself and his companions.

This wizards' duel—between Towser and Green-sleeves—had brought things crashing around them, too fast to encompass, so they could only react like bugs in a bottle. Now Towser renewed the attack, distracting them with rain and lightning. The wizard was stubborn, Gull knew, and veteran of several wizard duels.

Though he couldn't see it, Gull sensed a trap about to spring. More than ever, the sense they had to get away washed him like chilly rain.

Fighting panic, Gull made a quick count of their resources.

The elvish archers lingered, still with arrows nocked. Yet their captain shook her head as she warbled at Greensleeves. They'd depart soon, Gull could tell. More felt than seen, Liko and the rock hydra battled beyond the brambles. Thumps and draggings and hard-struck blows sent tremors through the ground. Gull feared the giant would lose another arm, but Liko had been enraged, angrier than Gull had ever seen: maybe his rage would sustain him. He wished Liko well, for that was all he could do. They had but three fighters, an unpracticed wizard girl, a boy, a mechanical animal—

Lightning made them flinch. It struck the clockwork beast again, sending that scorched stink through the air. Stiggur bleated, "He'll kill my beast!"

"It ain't alive!" said Kem.

"It is! I know it!"

"Greenie," said her brother, "can you conjure somewhat to push that cloud-man away? Arrows won't do! We need to move, get away from this spot! Towser'll drop something right on our heads!"

"We should stay put!" Kem barked. In the semi-darkness, the scarred side of his face glowed like fox-fire. "We're safe here, might not be elsewhere!"

"Don't argue! I know what I'm doing!"

"Since when does a woodcutter know about generaling?"

"Since when does an assassin?"

"You'll eat those words!"

"Makes me want to cry," put in Morven, "seeing you boys get along so nice. Warms the cockles of my old withered heart—"

Greensleeves murmured, "I th-think . . . I have . . . "

A flare like lightning lit the sky, but this brilliance lingered.

Once again, the nightmare rode the heavens.

The flaming horse billowed upward as from a green-brown cloud. It galloped from over the ocean, prancing on air. Gray body sleek as a seal's, fire trailed from its mane and tail and feet, flickering, guttering, but never quenching.

Gull thought that for such a horror, it was achingly beautiful. But then it made dreams, and dreams could be both beautiful and horrid at once.

"That's a girl!" he shouted. "It beat the djinn last time, smashed it like a rotten pumpkin!"

"That was at night!" Morven countered. "The sun ain't set yet! And this rain might douse its fire!"

"That's magic fire!" Kem argued. "It don't burn like wood! But that horse looks sickly!"

They had to agree. Colorful, the phantom yet looked filmy as a mist or rainbow, whereas the djinn looked solid as a thunderhead.

The nightmare whinnied, a high, piercing shriek

like a saw binding in oak that set everyone's teeth on edge. As it closed, the blue-cloud djinn, swelled up, head ballooning, and blew. The blast of air—Gull heard its roar—stalled the nightmare's charge, bowled it across the sky. The horse's flame all but extinguished, and its body grew paler, more ethereal. It coasted a hundred yards before finding its feet. Again it laid flaming hooves against an invisible road, and charged, and again the djinn puffed, sending it asail across the dark sky.

"The horse-demon's licked," muttered Kem.

Gull wiped his axe handle, but couldn't dry it for blood and water. He gestured inland, called above the noise of rain and sky battle. "Let's move while there's no lightning! We need to see who's out there! If it's those blue barbarians, maybe the archers can drive 'em off! We can rush the wagons! They'd make good shelter and Towser won't destroy them—"

"You forget the bodyguards!" Kem cut in. "They're better fighters than you are! I hired 'em!"

"Kem, if you can't help, belt up!" Gull hefted his axe. "We'll see what's what, flee if we must—"

Stiggur's cold hand grabbed Gull's arm. "Look!"

Atop the black, rain-slick monolith, Towser perched like a peacock.

Kneeling on the rounded top, the wizard clung with one hand. Gull could have pitched his axe and hit him.

With that thought, a score of elven black arrows whizzed through the night. Every one hit the wizard dead center—before bouncing off and disappearing into the dark eventide.

Damn that infernal magic shield! thought Gull. Damn all magic! The bastard wasn't even wet!

A white stripe flickered in Towser's hand. A silver wand aimed down at them.

Gull's body spasmed from head onto toe. His bad knee shot out and he crashed on the turf, almost braining Greensleeves with his axe. But she'd pitched backward into briars that held her like a prickly bed. Kem was down, crawling as if from bellyache, as did Morven. Stiggur lay on his side and twitched like a dog with nightmares.

Gull fought the jerky paralysis, but couldn't even clench his teeth without biting his tongue. His fingers hooked into claws, his arms shook, one leg kicked on its own.

The disrupting scepter, Gull agonized, that made a man's body betray him. But why hadn't Towser simply drained their energy? For Gull knew, somehow, it *had* been Towser who'd flown and stolen the life forces from his village. Yet Towser wanted Greensleeves's magic. Perhaps draining her would waste it? He didn't know—didn't know anything about magic, and cursed himself for his ignorance.

And his helplessness. For this was the snap of the trap. They lay exposed as baby mice in a spilled nest. Growing more vulnerable by the minute. The raging of Liko and the rock hydra had diminished, so one must have lost, and last time the victor had been the hydra. The flaming nightmare had vanished from the roiling sky. From the corner of his eye, Gull saw the elven captain crawl away, dragging her bow. Magic must affect them less, but still they were running.

Gull would have too, but it was too late. He tried to grab his axe, to sit up, but only flailed himself in the face and fell back. Towser could walk over unarmed, seize Gull's sister, stretch her on the altar . . .

A whispering came to him. Greensleeves's voice,

cooing as when she'd been simple. Maybe terror and exhaustion had twisted her mind to its earlier state. In the dimness he saw her white face staring upward, rain speckling her cheeks, blipping her eyes. Her small rough hands pressed flat against the earth as she whispered. Or chanted.

Then, deep under Gull's back, the earth groaned.

With his head against the wet grass, Gull's teeth rattled with the force of the earthquake. His vision danced until he thought his eyeballs would pop. Shock waves made his spine jiggle until he felt he'd break into pieces.

A roaring sounded as the earth shuddered, a strange grumbling and rushing as the dirt and rock of the bluff tore apart. Clickings and clackings and pingings told him rocks flaked from the cliff and bounced onto sea rocks below. Overhead, briars shivered and danced, flinging water droplets he could taste. The roaring increased until it filled his ears, his brain.

Then the black basalt monolith began to dance.

Towser found his perch swaying. Alarmed, he snatched at his grimoire. For his flying spell, Gull knew.

With a sliding grinding rush, a slab of the monolith split from the top, smashed dirt and rocks from the bluff's edge, and cascaded into the sea with a *boom*. The missing piece almost took Towser with it, but he launched into the air, flapping his arms, ungainly as a chicken.

A thought burned in Gull's brain. *My little sister did this?* She'd lived through one earthquake, back in White Ridge. But to conjure one . . . ? How much power did she wield?

The woodcutter heaved a shoulder, tried to clutch his axe, touched the haft with clumsy fingers. His whole body shook: he couldn't tell which juttered more, him or the earth. Gritting his teeth, he flipped over. The spasming spell must be wearing off.

Not soon enough.

Slowly, slowly, the huge monolith teetered toward the ocean, the unbalanced side, tilted farther—

—then the entire bluff collapsed under the shifting weight.

The sound of sliding, smashing, crashing stone striking the foamy, rocky shore was horrendous, ear-shattering. Aftershocks rippled up and down the beach and shorn bluff, spraying soil and grass like a snapped blanket. The ponderous clockwork beast, so heavy it sank into loam, went cartwheeling out to sea like a toy.

Through his hips and breastbone, Gull felt the earth slip farther. The earthquake and toppling monolith were too much. Before his eyes, a chasm split the bluff. The broken edge jumped at him in big bites, as if swallowed by an invisible monster. Grass and dirt disappeared at a hand's reach.

Halfway erect, Kem spit a bitter oath. Morven prayed. Stiggur went white with terror. Greensleeves just looked wide-eyed and amazed at the destruction she'd wrought.

Then, suddenly, as if they sat on a flying carpet, the earth dropped away, and they dropped, screaming.

Gull was unsure how far he fell, or how he survived the fall. He could only suppose their portion of bluff slid whole before bursting apart.

One second he sailed through space on the

earthern carpet, actually lifting from the wet grass, the next he plunged below icy salt waves, deep, deep, deep.

Blasts of icy water and panicked thoughts almost overwhelmed the woodcutter, buried in the sea. He had to retain his axe, his only weapon. He had to find Greensleeves. He had to get air.

The axe went immediately, his hand letting go on its own. He clutched water, clawing for the surface, unsure if he rose or sank. His lungs burned, ready to rupture, but then his head broke water. He gasped fresh salt air—and was buried anew in dirty churning waves. Down he went, but by kicking and clawing, found the surface again, was almost sucked under by another wave. The sea had been rough enough with the storm, but tons of plunging cliffside had set the ocean itself heaving.

Another wave batted his face, then his bare feet—his clogs were long gone—bashed against something first soft, then unyielding.

Wildly, the woodcutter grabbed for it. A seaweed-festooned rock. Slime disintegrated in his hands, then another wave mashed him against the rock. Climbing, spluttering, retching water, he got a foot wedged into a cleft—slicing skin on hidden barnacles—and hung on. Wracked, exhausted, he almost toppled into the next wave, but he hurled himself back up, wrapped around the rock.

But where was Greensleeves? He couldn't have protected her, come this far, only to lose her to drowning. And what of the others?

An explosive retching rang nearby. In the dim light, he saw Morven's gray head hang as he vomited water. Half-under him was Stiggur, like a drowned muskrat. That left—

"Gull, you bastard! Help me!"

Not far off, on a flatter expanse of seaweed, Kem struggled to land himself while towing Greensleeves by her hair. The girl waved her hands, protesting at the pain but, like a machine, the bodyguard hauled her higher up the slippery rock. Kem had lost his helmet, sword, one boot.

Tripping, sliding on sliced feet, Gull reached them, grabbed his sister around the shoulders.

Kem coughed hard enough to split a lung, but couldn't resist a snipe. "Don't—thank me."

Gull hugged his weeping sister. "Thank you, Kem. Thank you."

The ex-bodyguard snorted water out his nose, coughed anew.

Morven and Stiggur collapsed beside them. The boy sobbed, "I've had enough adventuring."

"Me, too, lad," gasped the sailor. "Thirty years afloat, and I come nearest drowning working for a wagon train. Neptune's after my soul—Oh, no . . . "

The heroes glanced around. The shattered cliff face was a stone's throw away, except now it sported a huge trough down its center, from the grass above to a massive cascade of dirt before them. High up, gazing down the trough, stood Towser. Waving both hands at the sea.

Where Morven gazed, horrified.

Silver shapes slipped in and out of waves. They flickered and flitted, vanishing, appearing, disappearing. A school of fish, Gull thought: that silver sheen was their backs. Yet the patches twisted, came together, formed coils . . .

A snaky head long as a ship broke from the waves, opened jaws with more teeth, with countless teeth. A crest like a ship's sail decorated the undulating head. The neck stretched on and on.

A fishy eye three feet across fixed on them, dipped through a wave, came out straight as an arrow, jaws agape.

"Sea serpent!" Morven shouted.

To pluck them off this rock like a robin gulping worms.

The serpent's head reared from the waves. The cavernous mouth yawned at half a bowshot. Then it split another wave, and Gull could have thrown a rock and hit it. He stared down the gullet, imagining the stink of long-dead fish. *Eaten*, he thought. *We're to be eaten, after surviving all this.*

In his arms, Greensleeves stirred. She lifted a hand, and the world went white.

A fungal glow loomed over them. The dank smell of musty mushrooms banished the salt tang for a moment, and Gull wondered where he'd seen this light before.

Ah, the battle of the burned forest. When the armored wizard seized Greensleeves, and was suddenly confronted by a mushroom beast the size of a barn, a fungusaur. Lily (where was she?) had pointed out that it was conjured by someone else, and of course, that had been Greensleeves. And Gull had been too dense to see her magical prowess.

Now she'd plucked this fungusaur from some deep cavern. Gray-white and glowing, with goggling yellow eyes, its mouth like a cave itself, the beast towered over them like a living wall—

—and the serpent struck it with mouth open.

Chunks of white, glowing with cold light, exploded through the air. The mushroom beast growled, bit at the serpent, whose long tail thrashed the water to foamy phosphorescence. The serpent snapped its head, tearing at the beast, whose pulpy muck-encrusted feet slipped on the slimy wet rocks. The fungusaur's growl dropped to a low rumble, then a grating squall. Though it was hard to see from below, Gull thought the serpent had torn a hunk from the fungusaur's spine, if it had such. Whatever, that sounded like a death keen from the white monster.

The heroes didn't wait. Grabbing one another, clutching for purchase, they scrambled across the spume-flecked rocks for the dirt cascade.

Within a dozen paces, they mired in soggy mud—loose dirt churned to slurry by seawater. In the lead, Kem sank to his hips in muck. He turned, yelled at the others to get back. But too late for Gull, who'd stumbled into a wallow, too. The others hung back, clinging to rocks, afraid to move for fear of water and mud.

"Where the hell now?" panted Morven as he gazed around. For the first time ever, he sounded old. Ancient. "I thought—the cliff—" He gave up, exhausted.

Sunk, wedged tight, Gull craned about. The sun was gone behind the clouds. It was almost completely black. Foam and flickering fungal light were no help. He felt they drowned in blackness. Even had he been free, he couldn't have picked a direction to go. Off to their left, the fallen monolith lay big as a barn and smothered in dirt. More cascade stretched to their right. Directly ahead was the huge trough, like a slue, that rose in fits and starts and jagged steps, all trickling loose dirt, up to the remains of the bluff.

Light showed up there. The wizard commanded the center. Ranged on either side were shaggy shapes with curved swords and torches. Blue barbarians, dozens of them.

The woodcutter looked seaward. Dimly, he saw the

fungusaur had been ripped to pieces that floated away.
Amidst the ruin thrashed the sea serpent, unharmed
and hungry and hunting them. It steamed back and
forth amidst the rocks, seeking a deep-enough channel
to close and swallow them. Rain still slashed down,
but Gull was so numb he couldn't feel it.

He'd feel nothing soon.

"Can't go, can't stay," muttered Kem. He threw
himself flat to try and swim out of his mudhole.

"Stabbed or eaten," gasped Morven. He instructed
Stiggur to hold his belt, leaned out across slurry for
Gull. "Or time permitting, we drown at high tide."

Gull stretched, and sailor and cook's boy hauled
him free to the rocks. Picking around the deeper pockets of mud, together they hauled Kem to safety.

Slapped by waves, by wind and rain, they huddled
inches above the sea. Kem muttered, "Hell of a place
to die."

"Let's hope we do," panted Morven. "I can use a rest."

Only Greensleeves peered around, sniffing like a
dog.

Gull asked, "Anything else, sister?" But he had little hope. Funny, he thought, ever since that first day
in White Ridge, he'd been running like a madman to
rescue his sister. Now overwhelmed, he could only ask
her to rescue them. Strange were the twists in the road
of life.

The girl swirled a hand in seawater. "Th-there's . . .
s-omething . . . s-singing to me. . . . S-something
st-stirred by the ear-earthquake. . . ."

The men watched glumly. Far above, Towser gave
orders. A score of barbarians hopped into the earth
scar, picked their way down sliding dirt toward the
captives. Not thirty feet out, the serpent hissed, louder
and louder.

Or . . . ?

It wasn't any beast hissing, Gull realized. It was the water, the ocean itself.

The surf pulsed all around, but each surge was weaker. They were no longer slapped by spume.

Curiosity made the men turn. Gull asked, "Greenie, is this your doing?" But the girl only stared oceanward.

Everywhere they looked, the water level dropped. Waves stopped licking at their heels, receded altogether. Rocks that had shown only seaweedy tips stood revealed. The water drained away so quickly flapping fish and clicking crabs were trapped in pools. The sea serpent, incredibly long and silvery, flopped amidst rocks.

Like a dream, the waves rolled away and away, clear to the horizon. The muck green seabed lay revealed, rocks and stranded fish and even a mossy shipwreck a quarter mile out.

"What is it?" breathed Kem.

Morven had gone white. He mumbled under his breath. "Oh, no. Oh, no. . . ."

Gull poked him. "What? What is it?"

"Tsunami," the sailor whispered.

"Su-what?"

"Run!" he shouted, startling them all. "Run! Ashore! Fast! Like you've never run before!"

Morven caught Stiggur, lifted him by main strength, then ran, galloping across rocks, fear making him light as a squirrel. Gull glanced at Kem, who stared back. But the panic was infectious. The woodcutter caught his sister's elbow, the bodyguard caught the other, and, hoisting her, they ran obliquely across rocks and thin mud for the shore.

Morven scrambled up the trough, pushing Stiggur by his backside. The men followed with Greensleeves, though they slid down as much as they climbed up. Panting, the sailor searched the blacker pockets. High up, a confused gurgle came from the backlit barbarians, who wondered why these men ran to their deaths, and what had happened to the ocean.

"What *is* it, Morven?" Gull hollered. "What's after us?"

"Tsunami!" the man shouted over his shoulder. "But we'll never outrun it, not on this slope, not ever! Look for a cave! It's our only chance!"

"But what the hell's a su-whatever you said?" demanded Kem.

"Here!" The sailor stopped at a cleft, just a blacker slash in the black hillside. He grabbed the boy's hair and mashed him into the cave. Stiggur yowled.

Gull swore. Morven had gone mad.

Yet the ocean was acting damned queer. Though Gull knew little about the sea, Lily had explained tides. But never that the water disappeared completely, rolled right over the horizon.

"Get in, get in, get in!" Morven plucked Greensleeves from the men's grasp, stuffed her in the hole. "In in in!"

"But *what* . . . ?"

For answer, the sailor pointed seaward.

Far far out, where the sunken sun cast an afterglow, a long low cloud had descended to earth. No, Gull corrected, it must be a mountain range uncovered by the water. Except it grew, higher and higher.

Then he knew what it was.

The ocean, returning in a single wave.

Gull recalled the town where they'd first seen the

ocean. His sister had splashed in the surf. Now she stirred it with her hands like a god.

Above them on the slope, barbarians babbled. Towser was gone, fled inland.

"What I tried to tell you!" bleated Morven. "A tidal wave!"

For a second, Gull couldn't move. Then Morven caught his hair and stuffed him into the hole after his sister. In pitch blackness, Gull smacked heads with her. Shifting, he banged Stiggur, made him grunt. "Crowd in, son!"

"I can't! This is all there is!" From the tiny squeak in his ear, Gull knew it was true. This cave was no bigger than a coffin.

Kem crammed in behind him, driving knees into Gull's back. "Move inside, idiot!"

Gull shuffled in the dark, squashing his sister. Kem wriggled against him, so tight the woodcutter felt scar tissue brush his neck. "This is it!"

"It can't be!" Kem grunted as Morven pressed behind.

The sailor wheezed. "Little Missy! Greensleeves! Raise that wall of wood! It's all that'll save you!"

"I—I—" Tearfully, Greensleeves stopped protesting to concentrate.

"No, wait!" From his voice, Gull could tell that Morven was outside the cave. There was no more room. "Morven! You—"

"*You,*" Morven interrupted to Greensleeves, "must conjure one of them walls of wood to block this cave! Tight as a curtain!"

"But—" Gull shouted. He flexed, tried to back out of the hole, but Kem was wedged in the entrance and the sailor leaned on him. *"Morven! You have to—"*

A rustling stirring chittering answered. Gull smelled the bitter tannin of oak leaves. The blackness got blacker, if that were possible. Kem grunted in pain as bark rasped his spine.

In seconds, Greensleeves's wall of wood sealed them off like a ship's hatch. Cut them off from Morven. Outside.

It was suddenly hard to breathe. And hot. Smells of earth and salt and bodies was strong. "How will we get out?" squeaked Stiggur.

"Will the cliff hold, I want to know," Kem gasped. "That wave might just suck this whole cliff *out to sea—*"

He shouted the last, for a roar louder than any windstorm was rushing howling pushing driving at them. The temperature plummeted, chilling. Gull supposed a hurricane's worth of fresh air was pushed before that mountainous sea.

Which must strike—

—the cliff—

—and Morven—

—any sec—

The world dissolved in water.

A wet hell gushed at them, around them, into them.

Gull's lungs were near bursting, but snatching a breath, he sucked water and mud and air in a devil's mix. Water pounded his face, mud filled his ears and eyepits and nose, roots ground at his head and spine. Hands aching, he clung to everyone, felt Greensleeves and Stiggur and Kem struggle as much as he.

Morven would have died right away, he thought. *We'll die slowly, gasping like those stranded fish.*

Dirt smothered him, water swirled it away, air

teased and then vanished. He was shaken like a rat in a barrel, battered on every inch of his body.

How long this went on, he could never recall. But suddenly there was more room. Kem's knees weren't gouging his kidneys. Swirling inside, he thought, the sea was tearing the cliff to flinders, as Kem feared. They'd be snatched into the giant wave in seconds, and drowned.

"*Gullll!!!!*" The bodyguard clutched so hard his fingers could have snapped Gull's collarbone. He was being sucked out the entrance.

With more room—too much—Gull reached behind, grabbed leather, hung on. He braced his feet against walls, but they dissolved into mud. Roots under one hand trickled away like sand. Gull reached for Greensleeves to brace her, keep her pinned so she wouldn't be washed out. But he missed her, found a muddy wall disintegrating.

The iron fingers on his collarbone let go.

Rather than pull me out, Gull thought, *Kem let himself be sucked away. He's saved us again. I'll never repay that, not if I live a thousand years.*

Pounded by new water and mud, Gull reached for Stiggur, jammed the boy's hands against Greensleeves. Maybe the two together—

Then Gull was toppling. Water gushed down his front, rinsing him clean, drowning him, sucking him into a dragon's maw—

He grabbed—

—found nothing—

—plummeted into a whirling watery waste.

CHAPTER
20

A sharp peck awoke Gull.

He pried open salt-crusty dirt-mucky eyes to find a sea gull backing away, wings flapping. Beady black eyes snapped, the yellow bill clacked a squawk. The bird had tested if he was dead. Indignant, it flew off.

An omen if there ever was one, the woodcutter thought. He hadn't expected to be awakened by his namesake. Not this side of the heavens.

Sun was hot on his face. His head throbbed because he lay upside down on the slope. Prying free of the mud, for he was sunk a foot, he took stock. Bruised, scratched, gouged, he was barefoot, tangle-haired, empty-handed. He'd even lost his leather kilt, had only his leather tunic hanging to mid-thigh.

But considering he should be dead, he had no complaints.

Rubbing crusted eyes with filthy hands, he peered around.

He wasn't far from their cave, only fifty feet above

the surf, which tussled and nuzzled the shore gently, as if the tidal wave had never been. Sunlight sparkling on waves made him squint. Sea gulls perched on the monolith lodged at the shoreline. The black stone absorbed heat, kept them warm. *It's serving a useful purpose at last*, the woodcutter thought groggily.

He wondered where Greensleeves was, surprised to miss the familiar jolt of panic. He'd lost his emotions somewhere. For now, he just existed, hungry and thirsty, like the sea gull that woke him.

He turned, faced the trough and bluff. Things looked different, for rough edges had been smoothed, large boulders plucked away. Their cave hideout was only a scratch. Gull thought of ants in a hill suddenly pissed on. Gods and nature did as they pleased, and people and animals lived or died, helpless.

Gull staggered up the slope toward a soggy brown and white lump. Stiggur, reborn like a potato dug up. The boy gasped and flexed, and mud crackled off.

Leaving him to peer about, he found a blob higher up. His sister, encased in mud. He chipped dirt from her face, nudged her. She murmured sleepily, as always, then woke up fast, like a cat. "Wh-what . . . ?"

Gull cast up and down the smooth mud slope. No one else.

The three limped down to the ocean, and squatting in the lapping waves, swabbed off mud. The salt tang aggravated their burning thirst.

When he arose, Gull saw Kem.

The ex-bodyguard lay facedown in a rock pool. The woodcutter waded out, brushed off crabs, hauled Kem's carcass above the tide line, laid him facedown so gulls wouldn't pick out his eyes. He told the dead man, "I'll return and bury you. I owe you that, at least."

Gull gazed at the blue vastness. Morven would be

out there, under the water. The sea had reclaimed him.

"Come," he told the survivors. "We'll see what's left up top."

Not a lot, it turned out.

The top of the bluff was swept clean. All signs of bramble walls and stone spears and walls of wood were gone, even the red earth under them. Crashing onto the shore, the tidal wave had sucked most everything seaward in its retreat.

But not everything.

Lying on the grass, as if dropped by a child, lay the pink stone *mana* vault. Greensleeves idly picked it up.

They walked inland.

Battered salt-poisoned grass stretched half a mile to a forest of beech and oak, the final barrier to the impossible tidal wave.

Now and then they passed dead barbarians. Their blue berry dye and clothes had been sucked off, so they lay scattered, tanned and tattooed, like children playing a game of statues. But none moved, and flies crawled on faces. Gull wondered if they'd died cursing Towser, the man who'd enslaved them.

Trees had lost leaves in the mad wave, but in some weird exchange, had been festooned with sea wrack. Kelp dangled from oaks. Driftwood had returned to the forest dragging beds of seaweed. A dying starfish clung to a beech tree as if a wharf piling. A codfish gasped in a nest of leaves. Sand glittered everywhere.

From a hollow jutted four pilings like a storm-tossed pier. But these pilings were jointed. Stiggur ran shouting, circled, found the clockwork beast's head half-buried in broken branches. With the energy of youth, he began to dig.

Shifting the *mana* vault, Greensleeves pointed into the forest. What looked like a white whale in a tree proved to be Liko's rump. Sail smock in shreds, the giant was fetched up in a forked oak twenty feet above the ground. Gull guessed he'd been climbing when the wave caught him. He was just too big to wash away. Too high to reach, Gull peered close, saw a toe large as a bushel basket twitch. They left the giant to wake on his own.

Traveling along the forest's edge, both stopped in shock. Greensleeves's knees gave out, and she sank, mewling like a lost kitten.

At the devastation she had caused.

Towser's entourage was spilled amidst trees like a shattered bird's nest.

For the first time that morning, Gull felt a spark in his breast. Surveying the wreckage, he breathed, "Lily . . . "

In her yellow clothes, Jonquil lay on the sward as if napping. A frown creased her coarse farm girl's face. She had no pulse, sleeping forever.

Stepping over Jonquil, they counted four wagons. Towser's, the heaviest, lay on its roof against an oak bole, one side splintered, four wheels smashed to pointed stars. The women's wagon had broken its back against a lichened boulder. The astrologer's wagon lay flat upside down, the hoops for the canvas roof crushed. The cook wagon had split, spilling ironware and soggy foodstuffs.

Horses and mules, left in the traces, were equally smashed and broken. Two of the horses, broken-backed, were still alive. Knothead and Flossy, Gull's mules, were dead, tangled in harness, wrapped around a tree. Gull stared a while, pronounced their epitaphs. "Flossy was sweet. Knothead was stubborn and cranky, but a good puller."

Searching, almost idly, for this new disaster was mind-numbing, Gull bumped a wine jug that sloshed invitingly. He hunted up a grill spike and chipped out the cork. He and his sister drank the sweet wine greedily, saved some for Stiggur.

Gull spiked the throats of the wounded horses.

Then counted the dead.

Felda, the fat cook, was wedged under her wagon, pierced by a broken wheel spoke. The bard, Ranon Spiritsinger, was nearby, horribly twisted, one arm rammed through her lyre strings. Rose and Peachblossom were dead inside the women's wagon, where they'd sought refuge. Under the astrologer's wagon, blue-clad legs marked Bluebonnet. There were no traces of the nurse, Haley, or the astrologer, Kakulina. Gull figured they had washed away, could be anywhere from deeper in the forest to deep in the ocean.

He tried to summon sorrow for these folks. He'd known them, eaten with them, talked of small things. But in the end they'd betrayed him, guarding their soft positions in the wizard's employ. They'd hunkered over a cooking fire and ignored a human sacrifice carried out by their master two hundred feet away. Ultimately, their master had failed to protect them.

Gull peered inside Towser's overturned wagon, all ajumble. Tangled blankets had fallen from the ornate bed, books and artifacts had rained from niches in the walls.

No trace of the three bodyguards, who would have stayed near Towser.

And, of course, Gull thought bitterly, no Towser. He

might have been killed, but the woodcutter doubted it. A wizard protected himself first and foremost.

And, finally, no Lily.

Then he heard a sigh.

The noise issued from under the collapsed bed.

Praying, pleading, Gull yanked aside salt-sopping blankets and tapestries.

His prayers were answered. It was Lily.

She lay on the upside-down roof, only an arm and her head showing. Face pale as her sundered clothes, she struggled to free herself.

"Lily! I was so worried!" He grabbed her arm to tug, but she shrieked.

"My arm!" Sweaty and cold, her body and voice shivered. "It's broken! I felt the bones grind together!"

Gull mopped his face, squatted to see inside the dark wagon. Up front, amidst smashed luggage and supplies, lay Knoton, the clerk. The woodcutter wondered how, with all these dead, Lily had survived.

Then he remembered. She too was a wizard.

"Don't fret, honey, I'll get you out! Lie still!" Greensleeves set down her *mana* vault and helped. Gently, tugging and winkling, they slid the dancing girl out, learned one leg was also broken. Lily hissed in agony, yet gasped they should search for green bottles in the red-lacquered case. Greensleeves poked in the wagon while Gull comforted the dancing girl.

"I thought I'd lost you." Gull cradled her head on his lap, smoothed her tousled hair. "I thought I'd lost you. I realized I didn't want to lose you. I want you with me forever. I want you to be my wife. I love you, Lily."

Grimacing, crying, smiling at the same time, the

girl pressed a finger on his lips. "Hush, Gull, please. Things aren't the—oh!—same all of a sudden."

"What?" Gull frowned, wiped his eyes. "What's wrong?"

"Nothing's wrong, exactly . . . It's just . . . How shall I explain—*ah*, it hurts! I—I never liked myself, Gull. I always thought I was unworthy, born of a whore, never knowing my father, a whore myself—"

"I don't care about that—"

"Hush. I know. You're a wonderful man, kind and loving. But things are different. Suddenly I'm a wizard. I don't know what that means."

"You don't have to be a wizard."

She smiled, winced with pain. Behind them, Greensleeves bustled, shifted boxes. "And a bird with wings needn't fly? Gull, when that giant wave hit us, I scrunched down and prayed not to die. And something—some tingling power—enwrapped me like a mother's arms. And I didn't die. Though I—*ow ow ow*—didn't protect myself *that* well. Still . . . oh, I love you so, but I can't marry you just yet. Do you see why?"

"No." He sounded petulant.

She sighed a feminine sigh, and suddenly Gull felt like a boy addressing a woman. "I need time. To think."

"You'll adopt wizardry, then." He was bitter. "And leave us mortals in the dust."

She shook her head, grunted as her arm moved. "No. I'll leave Lily in the dust, and find who I really am."

It was Gull's turn to sigh. "And that's not my wife? Ah, well. I shouldn't have let you dangle all this time. I should have reeled you in when I hooked you."

She chuckled, put a finger to her lips and kissed it, laid it against his lips. He smiled down at her.

Greensleeves crawled backward out of the wagon. Skirts more mud-stained and tattered than ever, she looked like a six-year-old making mud pies. But beholding the two lovers, her gaze became a woman's calculation. She offered an unstoppered beaker. "P-poppy seed e-extract and feverfew, I th-think. 'Twill e-ease the pain."

Lily nodded, drank the whole beaker. Before long, she nodded off and snored gently.

Greensleeves rummaged, found some slats, used scissors to cut a blanket. She handed them all to Gull. "Wh-while she sl-sleeps, you must s-set—s-set—"

"I know," said her brother. Strongest of the family, he'd been the one to set broken bones. "I'll tend her."

Late that afternoon, Lily lay in the shade of a chestnut tree while Gull and Greensleeves toted food and supplies.

Salvaging the wrecks, including Gull's woodcutting tools, they camped a half mile from the wagons. They couldn't bury the bodies today, so needed to move off before nightfall brought wolves and coyotes and raccoons. And ghosts.

As Gull arranged rocks for a firepit and Greensleeves aired blankets, Liko joined them. They'd heard a tremendous crash when he awoke and tumbled from the treetop. The earth shook as he staggered up, leaning to the one-armed side, sail clothing trailing in rags. Saying not a word, he flopped on his back, dozed off again. The humans had to talk above his dual snores.

Once the fire sent up smoke, thick gray because the branches were damp, a duo of voices hallooed. Helki and Holleb the centaurs trotted up, their shiny finery clattering, unaccustomed grins on their grim faces. Gull was so pleased to see them alive, he hugged each one, lifted clean off his feet by the forbidding Holleb. Everyone talked at once, including Greensleeves, and it was some while before the stories became clear.

But simple enough. From their greater height, the centaurs saw the water recede, and having lived near the sea, knew what it meant. They'd galloped inland, raced into the forest fast enough to burst their hearts. Seawater had lapped at their heels, but they'd topped a ridge and escaped harm.

"So we celebrate victory!" growled Holleb in his harsh accent.

Gull shook his head. "There's no victory, not with Towser escaping, not with all these dead. We survived, is all."

"We see. Is true," said Helki. "But where are others? Your friends who help you?"

Gull nodded down the tree line. "Stiggur has been digging and prying all day, trying to reach the controls for the clockwork beast, to see if it still works. Or is still alive. As for the others, there aren't any."

The centaurs looked around, saw only Lily, Liko, and Greensleeves. Helki said, "Oh."

By sundown, Gull had a meal together. He'd rescued an iron pot and unbroached cask of salt pork, put it on to boil. He'd found some flour, salted it, twined the dough in strips around green sticks to roast. They'd found several barrels of beer in the women's wagon, and crocks of Felda's pickles.

There was also plenty to feed the giant. Liko sat cross-legged and gobbled raw horseflesh while the centaurs nibbled from Towser's silver plates and tried not to watch. Greensleeves used twist bread to sop gravy. Gull fed Lily with clumsy fingers. She used her good arm to sip brandy for pain. Her other hung in a sling. Stiggur wolfed pickles and sniffed, remembering Felda's kindness.

After a night and day of privation, heartache, struggle, and sadness, it was a feast, though a quiet one. Everyone felt the absence of friends.

When people were sated, had fathomed one beer cask, Gull leaned back on his elbows, stared at the dancing campfire. "So what's—Hey!"

The woodcutter snapped down his flagon, hopped around the stack of supplies. Stabbing into darkness, he grabbed something that squealed, hoisted up the goblin thief, Egg Sucker. "What are you doing here? I threw you off the cliff!"

"Aye! And near broke me head!" Dangling again, the little pest rubbed his skunk-striped hair. "But you can let go, kind sir! I wasn't stealin'! I only saw a rat digging at your sacks, and—"

"Oh, hush up. Don't give me any stories. I should have let the elves feather you with arrows. Come here."

Back in the firelit circle, he propped the goblin on his feet, handed him his beer mug. Confused by kindness, Egg Sucker could only clutch it like a cask in his small crooked hands. Gull gave him a hank of salt pork, which the goblin tore into. But as soon as Gull sat down, he dashed into the night as if beset by dogs.

Gull sighed, reached for his mug, remembered it was gone. "Well, never mind. Where was I . . . ? Ah. So, what do we do tomorrow? After burying the dead, that is."

"We need get my clockwork beast upright. I tugged a lever and his leg kicked." Stiggur mumbled around a mouthful of bread, added suddenly, "I'll name him Knothead, if that's all right with you."

"It's fine," Gull chuckled. "If he has a name, he must be alive."

"We must find town," said Holleb. "Not much food here."

"Aye," Gull agreed. "There's somewhat else, too. Greensleeves or Lily, someone with magic, should fig-ure how to conjure, or summon, or whatever you call it, to fetch Tomas and Neith and Varrius and that pal-adin Bardo, and even those miserable orcs, off that tropical island. They deserve a chance to walk home, if they can find it." The women agreed.

"Home," sighed Helki. "Holleb and I need learn where is so can go there. Have been away long time . . . We miss it."

Greensleeves arose, walked over, laid her small callused hand on Helki's shoulder. "D-don't be s-sad, Hel-ki. We'll f-find your h-home. Y-you too, Li-ko." The giant nodded both somber heads. "M-maybe some of T-T-Towser's booty will h-help us." Probing the wagon, they'd found many bottles and artifacts smashed, but still acquired a stack of magical-seeming books and whatnots to study.

"Greenie's right. We'll see you *all* get home . . . " Gull was quiet a while, then murmured, "We lost our home . . . A whole village wiped out . . . in a *quarrel* between two wizards out to steal each other's *power*. They didn't care who they stepped on, as if we were ants on their battlefield . . . *That's* what we should do! We should stop *all* wizards from running roughshod over common folk!"

His voice had grown more animated, yet taken a hard edge.

Helki looked puzzled, as did the rest. "How?"

"I don't know." The woodcutter stared at the fire. "But there must be a way to halt them. If you could—assemble an army, and keep it together—a *volunteer* fighting force, not slaves—we could track these wizards down, somehow, then scatter their makeshift armies and make them submit. Then if you could, what? take away their power . . . ? I don't know. But there *must* be a way . . . "

Greensleeves had been toying with the pink stone box, which glinted in the firelight. Now she stopped. "I'll h-help, Gull."

Lily put her free hand on Gull's. "And I."

"And us!" shouted Holleb, as if accepting a challenge to a duel.

"Aye! Us too!" screamed Helki. The two sent a rollicking whinny war cry to the heavens.

When the echoes died, Liko's two heads spoke in unison for the first time. "Me too."

"Can I help?" asked Stiggur. "I can bring Knothead!"

Gull tousled the boy's hair so hard he fell over. "Of course, Stiggur. And bring your whip. We'll need that too."

Lily nodded toward the darkness. "What about Egg Sucker?"

Gull laughed. "Oh, aye. We'll need him for—something. But I wasn't proposing *we* form an army to stop wizards."

"Yes, you were," replied Lily. "It's something we've all wished, but couldn't voice."

Gull looked around the tiny battered group. "How odd. We were just a handful of strangers, each brought to grief because of wizards' greed. Now we're—an army, I guess. Wizards and warriors and—and clockwork beast riders and—woodcutters . . . "

A knot popped in the campfire, and sparks crackled

into the air. Gull watched them climb to join the stars that swept from horizon to horizon. "My father used to say the sky was never so clear as after a storm."

"So our future is bright," said Lily.

"I suppose. But are you all *sure* you want to do this? Dedicate yourselves to an army—a crusade—with no clue how to proceed? Battle wizards and thugs and fiends and hellions, risk life and limb, just to stop them razing villages and mucking up folks' lives, folks you've never even met? When you could instead just go home?"

He looked around again, searching each face, but everyone just nodded.

He reached out his toe, jiggled the fire brighter.

"Well, then. That's what we'll do."

CLAYTON EMERY has been a blacksmith, a dishwasher, a schoolteacher in Australia, a carpenter, a zookeeper, a farmhand, a land surveyor, and a volunteer firefighter, among other things. He was an award-winning technical writer for ten years. He's the author of several fantasy adventures, including *Tales of Robin Hood*, *Shadow World Book One: The Burning Goddess* and *Book Three: City of Assassins*; as well as an American Revolution novel, *Marines to the Tops!*; and "Robin & Marian" stories in *Ellery Queen's Mystery Magazine*. He lives in Rye, New Hampshire, in a house built in 1767 that needs LOTS of work.

FREE

UNIQUE CARD OFFER

To celebrate the launch of America's hottest new gaming fiction series, Wizards of the Coast, Inc. and HarperPrism are making available, for a limited time only, one new Magic: The Gathering™ card not for sale in any store.

Send a **stamped self-addressed envelope** and **proof of purchase** (cash register receipt attached to this coupon) to HarperPrism, Dept. WW, 10 East 53rd Street, New York, NY 10022.

No photocopies will be accepted.

Offer good in U.S. and Canada only. Please allow 8–10 weeks for delivery.

- -

Name: _____

Address: _____

City: _____ State: _____ Zip: _____

Age: _____ Sex: (M / F)

Store where book was purchased: _____

_____

Offer expires 1/96.

HarperPrism

#2